The Blue Path

BOOK TWO IN THE BLUSHING MOON TRILOGY

KITT LYNN

LUPO PUBLISHING

ISBN: 978-1-958309-01-8 (Paperback)

ISBN: 978-1-958309-00-1 (eBook)

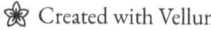 Created with Vellum

CONTENT WARNING

This book contains possibly triggering content.

If you are a survivor and need assistance or support, please call
the National Sexual Assault Hotline at
800-656-HOPE (4673)
https://hotline.rainn.org/

If you are in a dangerous situation and need help or support,
please call the National Domestic Abuse Hotline at
800-799-SAFE (7233)
https://www.thehotline.org/

Please do not struggle in silence. You are not alone.
If you need a more detailed list of the triggers within this
book, please reach out to me at misskittlynn@gmail.com.

I don't want to be the reason for someone to feel hurt, upset,
or traumatized.

- Kitt -

Creature Guide

Hannoth - Large, predatory mammals. They are covered in fur with large claws and fangs. When a hannoth attacks, flaps come away from the sides of its neck, projecting strings of acidic venom.

Kunzite crystals - Found throughout Havre. Pinkish crystals that grow in clusters underground and make everything from the land to the air very cold. But they also give the area a calm and serene atmosphere that anyone walking through them will find relaxing.

Lumenite crystals - Bright yellow crystals that emit a tremendous amount of heat. They are harvested and used frequently within villages.

Mountain Men - (aka, Rock men of Gygax). Men made of rocks that live within the mountains throughout Havre. Their origin is believed to be the result of witches and fairy folk that bewitched the mountains to aide during the Great War with the humans.

Punga - Bear-like mammal that has an unmatched speed, and can be vicious when cornered.

Rouges - Werewolves with no allegiance to a pack or village. Frequently they are banished from villages, and branded to prevent them from entering any other were-colonies. The actual brand varies based on the village, but traditionally a "R" on the neck or somewhere visible.

Sabbots - Magical humanoid creatures. Tend to tower over alphas. Blue in color with thick scales and barbs that jut out along their spine.

The Enchanted Lands of Havre

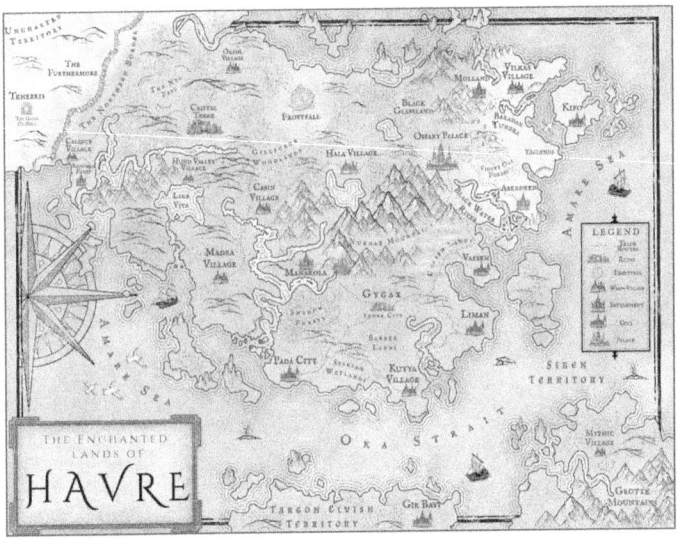

To see a larger version of the map of Havre, visit www. kittlynn.com.

Darkness

Joon

COMPLETE DARKNESS. It pulsed and swayed as if breathing around me. Sweat poured down my back as a shiver slipped up my spine. I swallowed convulsively against the urge to vomit.

I was so scared.

The occasional flit of a memory drifted into focus. It was the only reminder that I was still alive—or at least I hoped I was. Familiar faces lurched and screamed, making my temples pound before they faded again, leaving the harsh scent of ash in their wake.

Fennah's face pushed through the consuming black, twisting into Byna's evil smirk, then melting into Hida. I reached out, desperate to pull my mate back.

"Don't go!" I screamed, swiping through the vanishing figures.

Pain drummed against my chest and skittered across my

skin like wicked spiders. I couldn't even think. I could only feel white-hot pain wedged deep in my joints.

"Joon." Tzidal's voice was a slip of a whisper coming from somewhere behind me.

I spun to find her, but I couldn't stop. Everything rushed past me, spinning faster and faster, around and around, until I stumbled, falling onto my hands and knees into a puddle of slick, crimson water. The metallic stench of blood filled my lungs and coated the back of my throat.

I tried to move, but the thick, red water held me in place as it rushed over my skin. It grew dense and sticky, consuming my entire lower half. Then the hot pool of blood rose to my chest, squeezing so tight I could barely breathe. I strained, trying to push my feet forward. My thighs burned, but I didn't budge an inch.

I swiped at the shadows, looming just outside my vision, while I slowly sank into the earth. There was no one here to help me. I was all alone.

My nerves stretched tight, and fear finally overtook me.

Tilting my head back, I opened my mouth to scream, but nothing came out. The viscous swamp sucked me hard, swallowing me up. My ears pounded with my own frantic heartbeat as blood rushed over my face, flooding my throat and nose. It crept over my eyes, constricting and crushing me as the earth pulled me under.

Then everything went dark.

Tzidal's voice drifted to me from somewhere in the distance, "Joon, please wake up."

The Nukdae Mountains

Tzidal

MY DAGGER FLEW, slipping deep into the hannoth's silver fur. I needed to run to the bear-like creature and rip it free—continue my attack—but I was too exhausted.

Byriel's wolf-form dug his claws into the creature's back, sinking his teeth into the base of its skull. A wheezy breath left hannoth's snout as it jerked, trying to shake the Byriel's wolf free.

My hands trembled with overflowing adrenaline as I cupped Joon's face. Everything was too loud and sharp. The scent of tangy blood, acidic venom, and mud filled my lungs.

I wasn't sure how we'd make it out of this. It seemed as if we had been fighting since the moment we left Vaesen. Rain, harsh lands, vicious creatures, and determined rogues. Everything was trying to kill us.

The flaps on the side of the hannoth's face stripped open, exposing shiny pink flesh dripping with venom. Byriel's wolf pushed his fangs deeper into its throat, cutting off the hannoth's pained roar. A slurry of blood, venom, and saliva bubbled and poured from the maw where the its throat shredded apart.

Another rattling breath. Heavy pounding feet. A blue of something blue. Then the creature stilled.

A massive blue sabbot staggered toward me. Its arm bloody and mangled.

Slowly, the vicious, blue creature shrunk. The thick scales and jutting barbs along the sabbot's back pulled into its body. The vibrant color faded, going white as Lex phased back into the young man I was familiar with.

"Everyone okay?" Byriel panted.

His usually dark skin was ashen and sweaty, and his knees shook as he forced himself onto his feet. He was so weak, I was shocked he managed to shift into his wolf. My eyes fell to the wolfsbane charm around his neck, wondering if the enchantment within had helped him shift. Either way, I was thankful.

His wolf came through when we needed him.

"Tzi?" Lex leaned forward. "Are you okay?"

"I'm okay." I forced a smile. "Just rattled."

Looking down at Joon's unconscious form, laid out in the thick mud, I let out a thankful breath.

We were alive.

That's all I did lately—thank the Moon for allowing us to barely survive.

Today it was the hannoth, yesterday it was a territorial grizzly, and last week we were almost caught by a few determined rogues that tracked us for three days before finally giving up.

I was so tired. We all were.

"Let's find some shelter," Lex said. He stood and swayed on uneasy legs. He closed his eyes for a moment to steady himself.

"You're hurt," Byriel gritted out, pointing at Lex's wounded arm.

Black blood dripped in chunky clumps, and I panicked a bit, unsure what to do about it. I was good at finding herbs and flowers to speed up the healing process with wolves, but I had no idea if they would help a siren.

"We passed a shack not far back," I said, my hands resting just next to the wound on Joon's chest. His bandage was dirty, and red seeped through the center. It needed a good cleaning, but it was too late in the day to find a stream.

"I'll get Joon," Byriel said, pushing his massive body onto his feet. He staggered as he took his first step, and for a moment, I thought he would pass out. Sweat covered his dark skin, and his eyes were weary with exhaustion and hunger.

"Byriel," I lifted my hand as if it might help hold him up, "don't push yourself."

"I'm fine," he said a little too quickly, pulling in a long breath through his nose. He nodded again, "I'm fine."

Lex's face reflected my worry. We couldn't force the alpha to rest, and we did need to find shelter soon. It was probably best to let him push through his pain.

Byriel pointed at the dead hannoth. "Lex, can you collect a bit of meat from them?"

"Can we eat them?" Hope filled my chest. My stomach had never felt so empty.

"Legs only," Byriel warned as Lex knelt next to one of the lifeless creatures. "They have pockets of that damn venom along their neck and down their chests. One wrong cut, and it'll burn you up. Be careful."

"Legs only," Lex nodded, inspecting the hannoth's hind quarters.

Byriel grabbed Joon's upper arm and heaved him forward out of the thick mud. My alpha was wedged deep, the earth pushing up and over his legs.

It felt as if it had rained non-stop since we left Vaesen, and I decided I didn't care for northern Havre. Too wet and cold.

My body missed the soft, flat lands of Madra Village. It was dry this time of year back home, and I had never longed for a drought more than I did now.

"Grab your dagger, omega," Byriel said, taking forceful breaths as he steadied Joon over his shoulder.

Walking over to the hannoth, I pulled my blade from its throat. Yellow, sizzling venom shot out of its neck, spraying just past me. The hairs on the back of my neck raised, the close call making my skin crawl. Taking several steps back, I rubbed the coiling, purple mark that decorated my skin along my forearm.

While my journey had not been kind to my body, I was still thankful to be relatively unscathed. The Moon had been kind to me so far.

If only she'd give me back my alpha.

The Shack

❧

Tzidal

THE WHITE CLOTH bled dark red like a spilled cask of wine. The violent color spread outward across the fabric, consuming each thread until it was as soiled as we were. Removing it from Byriel's hip, I dipped it back into the bowl of water, before returning it to his wound.

"Don't look so worried, omega," he said. It was clear he was trying to sound stronger than he felt. "I'll heal." He glanced at Joon. "We all will."

I eyed the bite on his hip. The puncture marks had burst open again, exposing red, puffy flesh beneath his dark skin. His dark eyes moved down to the angry mark, and he pressed his lips together, understanding my fear.

A full cycle of the Moon had come and gone since Byriel had received the nasty bite in the cursed lands, and it had yet to heal, repeatedly ripping back open.

He and Joon should both have healed by now. It made no sense.

It was a miracle the stab wound to Joon's chest missed his heart. I was relieved when it started to heal the first few days after Vaesen. But the second we crossed the flat lands and entered the mountains north of the city, both he and Byriel became worse. Their wounds constantly wept blood and burned their bodies up with an unyielding fever.

Joon lost consciousness not long after, and I was terrified that Byriel would soon follow. Lex and I couldn't carry one alpha, let alone two.

"Does it look infected again?" Byriel asked, too tired to angle his head down to properly see.

"No. Not yet," I whispered. The damn thing kept gathering puss and was a chore to clean out. "At least we can end the day with a bit of luck." I forced a smile.

Byriel nodded. He never smiled, but it didn't stop my instinctual need to try to tend to the alpha. My wolf hated the distress and pain of others.

My hand moved over the dark bruise along Byriel's breastbone, adjusting the charm so it was out of the way. It was already a fierce purple, edging closer to black and very puffy. Looking at all the scratches, cuts, and bruises along his arms and legs, I pushed out a heavy sigh.

"I'll be fine," he said again. Our eyes met, and he grimaced. It was as close to a smile as I'd get. "We'll all be fine."

"You already said that," Lex groaned just behind me.

"The truth is worth repeating." Byriel raised a dark brow.

Lex snorted and rolled his eyes, tucking his wounded arm closer to his chest. It wasn't bleeding anymore, and the black skin was now a bright, shiny silver, but the design on his robes had yet to reappear.

I dabbed at Byriel's hip, making sure it was clean. He flinched, and it took everything in me not to cry. I needed help. I wasn't a witch or a healer; Byriel needed someone with the wisdom and greenery to fix him. Both alphas did.

Groaning, I rubbed my eyes hard with the heels of my hands. "Carrying Joon keeps splitting this back open, and I won't be able to fight off infection much longer. I'm amazed it looks as good as it does." I eyed his tight, blotchy skin. "Moving is making both of you worse."

Leaning back, I pressed my hand to Joon's cheek.

He had woken briefly two days ago, long enough to eat a bite or two, then he passed out again. He hadn't moved since. I didn't want to admit the fear that was starting to settle in my gut. Our journey for revenge had fallen into survival, and it looked like none of us were going to make it out.

The cold wind cut through a sizable hole in the worn roof. The slats were cracked and splintered, and I prayed it wouldn't rain again. However, there were no clouds tonight—just the stars glittering in the velvety black sky. Another small blessing.

Byriel stared at the whole with me. "We can't stay here."

"I agree," Lex said. What was left of our dinner sat not far from him, and he glared at it as if it had offended his creator. "The food here is terrible. Let's find somewhere with a nice hot spring and a sizable menu."

I nodded in agreement. The hannoth's grey-tinged meat tasted tart and sharp, like chewing on dandelion root. It was not the raw, clean taste of a fresh kill. My stomach growled at the memory of a proper feast, and Lex scrunched up his nose at the sound, making me smile.

"I'm sorry I've been too weak to hunt," Byriel said, a twinge of frustration making his features sharp, but it disappeared just as quickly. He swallowed hard and his stoic expression returned.

"You know," Lex said with a teasing lilt to his voice. He leaned forward, still cradling his arm. "If you both would drop the ridiculous attitude about not eating Weres, I could bring you a wonderfully fat meal. I may not hunt feathers or fur, but I could feed both of you quite well if you'd open your minds."

I curled my lip in disgust at the idea of eating my kind and turned back to Byriel, not bothering to respond.

"It's not your fault you haven't been able to shift," I said, resting my hand on his shoulder. He was burning with a fever again. "I'm just thankful your wolf was able to help with those monsters."

I knew of the creatures that roamed these lands, but I still wasn't prepared for how hard it was.

My mind drifted to a few Casin Village wolves I had met once when I was a pup. They looked so fierce and terrifying, covered in thick scars and telling wild tales of the beasts that roamed their lands. Mountain wolves really were something to be feared.

"We should be close to Aberdeen. Three or four days at most," Byriel said, his eyes on Joon's pale face. "What do you hope to find there?"

"It seemed like a safer place to hide than a were-village," I lied.

In truth I wanted to find the witch that had foreseen the prophecy.

That damn prophecy was the beginning of all of this, and if I could just get my hands on it, I was hopeful it might tell me how to end it. But I didn't want Byriel to know. While he had been true to his word, and had saved me more times than I could count, I still didn't trust that he wouldn't hurt that last wolf. It was clear his allegiances were still firmly with his King. *His father.*

"That's a good idea," Byriel nodded. "And they might be able to help with our injuries." He paused as if thinking. "The witches that live within the city aren't always friendly to outsiders, but I know one that lives at the base of the mountains. She could help us."

Hope bloomed in my chest. "Can a witch fix this?" I placed a hand on Joon's chest. He was so hot and clammy.

"They don't normally heal our people, but they are powerful." Byriel glanced down at his hip. "I think it's worth trying."

I nodded, a thick lump in my throat making it hard to speak. My wolf whimpered as I brushed Joon's dark hair out of his face. He was so pale, and his lips were dry and cracked.

"Don't worry, puppy," Lex said, grabbing my other hand and squeezing gently. "Joon's still in there. He'll wake up when he's ready."

I nodded again, my chest tight with so many emotions. Wrapping my arms around my chest, I eyed my dirty clothes. The once vibrant green robes with thick gold embroidery were now a dull brown, covered in so much dirt and grime they were hardly recognizable as the fancy Vaesen garments they once were.

Byriel pressed a clean cloth to his hip and carefully buckled his belt, securing the dressing in place. "We'll rest tonight," he said, trying to hide his labored breathing. "Then we'll make our way to the witch first thing in the morning. It's a day's journey from here. Maybe two"

Scooting closer to Joon, I snuggled into his side. His skin was sticky with sweat.

"He'll make it," Byriel said to me as if stating a fact. "Your alpha is strong, and he'll be okay. Have faith in the Moon to bring us through." He looked at me as if he could see the future, and all my worries were silly.

I wanted so badly to believe him.

The Next Morning

Byriel

I HEAVED Joon over my shoulder, making skin at my hip pull and pinch. Then pain radiated down my side. I didn't need to see it to know my wound had reopened. I stifled a grunt, not wanting Tzidal to know.

A trickle of blood rolled down my leg, and I was thankful my black leather pants hid it. It would surely upset the omega, and I didn't need to add to her worry. The fact that my body refused to heal scared me more than I was willing to let on. My wolf had never failed to fix me before.

"You feel okay?" Tzidal asked, looking me up and down.

Her gaze settled on my hip, and she pressed her lips together. It felt as if she could see right through me to the truth. Perhaps it was just guilt for killing her mate or the knowledge that I'd never be able to truly atone for my sins, but it didn't matter. Guilt was guilt, no matter how it came to you.

"I'm well," I gritted out, forcing my feet forward. I was so damn tired. "We shouldn't have to journey far, assuming I have my bearings, but my sense of direction is never wrong."

The siren rolled his eyes. "Lead the way," he huffed, motioning me forward.

My wolf bared his teeth but was ultimately too drained to be challenged by Lex's cutting tone. I was thankful. It was hard enough fighting off the pain in my body. I didn't need my beast's pride adding to my distractions.

"Tell me, wolf," Lex said, his voice already hinting at a snarky comment, "is there an alpha in all of Havre that doesn't have a perfect sense of direction?" I cut him a sideways glance as he spoke. "In addition to bragging about your scars and cocks, your kind are weirdly proud of your internal compass."

"Tell me, siren," I grunted, too tired to put up with his shit, "if you can phase into a sabbot, why didn't you do that the second that hannoth found us? It would have been a hell of a lot more helpful than sitting in the mud the entire time."

His smirk fell.

Tzidal pressed her lips together, her eyes moving slowly between us. She had spent the first few weeks of our journey begging Lex not to bicker and for me to not rise to his taunts, but lately, she just let us quarrel. She was done pouring her energy into us, instead focusing all her attention on Joon. I didn't blame her.

"I can project into anything that has thought and complex feelings. Oh, and alphas," Lex added in a mocking tone, "which have neither." He gave me a pointed smirk. "But I don't actually possess their talents or strength. I'm still limited by my form. I can only change what you see, not what I am."

"So you aren't stronger or...." Tzidal shook her head, not understanding.

Neither did I.

Sirens were a mystery not meant to be understood. They were feral animals with no honor or use; predators with a lust

13

for sex and blood that no smart being should trust. I didn't understand Tzidal's pull toward the dangerous creature. She wasn't simple, but her relationship with the siren made me question her just the same.

"Oh, I'm still strong," he said, giving the omega a playful pout. "All sirens are. Of course, my strength is nothing compared to an alpha or some of Havre's larger creatures, but if a smart beast sees a powerful enemy and expects to lose a fight, he'll submit to save his own skin."

"So the only real power you have is your bluff?" Tzidal asked in awe. She grabbed his arm and squeezed him close. His wound from yesterday was completely gone, and I looked at his smooth, pale skin longingly.

"Doesn't it scare you?" Tzidal asked him. "What if someone doesn't believe your trick?"

"He doesn't use his tricks for combat," I said, stifling a grunt as I shifted Joon's weight on my back. "He uses his tricks to fuck and eat."

Lex let out a loud laugh. "That's true."

I didn't want to admit how thankful I was for the siren's powers. His sabbot-form made the hannoth pause at seeing a mightier beast, and it gave my wolf the opportunity to take the bastard down. But it still would have been nice if Lex had pulled out his trick sooner.

"If I can get a fantasy just right," he continued, speaking sweetly to Tzidal, "a wolf will slit his own throat to bury his cock inside me. Then all I need to do is plant a quick kiss," he poked Tzidal's nose, making her smile, "and they fall over, ready to submit their beating hearts to my belly."

"You're gross," Tzidal snorted, wrinkling her nose.

A slight snap of a twig cracked just to my left, and I turned my head in the direction of the noise. The pair in front of me kept talking, unaware of the movement not far from us. I had sensed a presence the last few days, but I didn't know yet how much of a threat they were. Right now, it wouldn't take much.

A pained grunt left Joon's lips, and Tzidal stopped speaking mid-sentence, racing to him. I kept walking as the omega fussed behind me, trying to talk to the weak alpha. She placed a hand on the back of my arm but didn't ask me to stop walking. I was grateful. Joon's weight was pressing hard on my body and pulling me down. If I stopped, I wasn't confident my feet would move again.

"Is he okay?" Lex asked, dropping behind me to speak with Tzidal.

"He's not awake," she whispered, her tone sad and muted.

The two whispered as the siren comforted her, neither expecting me to add to the conversation.

"It'll be okay, puppy," Lex whispered. "Byriel will get him help. Joon will be okay."

"You think the witch can save him?" Tzidal asked, stepping up next to me. Her eyes repeatedly flickered back to her mate draped over my shoulder. I could smell the threat of tears on her, but she held firm, not succumbing to her softer emotions.

"Yes. Haxa is very good," I said. "If anyone can fix him, it's her."

I knew Haxa well, even though it had been years since I had been in her part of the forest. She was kind to me, supplying the King with herbs and spells. She was an excellent green witch. And I hoped she was stiff fond enough of me to help.

"Wolf," Lex snipped. My body went tight at the sharpness of his tone. He was full of fire today, his biting remarks pricking my skin and provoking my wolf.

If only I had a bit of my strength...

"What's the plan once we find the witch?" he asked carefully, moving his dark, wet eyes over the side of my face. My wolf growled, sensing something unsaid in his tight expression.

"Once she heals us, we'll need to find somewhere safe until we're back on our feet. There are several caves within the mountains along here," I said, trying to ignore the pain radiating down my hip and legs. Every step felt as if I was walking through fire. It was a fitting punishment for my sins. "I'm confident we'll find something decent that will allow us to gather our strength before pressing on."

"And then what?" he asked in a clipped tone, his eyes narrowed.

My wolf snarled. Whatever the siren was implying had woken my beast. The bit of energy my anger gave me put my wolf in the mood to fight. And I was on the verge of letting him.

"We sleep and hunt." I provided the obvious answer to the siren's stupid question.

"Why are you still here?" he asked bluntly, looking me up and down.

"Lex," Tzidal hissed. "Stop it."

"It's an honest question, Tzi," Lex said, turning his challenging glare back to me. "What's the old saying about plotting wolves?" He clicked his tongue. "It's madness to speak of peace when a wolf is hungry in his den."

I stopped and lowered Joon to the ground, being careful with his head. I swayed as I stood back up, tipping my head to the sky.

Everything hurt.

It hurt deep, hard, and long. Pulsing, ripping and screaming through me. I wanted to rip into something. I wanted to make someone feel just as horrid as I did. It was a shameful thought.

"You don't trust me, and I get it." My voice was strained and low, but it was too important to show my strength at Lex's pointed challenge, so I clenched my fists and held firm. Tzidal took a careful step toward Joon, her legs shaking as if trying to fight off the urge to run. "But I don't want to fight you, or hurt you, or force you to abandon your cause. Your path is your own, just like mine." My chest heaved, exhaustion pulling hard within me, but my anger was building, giving me strength.

"What do you want?" Lex challenged, tilting his chin up and looking me hard in the eye. My eyes pulsed red, and I grew dizzy, even the smallest shift pushing my body too far.

For a brief moment, fear took hold. What if Haxa couldn't help? What if I collapsed before we got there?

"There's no such thing as a lone wolf," Lex said. "Loyalty is in your blood. All you pack creatures follow someone or something. The tethers of obeying your Moon work against you in that regard. So, who do you follow?"

"Right now, I'm following a path to the witch. Once he's better," I flung a hand out toward Joon, "I can leave you with a clear conscience and follow the Black River home."

Lex snorted and shook his head. "You really expect me to believe you're just going to skip off into the night? Leave us to do whatever we want?"

Tzidal's eyes pulled down, unable to look at me any longer. She didn't trust me either.

My blood boiled, and my head spun. After everything we'd been through and the sacrifices I had made, they still saw me as a wolf with no honor. It shouldn't matter, but it did.

After all, I destroyed their lives—I killed her and Joon's mates. I deserved their hatred. But I had hoped to leave them, knowing I had done something right in this world to fix the pain I had caused. However, it appeared I had accomplished nothing. The torment I created would follow me forever and prevent me from seeing the stars after my passing.

I was bound to the earth by their rage, peace forever outside my grasp. It was a fitting end.

My exhaustion quickly muted my wolf, and my arms were suddenly too heavy. I needed to sit down, but I was scared I would never get back up. "What can I do to make you believe me?" I asked.

Lex's jaw jutted out a bit, his mouth held in a tight line. Tzidal's eyes stayed fixed on her alpha.

"I helped you kill Hida," I said softly, unable to take their silence. "I attacked palace guards, my brothers, my pack. I lied and deceived for you. I have tried to set things right." Tzidal shook her head slightly but didn't look up. "I know I can't fix what I have done, what I took from you, but I have no intention of hurting anymore innocents." The air swirled with Tzidal's guilt and anger. Lex simply looked murderous.

Exhausted and raw, I snapped, "What else can I do?"

"You could kill yourself," Joon moaned at my feet.

Tzidal jumped about a foot into the air, flinging herself onto the grass next to him. "Joon!" she gasped. "You're awake!" Her hands trembled as they moved carefully over his face.

"I'm awake," he smiled weakly, his words strained and soft. He raised a hand, and it swayed unsteadily for a moment before bringing it to the omega's cheek. "Mine," he whispered, looking into her eyes.

I took a few steps back and turned my back to them. This was too private for an audience.

The siren kept his eyes firmly on the pair, his hands clasped under his chin. I swiped a hand at him, trying to get him to look away, but he only scoffed and turned his blissful expression back to the two wolves. I did not understand the three of them in the least.

"We're taking you to a witch," Tzidal said softly. "We should be there soon." There was a pause. "Right, Byriel? We're almost there?"

"Almost there," I said to the grass at my feet.

"Where," Joon sucked in a sharp breath, "are we?"

"North of Vaesen, west of Aberdeen," I answered.

"Far," he rasped out.

"Yes," Tzidal gave a breathy laugh. "We made it far. But we need to find you help. Your wound isn't healing as it should. Byriel is hurt too."

Joon grunted, and I turned to see him rolling slightly in an effort to sit up. Tzidal quickly placed a hand on his chest, careful not to touch his bandages, easing him back down.

"Don't move too much," Lex said, kneeling next to Tzidal and handing her the canister of water. She took it and immediately brought it to Joon's lips.

He drank deep, gulping as much as he could. Once he got his fill, Joon let his head fall back onto the grass and took several deep breaths. The simple movement drained him of his energy so quickly. The fact that he was awake was good for now, but it wasn't as promising as the omega had hoped. Joon was still very weak and needed help fast.

A twig snapped, and I jerked to the sound.

Listening carefully, I scented the air. There were no out-of-place aromas and no beat of hooves or scurry of wildlife that came with the sound, which meant it wasn't wild-game. My eyes fell to Lex's shiny skin along his arm, and I wondered if he'd be able to fight if I couldn't.

Outside of one small—albeit fierce—omega, we were defenseless.

My instincts tingled, and I reached for Joon. I heaved him over my shoulder again, every muscle in my body screaming out at once. The alpha mumbled a few protests but didn't attempt to fight me off, his body going limp the second I had him in place. He was soaked with sweat. We both were.

"Byriel!" Tzidal yelled, her voice high-pitched. "He was in the middle of saying something!"

"We need to move." I walked, my feet like lead. I marched past the furious omega, but she kept pace, trying to scold me.

The urge to smack her mouth for speaking to an alpha in such a way surged through me, but I beat it down. Instead, I concentrated on the pain throbbing through my body and the sound of delicate movement in the trees around us.

Whoever was tracking us was close.

We needed to get to the witch's hovel. And fast.

The Willow Tree

Tzidal

I KEPT PACE BEHIND BYRIEL, my eyes never leaving Joon. He passed out again, his arms swaying gently with each of Byriel's steps.

I clung to the fact that Joon had not just woken up, he had spoken as well. It was only for a few moments, but he spoke in full sentences with his eyes focused on mine. It was more than I had gotten out of him in weeks, and my heart was bursting with hope.

"Only a witch would live inside a fucking tree," Lex sighed, glaring straight ahead with his hands on his hips. "It's a little cliche if you ask me."

I stepped around Byriel to see what they were looking at.

An old, cracked willow tree sat just off in the distance. A few evergreens and massive oaks grew near it, as did some bushes and flowers that were a little too lush for the colder weather. A hazy puff of blue smoke drifted up from the center of a few mistflowers, painting the air a gentle shade before being carried off by the wind.

It all looked normal.

"Is she inside the tree?" I asked, still not seeing whatever told him it was a house. "How do you know?"

Lex smiled sweetly, then pulled me close to him. "Look through the mistflower smoke." He angled down so his head was level with mine, then moved my shoulders a bit, forcing me to look directly through the mist.

The blue haze twisted upward in the breeze, and the longer I looked through it, the clearer it became. The movement of the wind seemed to pull at the bark on the willow tree in the distance, somehow shifting it. The rough texture of the tree swirled, then drifted with the wind, displaying a perfect, little yellow door.

I straightened my back and looked at the tree. The yellow door stayed in place, greeting me brightly. "How?" I asked, my mouth open in awe.

"You have to know it's there to see it," Byriel groaned, adjusting Joon before walking forward.

"But I didn't know," I said, still not understanding. "So why do I see it?"

"The flowers told her secret," Lex smiled.

"That makes no sense."

He winked at me, then moved toward tree. Moments like these made me miss the simple world of my old life: werewolves, status, and a clear order of things. My life was so neat and simple then. But outside my village's borders, everything was confusing and painful—even getting an answer to a simple question was more work than it was worth. How the hell did flowers share secrets?

Byriel worked quickly to pull the enchanted charm off his neck, then he stuffed it into his pocket. I wanted to ask him why he had taken it off, but before I could speak, he knocked loudly on the little door with a fierce boom. The aggressive pounding of his fist made me jump. If I lived here, I would never open the door to such a hostile greeting.

"What do you want?" a woman's voice yelled from the other side. She sounded a little raspy and irritated.

"Help," Byriel barked.

"With?"

"Just open the fucking door, Haxa."

"Byriel?"

Slowly the door creaked open, revealing a tiny flit of a woman. She had friendly wrinkles around her eyes, frizzy blonde hair with streaks of grey framing her face, and she stood just barely taller than me. She smiled at Byriel, her whole presence warming at the sight of him. My worry that she'd send us away quickly faded.

"You look like shit, wolf," she snorted. Her eyes moved to each one of us, her smile growing. "And you brought a party."

"My friend is hurt." Byriel patted the back of Joon's leg. "Can you help?"

"Put him on the table," she said as if this was a common occurrence, stepping aside to allow us in. Byriel ducked his head under the doorframe and lumbered inside. "I've never had a siren in my home before." Her bright eyes moved over Lex. "Will you behave? Or do I need to prepare something to calm you?"

Lex leaned in with his usual flirty energy. "I'd promise to behave, but I try not to lie."

I groaned, ready to scold him, but before I could open my mouth, the witch tipped her head back and let out a hearty chuckle.

"Come on, you two." She motioned for us to enter. "Byriel never brings friends, and I'm far too intrigued to make you sit under the switches." She pointed to long, whip-like branches.

Lex hurried in after her, but I stayed frozen in the doorway, shocked at the sight before me.

Her home appeared to be a normal, average-sized dwelling. I took half a step back to make sure the outside of the tree was still just a tree. The trunk was very fat and broad, fitting the little door comfortably, but there was no way it could hold the cozy room before me. I knew it was a trick, but it hurt my head to think of how.

Too tired, I let it go, and stepped inside. Walking to the colorful kitchen in the back, I took in the cozy dwelling. The scent of cloves, mint, and soot warmed my chest as I moved through the cluttered living room, passing a wicker rocking chair and an old sewing table.

Joon's big body consumed the large wooden table, his feet dangling off the end. A few books and loose scrolls of parchment lay at his head. In fact, stacks of books and paper littered the floor, countertops, and chairs. They were everywhere.

Byriel grunted as he settled into a kitchen chair, stretching his long legs out. He looked to be on the verge of passing out. My nerves flared at what we might do if this witch couldn't help.

"You hurt too?" Haxa asked Byriel.

He nodded, undoing his belt to expose his blood-soaked bandage.

"Let's see," she huffed, moving to him.

He motioned to Joon. "My friend—"

"He's not going anywhere," she cut him off, giving a lazy wave of her hand.

Byriel stiffened at her interruption but didn't say anything. Nothing set an alpha off like an interrupted thought, and, for some reason, it made me like the witch even more.

Haxa pulled at the bandage stuck to Byriel's skin. He hissed as it slowly pulled free. "Did a wolf do this to you?" she asked, pressing at the edges of his puffy skin.

"No. Something wild got me," he gritted out, his chest rising and falling as she pressed harder.

She pulled her lips together in a pout, thinking. "And this one?" She moved to Joon.

"He was stabbed." I gently laid my hand next to the wound in the center of his chest. His usually tan skin was so pale, and he was shiny with sweat.

Haxa peered at his chest for a moment, then ripped the dressing off in one quick jerk, startling me. Some of the tree sap holding it in place stuck to his raw skin. I frowned at the witch, biting my tongue to keep from snapping at her; there was no need to be anything but gentle with my alpha. But I kept quiet, not wanting to be ungrateful.

She examined Joon's wound, leaning very close to his chest and running her nose along the torn skin. For a moment, I thought she might lick him.

Lex stared at the witch with such fascination, leaning forward a bit as she smell the cut. I relaxed a bit, seeing his soft but curious eyes move over her. If he wasn't on alert, I didn't need to be either.

"Both alphas were injured over a month back," Lex said, settling into a chair at Joon's head. He absentmindedly twirled his finger around a strand of Joon's hair. "All their other injuries have healed except these. I think they're doing it for attention."

I smacked the siren's arm, earning a pouty glare from him. Now wasn't the time for his sass.

"What is that?" Haxa whispered to herself. She cupped her hands over Joon's chest and peaked between a crack in her fingers. She stayed in that position so long, it made me jump when she suddenly spun and did the same thing to Byriel's hip. He closed his eyes and tipped his head back, exhausted.

"What creature got you two?" she asked.

"I told you." Byriel peaked his eyes open. "Mine was a creature, a snake of some kind. But his was a dagger. Nothing cursed or enchanted. Just a regular blade."

"No." She pulled out a cream-colored handkerchief, rubbing the end of her nose in a quick, forceful manner. "Before that. What got him?"

Byriel moved his eyes over the floorboards as if they might provide the answer he needed. "I don't know." He shook his head.

"A lizard in the cursed lands!" I yelled, suddenly remembering that awful night. Joon and Lex were unconscious and huddled under a tree while I did my best fighting for our lives. "Joon was scratched on his arm by a lizard-like creature, but it was only skin deep. It barely bled and only for a moment."

"Was your snake in the cursed lands as well?" she asked Byriel. "Or in the wildlands?"

"Cursed," I answered for him, remembering when we first found Byriel by the river. "You said you were bitten in the cursed lands. Right?"

Byriel nodded, and Haxa hummed. "Yup," she clicked her tongue, "that'll do it."

She crossed the room to a cluster of bookshelves on the other side of her living room. The heavy, wooden shelves were covered in a mess of little boxes of various sizes and glass jars filled with flowers, plants, and some that had tiny bones and stones.

"The wounds are simple to explain," Haxa said as she returned. She held a small, black tin in her hands. "Rain from the cursed lands entered your bodies when you were attacked, and the curse seeped in. It makes deep injuries—ones that are more than a scratch—almost impossible to heal. If you look at it without any light," she motioned to Joon's chest, "you can see the dark magic in the torn skin."

I leaned over Joon, cupping my hands. Faint traces of

green, shimmering dust lit up the edges of his cut. It would have been hard to see even on the darkest night.

"Is this permanent?" Byriel asked, eyeing the ugly mark on his hip. The muscles in his jaw ticked as he waited for her to answer. I understood his fear. An alpha that couldn't heal, couldn't fight. And an alpha that couldn't fight wasn't an alpha at all.

"It's not permanent," Haxa said confidently. "I can fix you, but I want answers."

"Answers? Answers to what?"

Haxa eyed Byriel for a moment before twisting her hips in an almost playful manner. "I think you need some tea."

A low, deep growl pushed from Byriel's chest. "You cannot be serious."

"I am," she said, tipping her chin up. "You can be as huffy as you want, but I need to know the answers you give me are truthful. I need to protect my people just like you."

"I've never lied to you before." Byriel leaned forward, his eyes almost wounded. "Why would I start now?"

"Byriel," her voice slipped into a careful, soft tone. "The trail of bodies in your wake is too strong, and spilling that kind of blood changes someone in ways that can be shocking."

Byriel's eyes widened with shock. "How do you know?"

"We know many things." She placed a hand on her chest. "Witches see more than we want."

She set the black tin on the table, not even a foot from me. I stared at it, wanting to snatch it up and dump the contents onto Joon's chest before she could change her mind.

The clink of teacups pulled me from my thoughts, and I forced my eyes away from the tin.

The steaming brown liquid Haxa poured had a sweet aroma and tickled my nose with notes of peppermint and something spicy. Byriel gave her a pointed look as she handed over a cup. He pushed out a heavy sigh, then downed it in one go. I stared at the alpha, waiting for him to scream or die or turn into a toad. But nothing happened.

"What's it do?" I asked Haxa.

"It makes the very idea of telling the truth so wonderfully tempting, your toes curl, and your spine sings," she said with a melodic lift.

"Really?" Lex gasped, a mischievous glint in his eyes. "Can I get a cup as well?"

Haxa looked down at the kettle still in her hand. "But... it's got a spell," she said, confusion twisting her brow.

"That's okay." Lex smiled brilliantly, holding out his hands to accept a cup.

She gave a quick shrug and grabbed another teacup. This one was bright yellow and had a distinctive crack down the side. I half expected tea to seep through the jagged line.

Lex took a long sip and hummed. "Lovely!" He placed his hand over his heart. "It's simply been too long since I had a good herbal tea."

Haxa scrunched her nose up before turning to me with the biggest smile. "He's so cute!"

"He's adorable," I said with a quick smile before my eyes pulled back to the tin. I couldn't help it.

Haxa followed my gaze and nodded. "Go ahead."

My hands jerked, hovering just at the container. "Are you sure?" I asked. My desire not to be rude was stupid, but I couldn't help it. She was being so kind, and the omega in me demanded it.

"Of course." She nudged it toward me with her fingertips.

I whispered a quick *thank you* before snatching it up and turning my attention to Joon.

My fingers trembled as I worked the tight lid off to reveal a smooth, slippery substance that shimmered at me. It smelled milky and wet. I dipped my fingers in it, then looked at Joon's face. His eyes were sunken with dark circles, and his breath was labored.

This had to work. I needed it to work.

Saying a quick prayer to the Moon, I scooped up a decent glob and immediately set to work, pushing it deep into his wound as gently as possible. The muscles along Joon's neck and jaw strained, but he didn't wake. The oily cream mixed with a fresh swirl of blood, then bubbled around the edges. I stared at his face, willing him to open his eyes, but nothing happened.

Fear slipped down my spine.

I didn't have the strength to survive the loss of another wolf I loved so dearly.

If this didn't work, I'd curl up and die with him.

The Witch's Kitchen

Byriel

Tzidal stared at her alpha, her lips pressing tighter and tighter with each passing second.

"Give it a few, sweetie. It works quickly, but he's fairly sick. He just needs a moment." Haxa squeezed her shoulder. I didn't miss the way Tzidal leaned into her touch. Even with Lex's affections, I was sure the omega was desperate for contact. Omega's always were when distressed. And while Tzidal's scent hadn't spiraled completely, her usual sugary perfume was hanging a little thick lately.

Tzidal let out a soft sigh, then pulled herself away from Joon. She scooped up a sizable glob of the witch's potion and pushed it into my hip. The salve immediately set to work, making the tight skin ease and the pain cool. For the first time in weeks, I could breathe.

"Now, Byriel," Haxa turned her glassy eyes to me. I always thought they looked like crystal balls, the kind seerers used in shady markets to rob simpletons of their gold. "I know what your father tasked you with," she gave me a pained, half-hearted smile, "but I don't know why he's now harassing my people. What's going on?"

"I failed," I blurted out.

My wolf jerked within me, disgusted that I would admit to anything the King had commanded me to do. My missions were something I was forbidden to share with others. The only reason Tzidal and Joon knew was because they were there when I ended their mates' lives.

A soft tingling sensation warmed my belly, spreading outward into my chest and arms. Haxa was a powerful, green witch. A kind of sorcery most handwaved as a weak bit of magic, but I doubted there was a creature in all of Havre she couldn't convince to do her bidding.

Pulling a deep breath, I was resolved that I had no control over this situation. My wolf warred within me, urging me to fight and flee. I dug my claws into my thighs, trying to stay in control. The scent of wolfsbane hidden somewhere in Haxa's little home burned the inside of my nose, but the charm in my pocket made the weed useless. If I slipped it on, I could shift, and my wolf knew it. But I took it off for a reason. Shifting in Haxa's home would be inexcusably rude.

"You failed what?" Haxa sat in the rickety chair next to me, placing her hand on my knee. I hadn't realized my leg was shaking up and down, making the glass jars clink throughout the house.

"Finding the marked wolves," I said. "I failed my King."

I needed to shut up, but the sleepy, soft feeling pouring over me made my lips loose. I would share whatever anyone wanted to hear, then bathe in the joy of the crystal, clean relief it was sure to provide.

Haxa leaned in, asking softly, "How many are left?"

"One." Tzidal and I said in unison.

"There's only one," Tzidal whispered. She smoothed her hand over Joon's stomach, then turned to Haxa. "You couldn't help us find them? Could you?"

"No." Haxa jerked at her words, her expression tight with anger and disgust.

"She doesn't want to hurt them," I said, squeezing Haxa's hand. "Omega Tzidal means to help them. To keep them safe from me and the King and his guards."

"Oh," the witch let out a soft breath of understanding. "Sorry. I didn't think gentle wolves like yourself were capable of hurting others, but you never know."

"She hates being seen as weak," I said, pointing to Tzidal's tight smile. "Even though her kind are weak, she's very strong. At least in spirit." I nodded, knowing my assessment was true. "She's a very determined omega." Tzidal's cheeks went pink, staring at me as if not sure what to say.

After a moment of silence, Haxa spoke up, "I'm afraid I still can't help. I'm a green witch. I don't do visions."

"But you read the prophecy for the King, right?" I asked.

Tzidal's eyes went wide, and she hurried around the table. Her energy doubled by the time she made it to Haxa. She clutched the witch's hand tight. "You did? Do you still know it? What's it say?"

A wash of understanding moved across Haxa's face, and she turned to me. "Is he looking for the children of the blushing Moon in Aberdeen?"

"He's probably looking for them everywhere," I said, the words flowing from my consciousness like a bubbly, clear spring. "But I don't believe the King would send a full battalion to march through a city, especially a non-wolf settlement. The King has always been careful in searching for wolves across Havre. He doesn't like to upset the packs. When the packs are in unrest, the alphas go a bit wildling, and the next thing you know, there's war all across the lands. It happened not that long ago, during the elvish-era. It was why they were the dominant creatures in Havre for so long. They—"

"My stars," Lex blurted out. "I don't think I've heard Byriel talk so much the entire time we've been with the alpha."

Tzidal nodded, her mouth open and her brow lifted in disbelief. "That's some powerful tea."

"Hey, By'," Lex leaned in with a mischievous glint in his eye. "Do you think Tzidal is a tasty little wolf?"

"Lex!" Tzidal snapped. "How would you like it if I started asking you a bunch of questions?"

"Ask away, puppy." He winked. "But unfortunately for you, I'm not bound to this witch's magic. I'm a siren. My very essence is built on death and deception. These spells can't sway me, but the tea was still lovely. Now Byriel," he turned to me with a shocking amount of energy, "Tzidal. Is she desirable?"

"Yes," I said with a nod. "Although, she'd be more desirable if she were obedient." I turned to the omega. "You have far too much lip for someone of your status. I don't understand how an alpha hasn't killed you yet."

Tzidal crossed her arms with an angry huff, and Lex burst out laughing.

"He's right," Joon mumbled.

Tzidal jerked, then rushed to her alpha. She cupped his cheeks, staring at him as if he were a ghost. "You're awake!" Joon groaned, then moved to sit up. "No!" Tzidal tried easing him back down, pressing on his shoulders.

"Actually, it'll be good for him to move," Haxa said. "Get the blood pumping."

I leaned forward, then twisted slightly, feeling not an ounce of pain. "Thank you, Haxa," I said with a breath of relief. "I knew you'd be able to help. Green witches really are superior."

The older woman beamed, pinching my chin between her thumb and forefinger. "You were always my favorite amongst the wolves."

"I hate to be rude," I said, feeling my face warm at her praise, "but I was wondering if you remembered any bit of that prophecy. It might help my friends."

"Actually," she smiled wide, standing up. "I can do you one better. I still have it."

On The Table

Joon

THE TINY WOMAN disappeared behind a row of shelves.

My muscles ached as I pulled myself into a sitting position, but I still felt better than I had in a very long time. Tzidal repeatedly whispered the word 'easy' as if I might shatter at any moment. The second I was upright, Tzidal moved between my legs, pressing her nose into the crook of my neck. It felt so good to have her safe and pressed against me.

Moving her lips to my ear, she whispered, "I thought you were going to die. You said I was yours, and you were mine, then you...." Her words grew thick, and a shuddering breath lifted her sweet lips.

"I'm sorry, my omega," I whispered, holding her tight. "I'm not going anywhere."

Tzidal caressed the skin around my quickly healing wound as if to wipe the curse from my body. It felt good to have her hands on me.

Lex gave me a playful wink, and I couldn't help but smile. Byriel, on the other hand, kept his head down, pretending he couldn't hear us.

"Byriel!" Lex said with far too much energy, making Tzidal flinch. "Since this lovely tea is keeping you honest and chatty, I think I might have a few questions."

Looking around the cluttered space, filled with plants, jars, and a library's worth of books, I could only assume we were in the home of a healer, but more likely a witch. It was common for the magical humans to poison visitors, and it made me smirk to know Byriel had been forced to drink a spell.

"I don't suppose you'd offer me mercy?" Byriel asked in a gruff voice, making Lex snort.

"Mercy is for the divine and the boring. I am neither." Lex crossed one leg over the other, eyeing Byriel with a devilish smirk. "Now," he paused, letting his impending question hang in the air. The muscles in Byriel's jaw twitched as he waited for Lex to continue. "Do you plan on killing us?"

"No," he said without a moment's hesitation. "Of course not. Why would I do so much to help you just to kill you?"

Lex raised a brow. "Fair point. Do you plan to kill that last wolf you've worked so hard to find?"

"No," he said much softer this time, then his eyes widened as if he hadn't realized it himself.

"Do you still want to save the King?" Tzidal whispered, still pressed to my chest, her hands resting on either side of my goopy wound.

"I do." Byriel looked deep into my omega's eyes. It wasn't an angry or challenging look—just one filled with honesty. "I'm sorry if that upsets you. I have no intention of killing innocents, and I know what that might mean for my father's reign, but I will find another way to save him." He inhaled deeply, squaring his shoulders. "It's my duty."

"You've got to be fucking kidding me," I snapped, unable to help it.

"Joon," Tzidal squeezed my bicep, "the King is still his father. Byriel has kept his word. He helped us find Hida, and he helped us navigate the mountains. Let him deal with his kin. We'll deal with the last wolf."

Shock stole my ability to speak, and I nodded, not wanting to upset her. I couldn't deny that I owed Byriel a great debt—a fact that left a bitter taste in my mouth—but his allegiance to a murderous King wasn't something I could just ignore.

Tzidal tipped her head back, looking me over. There was so much fear and relief in her beautiful, golden eyes. I hated that I hadn't been able to watch over her and protect her these last few weeks, lost to a fever and the horrible visions in my mind.

"Here!" the small woman returned, handing a slip of weathered paper to Byriel. He immediately gave it to Tzidal. It was stiff and faded, and the lettering bled as if it had sat in a puddle for several days.

"I read it for the King well over a year ago," Haxa said. "I don't do prophecies. I'm a green witch. But when Mother Nature fills you with vision, you must share it, or it will tear you apart." Her voice dropped, sadness pulling her brows together. "I'm just sorry for my part in this."

Lex clapped his hands, ignoring her somber words. "Read it," he squealed.

Tzidal cleared her throat and read it slowly.

Marked children of the blushing moon,
their end to start it all
The dawn of a new era,
sparks the reason for the fall
Trust the blue path paved in grief,
to free the fractured King

I was enraged. And I could tell from the look on my omega's face that she was too.

The words on this paper had condemned so many to death; they had changed my life, Tzidal's life, and so many others. I wanted them to be a bold proclamation of the end of times, something so horrible that only the death of the marked wolves could save Havre. I wanted it to spell out Fennah's name, explicitly condemning my mate to death.

But this was just a jumble of words that didn't mean anything.

"It doesn't even rhyme." Lex grimaced, glaring at the paper in Tzidal's hand.

"I have to admit," Byriel said. "It's...disappointing."

"That's a fucking understatement," I snapped.

Tzidal smacked my pec, hitting a bit too close to my cut. I grunted, then smiled at her scowl. Unable to hold onto her anger, she smiled at me. *Fuck*, her smile was gorgeous.

"Haxa, my friend," Byriel bowed his head, "what do I owe you for your kindness?"

"Tell me what you're going to do?" There was a lot of sympathy in the older woman's eyes. "I want nothing from you. I just want to know," she squeezed her fingers, "how will you stop your father from this madness?"

"There's nothing I can do." Byriel stood like a soldier, tall and straight. The top of his head brushed the beams along the ceiling. "While I am not convinced guards are storming the cities on the King's orders, I am eager to get home and find out what is happening. My father is careful in his plans, and waging war on his own people makes no sense."

Haxa gave him a pained groan, closing the space between them. She was so tiny, tipping her head back to look the alpha in the eye. "I can feel it, Byriel. I may be a green witch. Prophecies and such are beyond me, but change is thick in the air these days. It's cold and cutting, and it will take a powerful wolf to fix this."

Something like sadness cut through Byriel's eyes, and he leaned down to the woman, whispering, "I have no power here." Swallowing hard, he stood back up, his eyes not quite meeting hers.

Feeling stronger, I stretched, eager to leave. My skin tingled, and soft energy flowed from my chest. Even though I was still a little unsteady, I felt really fucking good all of a sudden.

The wound on my chest was no longer puffy and had stopped bleeding. I could also feel my fever was gone. At this rate, I would be completely healed by sunset, if not sooner; nothing but a scar left to warn other wolves what I was capable of surviving.

"We should go," I said, wrapping an arm around Tzidal's waist and pulling her to my side. Even in sleep, I had missed her, and my wolf demanded I keep her as close as possible.

Byriel paused in the doorway, turning back to the witch. "How long until the tea wears off?"

"Not long. Hour at most." She pointed to a small yellow door. "I hope to see you soon, Byriel." There was clearly a lot she left unsaid, but the alpha simply bowed low to her, then left.

Lex quickly followed, pausing to take Haxa's hand. "It was so lovely to meet you, Haxa. I look forward to our paths crossing again. I just adore the hospitality of witches."

"Of course," she patted his cheek. "Be careful out there, siren. There are many that would love to make a trophy of your head."

"There always are," he smiled brightly before flitting out the door.

WE WALKED IN UTTER SILENCE, not speaking about the prophecy or what was to come next. We simply looked for somewhere decent to make camp. Honestly, I didn't care what came next as long as I was with my omega.

As evening fell into night, Byriel decided to let his wolf run and hunt. His injury looked good. Only twin scars and a fading bruise remained. My wolf was happy my wound would leave a much more impressive mark. Suffering came with bragging rights, and scars were the best way to prove your battles.

Tzidal prepared a small circle of rocks for a fire pit. With autumn settling in, the grass around us was dry. She pulled at the tufts, setting the clumps in the center of the rocks. She was insistent on boiling water to clean our wounds. There was no need, but I was happy to do whatever her heart desired.

"Are you going to shift too?" Tzidal asked.

"I'm not shifting today," I said, pulling her away from her task and into my arms. "I want to be with you." My wolf was restless and begged me to let him run, but the thought of leaving my omega was unacceptable. I had no intention of letting her go until I absolutely had to.

Tzidal moved to straddle my lap, snuggling into my arms. Her long, dark hair moved softly in the breeze, and her eyes...those perfect, golden eyes...they looked at me with so much love. It was a look that gave me life and purpose and a raging hard-on. Fuck, I missed her.

"Please don't ever scare me like that again," she whispered, her fingertips brushing down the side of my face.

"Promise." I ran my nose over her old mating bite and the edge of her jaw. Inhaling deeply, I moved to her perfect, pink lips, ghosting mine over them. "I promise, my omega. Never again."

Gripping her hips, I pulled her to me as I claimed her mouth, moving slowly at first. She let out a delicate, little gasp against my tongue, and I growled long and deep.

Pulling her tighter to my body, I kissed the breath out of her, tasting every surface of her sweet mouth. I wanted to pour every emotion that pulsed within me into her soft body, fill her up with my lust and love, and consume her from the inside out.

Tzidal rolled her hips into my rock-hard cock, and I let out a deep rumble. I was alive with an electric energy that could power all of Vaesen, and I wanted to use all of it to pull more soft moans from her throat.

"Alpha," she whispered, her eyes hooded with a lust that made my fangs tingle. I grabbed her ass and squeezed, moving her small body against my straining cock. "We shouldn't," she moaned, tilting her head back to expose the perfect column of her throat. "You're not well."

"I am very well," I growled, pushing the vibrations from my chest into her soft body. She shivered, and my wolf leaned in possessively.

"You're not fucking out here," Lex yelled as he walked up to the camp.

Tzidal hurried off my lap, and my body flashed with rage at the loss of her warmth. My wolf snarled, desperate for either my omega on my cock, or Lex's blood on my hands.

"We're not doing anything," she mumbled, bunching up the front of her shirt in her fists. It was unnecessary as not a single button had been undone, but she still held the fabric firmly in place. "We were just—"

"Fucking each other's mouths?" Lex gave her a pointed look, dropping a small bundle of sticks onto the mess of rocks.

The soft movement of leaves in the distance caught my attention, and I glanced at the siren. He gave me a knowing look.

We were being followed and had been since leaving the witch's house. I wasn't sure at first. Whoever it was, was very good at masking their scent, but the sounds were unmistakable. This wasn't wildlife.

"I found a stream so we can bathe," Byriel said, appearing just around a cluster of trees.

He was naked—except for the enchanted charm hanging from his neck—and his hair was wet. His chest moved rapidly as he carried a sizable mountain cat over his shoulder. I envied him. My pent-up energy had no outlet with my omega now keeping her distance. I eyed her soft curves, wanting to snatch her up and carry her somewhere secluded to fuck her hard.

Feeling my eyes on her, Tzidal glanced at me, then my wound, smoothing her hand over my healed flesh. It was very bruised, a puffy scar already forming.

"Did you see whoever's on our trail?" I asked Byriel, trying to distract myself.

Tzidal's head snapped at my words, and she suddenly looked frightened and a bit overwhelmed. I tucked her into my side, letting my scent soothe her.

"No," he said, pulling on his pants. "Their scent is very slight. It's not an alpha, that much I know."

"How long have they been on us?"

"A few days, but I'm not entirely sure." Byriel shook his head. "They're quiet and careful. Whoever they are."

"We're being followed?" Tzidal asked with an angry lift to her voice as she eyed all three of us. "Did you all know? Why didn't anyone tell me?"

"We're the threat. Not them," Byriel said, sitting down and working to arrange the fire pit.

"You don't know that," she snapped, pulling away from me. I circled my hand around her slender arm and pulled her back to me. She didn't fight.

"If they wanted to hurt us," I said, wrapping her long hair around my fist, "they would have attacked while I was unconscious. They might be traveling in the same direction as us by coincidence, or they're hoping to steal supplies. Either way, it's not someone looking for a fight. They're being too careful."

"Or maybe they're tracking us to lead the King's guards to us." She narrowed her eyes.

"Or that, too," I sighed, not wanting to admit how likely it could be.

"I highly doubt it's the King's guards," Byriel said, pulling the flint from the satchel.

"How can you say that?" Tzidal jerked away from me, making my wolf snarl. She tried to hide her temper, but her clenched fists gave her away. "The King wants you dead, in case you forgot."

"No," he said in a harsh whisper. I didn't care for the look in his eyes directed at my omega, and I flashed my teeth. "I already told you. Hida didn't act on the King's orders. Those were either my sister's words or an outright lie. I'm sure of it."

"What does the prophecy mean?" I asked, not interested in hearing his delusions of how honorable his father was.

Lines settled between his brows. "I don't know."

His words almost knocked me over. "You don't know?" My voice rose. "How the fuck do you not know? Didn't the King explain it before sending you to kill your people?"

Byriel's chin jutted forward, squaring his shoulders. "My King gave me my orders, and, as a member of his guard, I did what I was told."

"That lunatic told you to kill innocents, and you just skipped off on your merry way without a single question?"

Tzidal shook her head, her anger softer than mine but just as clear. "How can you blindly follow a wolf that would ask something so horrible of you? Is the King's grip on you that unyielding?"

Byriel stood, curling his fists hard around the flint. His

angry gaze moved over Tzidal's slight form, and I stood, ready to attack if necessary. With obvious force, Byriel turned his glare to me. "One day, an alpha is going to kill her for her lip. You aren't doing her any favors by letting her act like this."

Tzidal shivered at his threat but held firm, keeping her head up.

I lowered my voice, forcing myself to be as calm as possible to keep from upsetting her further. "If you even think of laying a single finger on her, I will present your head as a gift to your beloved sister. Do you understand me?" My fangs lengthened, and my wolf paced, ready for a fucking fight.

"I think Byriel's right." Lex's cheerful tone cut through the tension. He walked up to Tzidal and wrapped his arms around her shoulders, completely unaffected by the rage that hung in the air. "Obviously, his sister has some guards on her side, but the wolves at Vaesen weren't aware of any orders from the King."

Byriel gave Lex a curt nod, obviously thankful to have someone on his side. Then he looked Tzidal hard in the eye before dropping the flint on the ground. "The King would never kill me. He believes in the sanctity of royal blood."

"Royal blood," Lex snorted. "As if your flesh would taste any sweeter than a maid's."

Byriel's expression was pinched as he narrowed his eyes at Lex. "For someone that lives and hunts in wolf-territory, you seem very comfortable mocking our ways. I don't care for it."

"I'm comfortable saying whatever the hell I want, sunshine." Lex tipped his chin up, giving the alpha a piercing glare. "But I'm done talking about this today. It's boring, and I'm hungry."

Lex stepped past me, stopping just next to Byriel. "If you have a problem with my attitude, you know where to find me. You may think you're at the top of the food chain, but when the sun sets, the real monsters of Havre come out to play, and I would love to see if your royal blood soaks into the dirt any slower."

Byriel lowered his chin to look down at the smirking siren. "I look forward to both of us bleeding for our cause."

The Cave

Tzidal

"This is a good one," I yelled over my shoulder as I entered the small cave.

This part of the mountains had many caves for us to take shelter. Some were too small or already occupied by other wildlife, but we didn't have to look too far to find a decent place to sleep for the night.

Byriel stepped inside and dropped the satchel. He kicked at a few old, burnt logs in the center of a poorly made fire pit. "I think we should go without a fire tonight, but I leave it up to you," the alpha said. "I plan to keep vigil outside the cave. I want to see if our shadow shows their face."

"Be careful. We just got you and Joon back to good health, and I don't want to throw that away with a sleepy fall from a tree." I settled on the soft dirt. There were very few pebbles or stones, and I was confident it would be a fairly comfortable night's sleep. "If you see Lex, will you tell him where we're camping? I'm sure he'll be out all night, but I don't want him to worry."

Byriel rolled his eyes, making me smile. It was a rather animated reaction for the usually stoic wolf. "I'm sure the siren will be fine. He's at the top of the food chain after all."

Before Vaesen, Byriel had seemed almost relaxed, but since the battle with Hida, he had pulled into himself. I couldn't blame him. Hida said so many horrible things about the King hating Bryiel. It would have broken my heart, too, to think my father wanted me dead.

Bryriel turned toward the cave's entrance, but I yelled out, stopping him. "About what we said at the witch's house." Guilt twisted in my gut. "I know this can't be easy for you. And I'm sorry for not trusting you before. I just—"

"Please don't apologize, omega." He lowered his head, bringing himself to my level. His green eyes were rather striking, even in the dim light. "I understand your mistrust. I deserve it. Please know, I would never hold it against you for being honest."

"I just want to say that while I know our paths are going in different directions, I appreciate your help so far. I feel that." I swallowed hard, gathering all the mercy in my bones, "you've fulfilled your debt to me. I forgive you for your part in killing my mate. My Korban."

Byriel stared at me. His dark eyes went a little glassy, but there was no other indication he had heard me. Finally, he cleared his throat. "Thank you," he whispered, his voice gruff. "That means...very much to me."

His mouth curved slightly, almost resembling a smile. It made him appear younger and kind. While he was always polite—sometimes to the point of annoyance—he never came across as especially friendly. Or perhaps he had just been too exhausted for the emotion. I understand that. I was sure I hadn't been very friendly either.

"You have been nothing but courteous with me even though you have no reason," he said. "That is not something I will soon forget."

He gave a quick nod, then disappeared into the forest, not giving me a chance to respond. The gentle movement of leaves and the groan of a few branches drifted toward me. Then it went quiet.

"I think this will help," Joon said as he entered the cave.

He carried something wrapped tightly in a black shirt. I glanced at the garment, deciding it was probably time to switch out my dirty, green robes for one of the uniforms we had swiped from Vaesen.

Moving cautiously, Joon dumped a bright crystal into the center of the fire pit. A chunk of luminite gave off a soft yellow glow. It was warm and cozy, and so tempting to touch. I reached out, but Joon pulled my hand back quickly.

"It's *very* hot," he said, placing the shirt in my hand so I could feel the heat that had soaked into the fabric. I hugged it to my chest, soaking up the heat.

Joon settled beside me. His scent was smokey and sweet as it wrapped completely around me in the small space. It was bliss. Rustling through the satchel, he pulled something out, then took my hand. "I want you to wear this."

Looking down, my heart squeezed. The pendant Joon had once given to his mate, Fennah, sat in the center of my palm.

"Joon," I whispered, "this is so personal. I can't—"

"You can," he said, taking the necklace from me and clasping it around my neck. "I got this for my first mate. She wore it every day as a symbol of my love. I thought my heart died with her, but then the Moon brought you to me. And while I will love Fennah forever, just like you will love

48

Korban," he touched the blue pearl tied around my wrist, "I want to look at this pendant and think of the beautiful wolves I have been lucky enough to love in my life."

I swallowed hard, not wanting to cry but unable to help the tears that burned the back of my eyes. "Thank you," I whispered, touching the pendant.

He kissed my lips softly before looking around the cave. "Where is everyone?"

"It's just us tonight," I said, looking forward to snuggling my sweet alpha without Lex's sassy commentary or Byriel's stuffy presence.

"Thank the Moon." Joon let out a gravelly moan, pushing me gently onto my back. "I want to bury myself between your legs and drown in your slick," he growled into my neck.

I pushed at his shoulders, making him lean up a bit. "You are still healing," I said firmly. His eyes flashed red before filling with soft rejection that pulled at my heart. But not enough to make me cave. "Joon, I'm serious. I need you better."

He let out a defeated sigh but didn't roll off me. "Can I scent you at least?" He moved his big hands through my hair, trailing his thumb over the shell of my ear. "I need something of you coursing through my veins, and if I can't have your passion, let me have your comfort."

It was such a romantic thing to say, but I knew the alpha too well. "I feel like you practiced that." I arched a brow.

"I did." His perfect dimple teased me, begging me to touch it. *How I missed his smile.*

"You are horrible. You know that?"

"Admit it," he growled, deep and sexy, "you love me."

"I will admit only to tolerating you," I teased.

"I'll take it."

He shifted onto his forearms, and I instinctively wrapped my ankles around his hips, loving his weight on top of me. It was a dangerous position, and my resolve might not last, but I had missed him too much.

I tipped my head back, giving him ample access to my neck, and closed my eyes in anticipation. Slowly, he nuzzled gently over my throat and inhaled deeply, making my tummy flutter.

He hummed, the vibrations from his chest pushing into me. "You smell so good." His deep baritone danced across my skin, and my wolf purred.

Joon mouthed just beneath my ear, licking and sucking gently. He stopped every few moments to inhale, a rolling growl leaving his chest each time. He moved over my body slowly, his strong arms holding him just above me as he kissed from one side of my neck to the other, nipping at my earlobe.

Slick gathered between my thighs, and my body hummed as he sucked especially hard just beneath my ear. The rich earthy scent that rolled off my alpha made me feel as if I were floating.

"You taste so fucking sweet," he whispered. Everything about his touch made me feel light, flirty, and a little stupid.

Pulling at his shoulders, I brought him closer, his chest flush against mine. Joon wrapped an arm around my waist, then lifted me slightly off the ground. His hard length pressed tight against my wet center, and my head swirled with his scent and touch.

I really did want to hold firm. To force him to rest and sleep. But I needed Joon right now more than anything else in Havre. I wanted to feel and taste and love him.

I needed to feel alive.

I let out a breathy gasp, and Joon lifted my body off the ground, plunging into my neck with sloppy, open-mouthed kisses and long, slow licks. His hips pressed so firmly against mine I could feel every inch of his thick, hard cock.

I needed him inside me.

Channeling his fingers through my hair, he licked my old mating bite, causing me to moan and thrust up. I was lost in a pleasure I didn't know was possible while fully clothed. Joon leaned up and scented the air. His eyes dilated, and his breath hitched at the smell of my arousal.

I wanted to blush at the intense look in his eyes, to be his sweet, innocent omega, desperate for him to ruin me, but I was too turned on. I wanted him to fuck me like the animal he was, and I wanted him to know I craved it.

A deep growl pushed from his chest, then he leaned forward ever so slowly, ghosting his lips over mine. "Let me have you," he whispered, but it wasn't a request. It was a command. "Give me what's mine."

I nodded, hating him for proving just how weak I was, but loving every second at the same time.

His lips crashed against my mouth, his firm chest pressed against me as his tongue moved and twisted with mine. I gave up all control, letting my alpha dominate me with his powerful kiss. Joon sucked at my bottom lip and tongue, drinking down every moan and gasp I gave him.

Pinning my wrists above my head with one hand, he slowly began unfastening my robes with the other. He pushed the fabric away, revealing my breasts. Looking down at my exposed flesh, he hummed before ducking his head to my nipples.

He mouthed a pert bud, sucking and flicking his tongue over me. My core twisted, and I pushed my hips up in a desperate hunt for friction.

"Someone's needy." His voice was smooth and deep. The sound alone made my nipples harden even more.

"Don't tease me," I gasped as he sucked my nipple especially hard, letting it snap out of his mouth with a soft pop. "Give me what's mine." My voice was a throaty purr, and I loved the red that pulsed within his brown irises as I spoke.

"Am I yours?" Joon whispered against the peak of my breast, palming the other one in his big hand. "Is my little omega staking her claim?" He flicked his tongue over a nipple, then blew cool air onto my skin.

I let out a quick snarl and pushed him, rolling us. He moved easily, letting me control him. "You are *mine*, Seonjoon. And if you ever forget it, I'll rip your throat out." I bared my teeth and pinned his hands over his head. He let me pretend I could dominate him, and I loved it.

Joon thrust his hips up against me, a smile teasing his lips. "You gonna put me in my place, little beast?"

I dragged my nails down his shoulders, moving over his pecs and along the soft grooves of his abs. "Yes," I whispered, rolling my hips over his thick shaft.

I hated that we were both wearing pants, but something about it was a little thrilling. The soft barrier of fabric between his steely member and my wet center made my clit swell.

I let my robes fall off my shoulders, then squeezed my breasts for him, making my nipples pucker out—the pendant nestled snugly between my soft mounds. Joon's eyes fell to my hands, and he grabbed my hips, helping me grind over his bulge while I palmed and squeezed my breasts.

"Pull your nipples," he commanded, alpha slipping into his words.

I pinched them softly and pulled them out, letting my breasts jiggle as they bounced back.

"Again." His dark eyes pulsed red.

I did as I was told and circled my hips over his cock, making my clit throb. A breathy pant left my lips, and I was suddenly on my back. Joon's massive body hovered over me, trapping me in place. He ripped my pants off in one quick motion, then cupped my sensitive core.

Pushing his palm over my clit, he moved in slow, deliberate circles. He looked deep into my eyes as he rubbed my sex in the most unimaginable way. Then slowly, he pushed two thick fingers into me, and I closed my eyes.

"Open," he ordered, his wolf inching forward.

I obeyed, looking deep into his eyes, unable to defy him even if I wanted to. But I wanted his dominance. I wanted him to own me, fill me, fuck me, take me. Force me to do whatever the hell he wanted.

I was his to control.

Joon thrust his fingers deep inside me, filling the cave with a wet, squelching sound, followed by my breathy moans. All too soon, my pussy tightened, tipping me over that blissful edge.

"That's it," he growled, curling his fingers wildly inside me. "Show me how hard this pussy can come."

My orgasm ripped through me, flashing across my skin and up my spine. I pushed my hips into his hand, not stopping until every swimming pulse of pleasure within me stopped.

Once my body calmed, I dropped my knees, letting my legs fall open. Joon brought his hand up, looking at my slick coating his fingers. I expected him to suck them, but instead, he brought his hand to my mouth and wiped my fluids all over my lips and chin.

He let out a deep growl, then leaned into me, licking the slick off my face. "Do you like the way you taste?" he asked, kissing the tip of my tongue.

"I like the way I taste on your lips," I whispered, breathy and desperate.

Joon thrust his tongue into my mouth and rolled his hips forward, filling me completely. His cock was so hard, and the stretch burned for a moment before bliss took over. He slammed his hips repeatedly, fucking me wild. His feral thrusts pushed me quickly to the edge of another climax, and my body spun out of control, falling apart around him. His eyes flashed red, and he bared his pointed teeth.

Without thinking, I gripped him by the hair and shoved his face into the crook of my neck. Then I demanded, "Mark me."

Then I closed my eyes as he sunk his teeth deep into my flesh, right over Korban's mark.

The Cave Floor

❧

Joon

MY FANGS PUSHED into Tzidal's soft throat, and my mouth flooded with the sharp tang of blood, followed quickly by the sugared taste of her honey scent. My knot immediately expanded, and I thrust forward, lodging inside her sweet cunt as I came.

My cock pulsed in time to my omega's fluttering heartbeat pressed against my tongue. I was floating in a sea of honey and slick and sex and love.

It was so fucking hard to breathe, and I thought I might pass out for a moment.

Taking a few steady breaths, I sucked hard at Tzidal's throat, causing more of her sugared scent to push into me. The soft taste of cedar followed, then faded, and I finally removed my fangs. I immediately lapped, sucked, and kissed, trying to soothe the torn flesh. My body still thrummed as I worked, holding my mate close.

Tzidal placed her trembling hands on my shoulders. I could already feel the love and happiness within her surge through our mating bond, mixed with fear and sadness. I understood her torment. The last of her mate—the small bit of his essence that lived inside her—was washed out and replaced by my own. All of him was truly gone for her now, and only her memories of him would remain.

There were many moments since my mate died when I wished betas and omegas could mark their alphas in a similar way so that I could have kept Fennah with me. But now, I was thankful they couldn't. My beautiful Fennah had been gone from me for a very long time, and having her bond in my blood would have been more than I could have survived.

For Tzidal, the last piece of her mate just died. His cedar scent—an aroma that was always weak on her, mostly washed out by her vibrant sugar flavor—was gone.

I looked over my mark, making sure it was no longer bleeding. Once satisfied it was clean, I moved my hands, tilting Tzidal's face to better see her. Tears clung to her eyelashes, and her lips trembled.

"Are you okay?" I whispered, trying to push my calm through our slowly forming bond. My mind expanded into hers. A tingle in the back of my mind spread, filling every inch of me with my omega's being. It was a connection I hadn't felt in so long, and my wolf settled, bonding deeply with our new, perfect mate.

She nodded weakly. "I'm really happy." She forced a smile as tears spilled over, dripping down the sides of her sweet face.

"I know," I whispered, rubbing her temples with my thumbs and pressing my forehead to hers. She was happy, but she was grieving too. And it broke my heart for her. "I'm really happy, too."

Tzidal wrapped her arms around my neck and held me tight. Her body gently shook as she cried, pressing her nose into my cheek. "I'm sorry," she mumbled. "I didn't think it would be this hard."

"Hey," I leaned up, looking into her golden eyes. "Don't apologize, my omega. It's okay if it's hard. I'm right here with you. You aren't alone. Okay?"

She nodded, then gave me a brilliant smile, happiness edging out a bit of her sorrow. "You mated me." She let out a breathy laugh through her tears.

"I did." I returned her smile, loving how her eyes sparkled even while glazed with tears. "You're stuck with me now."

She let out a musical giggle, and I pressed my nose into her hair. "I think I was stuck with you no matter what," she sighed, holding me tight.

"HOW DID you get cum in my hair?" Tzidal groaned. Trying to brush out the dried mess with her fingers. She grimaced as they became stuck in a particularly wet tangle.

"I don't know, but I like it." I smiled at the sight of her. She was covered in deep love bites, soft bruises from my fingertips, and her knees were still bright red from the best morning I could ever remember.

"I think I just need to wash properly in the stream," she sighed, abandoning her hair and grabbing my black shirt. "I'm sure Lex will have lots to say when he sees what you've done to me. Probably Byriel too."

"I don't want that alpha to see you bathe," I snapped. My voice was instantly possessive and sharp, but I didn't give a shit. This was my omega, and no one was allowed to see what was mine.

"Oh, I do love a newly mated alpha," Tzidal teased, gently pinching my lips with her fingertips. She pulled the oversized shirt on, not bothering to button it, and grabbed her pants, tucking them beneath her arm.

"I'm serious, omega." I followed her out of the cave toward the stream on the other side of the ridge. "I might not have had a right to command you before, but you're my mate now. And I forbid it."

She released the front of her shirt, letting it fall open so I could see her breasts and soft cunt hidden behind dark curls. "Do you forbid it?" she asked in a breathy whisper, her eyes teasing me with defiance.

My cock jutted out, thick and ready. "Tzidal," I growled in warning. "Do I need to remind you of your place?"

"Are you going to punish me, Alpha?" A coy smile pulled at her lips as she moved to slip the shirt off.

I grabbed the fabric and pulled it back over her shoulders. "I mean it, omega. I will fuck you into submission if I have to."

Our mating bond danced with her arousal, and her eyes fell half-hooded.

The soft sound of movement near the cave drifted toward me, and I turned to it. Disappointment flitted across Tzidal's face.

"I'm sure it's Lex," I said. "Come. You can wash later. I'll find somewhere more secluded."

She hesitated, not moving.

"I just need a drink," she said, stepping into the water. A chill worked through her as she crouched down. She cupped her hands and dipped them beneath the surface. "Joon," she smiled at me as if I were being ridiculous. "Go. I'll be fine."

I glanced back at the camp behind me, then at my mate again. She sat happily, stretching her legs out, the water moving slowly over her pale thighs. The bruised love bites along the sensitive inner thighs made my teeth tingle.

Leaves rustled, and I groaned. "I mean it." I pointed a

finger at her. "You are not to bathe here. Anyone could see you."

She nodded, waving me away.

I didn't trust her to obey, but I needed to let Lex know where we were. As a predator, he had a decent sense of smell, but it wasn't as good as an alpha. More than once, he had wandered off in a huff when he couldn't find us. It was better to find him before he got too worked up.

And I was also eager to know if he came across our shadow in his hunt.

Walking through our campsite, I kicked some dirt over the remnants of an old fire. Our flint rocks sat carefully next to it. That had to be Lex's doing. The siren was shit at remembering to pack up our supplies after using them.

Lex stepped out of the cave, his new appearance startling me. He wore the face of a young male omega with very dark blue-ish, black hair that hit his shoulders, and his skin was so white it had an almost blue hue.

The sun hit his face throwing off an odd sheen, and I shook my head at how ethereal he looked. I couldn't understand how a siren could trick anyone. They never quite looked right. Always just a little too perfect to be real.

The blue-haired Lex pulled the satchel's strap over his head, settling it flat against his chest. He looked up at me and then froze, his dark eyes locked on my face.

"How was your hunt?" I asked, picking up the flint.

Lex nodded, his body stiff and fists tightening around the strap just over his heart.

I held out the flint, waiting for him to take them. "We're probably another day or so from Aberdeen, but the land will level out between here and there, so hunting will be easier. More hooved creatures, less predatory ones."

I continued holding the flint, but the siren didn't move to

take them. He didn't even look at my hand, his wide eyes still firmly on my face. It was as if he was in a trance.

"Lex?" I said a little louder than I intended.

"What?"

I spun to the sound of the siren's voice. He stepped over the ridge behind me, hand in hand with Tzidal, her hair wet and body shaking slightly from the chill in the air.

I cut my eyes back to the blue-haired boy. He let out a frightened whimper.

Then he ran.

The Forest

❦

Byriel

JOON'S VOICE boomed through the forest before the unmistakable sound of a chase hit my ears. The wind shifted, and the softest scent hit my nose. It was impossible to place, but it wasn't anyone from our group. It had to be whoever had been trailing us these last few days.

I took off, running as fast as I could toward the sound of crunching leaves and snapping twigs. My wolf edged forward, prepared to shift if our shadow appeared to be an equal in a fight. Otherwise, my fists would be more than enough to pull their purpose from their lips.

Jumping over a wide-set break in the rough terrain, I landed softly, then darted toward the base of the hillside. Joon appeared in the distance chasing someone small and fast. The creature raced quickly, his movements seemingly graceful but too panicked to avoid the branches that kept smacking him every time he looked over his shoulder at the enraged alpha on his heels.

I angled my body and made a line straight for the young man. I was within arm's reach of him when he turned just in time for his frightened eyes to see me crash right into his middle, tackling him to the ground. He fell beneath me with a thump and let out a soft whimper.

My wolf panicked, the sound too familiar to be ignored.

I rolled him onto his back, and his face scrunched with pain. Leaning into his hair, I inhaled the air around him. He smelled soft and clean, not as strong as others of his status, but it was still very clear. He was an omega. But he had incredibly white skin and dark blue hair. Almost black.

What was he?

His lips trembled, and tears dripped out of the corners of his eyes as he held his ribs. I leaned away from him. My wolf was enraged that I would treat a delicate creature in such a needlessly violent way.

"Are you alright?" I whispered, ghosting my hands over his slender arms. My need to soothe him was overwhelming, but I had no idea what to do. I was never great at offering comfort.

He gave a quick nod, his big eyes fixed in the distance, too scared to look at me. I stared at him, unable to help myself. His nose was long and straight, and his lips bowed upward in a slight pout. But his eyes were what made it so damn hard to look away. They were blue and green and everything in between, the colors swirling ever so slowly together. They were the most hypnotizing eyes I had ever seen.

"I apologize," I said, trying like hell to figure out how to calm the fragile creature. Leaning down, I scented him properly, trying to find any injuries from my rough handling. My lungs flooded with his fresh scent, and my mouth watered.

A deep growl pushed from my chest, and I settled more of my weight on him, loving the feel of his warmth pinned beneath me. He whimpered, displaying the long column of his neck. He was so submissive and pliant to my dominance without me even having to say a word. My cock grew hard, and my wolf edged closer.

"Byriel!" Tzidal yelled as she hurried down the hillside, wet hair flying wildly behind her.

The urge to snatch the male omega up and run pulsed hard within me, but I kept myself in place, fighting against every instinct.

I raised my hand to wave Tzidal over, then curled into myself as a swift blow hit me right in the balls. The omega shimmied out from beneath me, racing off while I grunted and heaved onto the forest floor. Sharp pain shot from my groin and settled deep in my gut, blurring my vision.

Looking up, I tried like hell to focus on the fleeing omega. Joon caught up to him and wrapped his arms firmly around the creature, bringing him to a stop.

Lex walked quickly down the hill, his eyes fixed on me, laughing long and hard. "Are you," he spoke between loud burst of laughter, "are you okay?" I glared at him as he continued to cackle at my expense.

Tzidal knelt next to me, placing a careful hand on my shoulder. "Are you seriously injured or just your pride?" she smiled sweetly.

I pushed myself off the forest floor, then zeroed in on the little shit struggling in Joon's arms.

"Our shadow?" I asked, my voice strained. Swallowing hard, I tried to force away the dull ache in my balls and the pulse of nausea in my throat. My wolf whimpered and curled into himself, too wounded to help me walk it off.

"I think so," Joon grunted, heaving the flailing boy toward us. "Stop!" he ordered, pushing his alpha deep into the demand, and the omega went limp.

My wolf inched forward at the display, and an urge to rip

him from Joon's arms surged within me. I crossed my arms to hold myself back.

"Woah," Lex said, eyeing the boy's slack body. "Why doesn't that happen to you?" he asked Tzidal.

"Young omegas struggle to defy alphas. It takes a lot of practice," she said, moving to Joon's side and helping him situate the boy on the ground. "And even then, some omegas never master the ability."

The omega eyed Tzidal as she ran a hand through his hair and down his arm. He seemed to relax at the gesture, and she leaned in, her voice soft and motherly. "How old are you, pup?"

"I'm of age," he whispered, wide eyes darting widely between me, Joon, and Lex. The need to comfort and scent him burned my flesh from the inside out. "I'm twenty," he said to Tzidal. "Just this last spring."

"Well, that's old enough to push back a bit on an alpha's orders when in danger," she smiled sweetly. "Are you really of age?"

The omega eyed Joon and me carefully before leaning into Tzidal's hair and whispering. Her mouth fell open as he spoke, and her eyes widened. When he finished speaking, he stayed pressed to her side, continuing to move his hypnotizing eyes between the three of us.

"What's your name?" she asked.

He whispered again.

Tzidal smiled and ran a hand through his dark, silky hair, tucking it behind his ear. "This is Blue," she said, "and he has never met an alpha before."

The Hillside

Tzidal

BLUE'S CHIN quivered as he pushed his slight body into my side. I hummed softly, trying to calm his wolf. The thick stench of angry alpha was enough to put the most seasoned omega on edge, and Blue, with his lack of exposure to the aggressive wolves, was struggling to breathe properly.

The youngling was tall for an Omega, an inch or two bigger than Lex and just as slender. His scent was also the softest I had ever pulled from someone of our status.

Omegas tended to have strong, perfumed scents, meant to entice mates and make us easier to track should we get lost or kidnapped. It was a gift from the Moon to keep us safe, even if it put us in danger outside our villages. But Blue's wolf smelled so slight and clean. It was unusual and lovely.

Running my fingers over the omega's arm, I looked over his stunning features. His heart-shaped face and soft cheeks made him look very young, and his coloring was unique.

While Lex's pale complexion held a shimmering quality, Blue's white skin was velvety and gave off a subtle, light blue sheen—almost as if it were a trick of the light. His deep blue-ish black hair was stark in comparison to his complexion, and I ran my fingers through it, noticing a thick streak of purple that curled slightly next to one ear.

"Where did you come from?" Joon asked the omega. He was still pushing his dominance into every word, which was unnecessary. It made the poor boy shake and stammer as he was forced to answer.

"My, my village," he said softly. Blue's wide eyes shot to me, and I noticed the beautiful colors gently swirl within them. He looked like a living spell—something the witches sat down in the middle of the forest, meant to live among flowers and fairies.

"There's no village out here," Joon barked. Hearing his tone, I gave my mate a stern look. He let out a sharp groan, then cleared his throat. "Is your village close?" he asked in a forcefully kind manner.

"Yes, but..." Blue's eyes darted between the two alphas.

"But what, sweetie?" I asked, smoothing the fabric of his shoulder down his arms. His clothes were clean and well made and while thin, he was clearly well-fed. This boy was no rogue. He had a proper home, and I wanted to make sure he got back to it safely.

Blue leaned into my ear and whispered. "I can't tell you. We have no alphas there, and the elders would be very cross if I brought them inside the borders."

"What about Lex?" I motioned to the siren. "Can he know?"

Lex stepped forward and knelt next to us. I could feel a spell pushing off him, making my chest feel soft and fuzzy. Blue leaned into Lex's magic and smiled. He sat up with big, curious eyes, his fear forgotten.

Scooting closer, Blue reached for Lex's fluffy, white hair. "You're so pretty," the omega whispered, running the tips of his fingers down the side of Lex's cheek.

"Thank you, little one," Lex beamed.

"What the hell is wrong with omegas?" Byriel said to no one in particular. "Can they not feel the threat within sirens?"

"I'm not a threat to them," Lex said softly, smiling wider as Blue ran his hands over the sleeves of his robes. "Sirens are tasked with cutting out evil from this world. Not good. And omegas are very good. They're nurturing."

Joon snorted and shook his head.

"Are you saying alphas are evil?" Byriel raised his brow.

"Just you," Joon shot, giving him a pointed look.

Tipping his head back, Byriel turned his big body toward Joon, and I instantly jumped up before either one of them could start bickering. I grabbed my mate's hand and pulled him away from everyone.

The second I was sure no one could hear us, I turned to my mate. "We can't just leave him here."

"Agreed," Joon said, keeping an eye on Byriel. Thankfully the other alpha was busy watching Lex and Blue giggle. Lex's spells were like no other and could calm a rogue in a temple fire.

"I want to make sure he makes it home," I said, "and that his parents know he got out of their village."

"There's no village here, Tzidal," Joon said with an edge in his tone.

"Fine. I want to get him home. Wherever that is." I crossed my arms. His pride was clearly still wounded at the omega's ability to almost escape him. Blue's speed was both startling and impressive. Had Byriel not shown up when he did, we would have lost the omega within the trees.

I shook my head, still stunned the youngling was out here.

"I can't leave knowing he's just wandering around the forest all by himself. I won't sleep until he's home."

Joon nodded.

"If he doesn't want you and Byriel to know where he lives, Lex and I—"

"No," he snapped, giving me a stern, commanding glare. I swallowed thickly to keep from baring my neck in submission. "I will not let my mate wander through the forest without me to an unknown location. Do not ask again. It will not be happening."

My wolf shivered, and I instinctively reached for his hand, needing to ease his temper. "Why are you so mad?"

He took a step toward me, his expression hard. He held a strand of my still wet hair between his fingers. "I told you not to bathe in that stream." His voice was a deep, dominating growl. It both frightened and aroused me, making me tremble and slick at the same time.

"What do you think?" Byriel asked, suddenly at my side. His deep voice startled me, and I jerked, hating how silent and quick alphas were.

"We're going to take him home," I whispered. Lex and Blue were busy talking softly amongst themselves, but I still didn't want the frightened omega to overhear. He was already so upset.

"I can escort him home," Byriel said. "I'm headed back to Ossory, and he glanced in that direction when he spoke of his village. Even if it's a little out of my way, I don't mind."

"No," Joon shot. I could feel something cautious push through our bond. Byriel had him on edge—or more on edge than he already was. "Tzidal wants to see him home. We'll take him."

"I really don't mind," Byriel said, giving an agreeable shake of his head.

Joon angled his shoulders forward, his expression as tight as his fists.

The unusually sharp look in Byriel's eyes made me take a step back. A not-so-subtle challenge passed between the two alphas, making the hair on the back of my neck stand up.

Byriel glanced back at Blue, and rage burst from Joon's chest, making my eyes water.

I took a step back, not interested in putting myself between the two alphas. I hated it when they worked each other up. "What's wrong?" I asked Joon.

"Tell her," my mate demanded, keeping his red eyes on the dark wolf.

Byriel shook his head in confusion. "Tell her what?" He pushed his hands into his pockets. He was trying very hard to look relaxed, and it didn't suit him. I had spent several months with the alpha, and he always looked tense. This was odd.

"He's blue," Joon said as if that explained everything.

"Okay?" I didn't understand. Then the prophecy's words hit me like a rolling boulder, and I pulled the parchment out of my pocket, re-reading it.

'Trust the blue path...'

"Do you think he's the blue path?" I asked Joon, my eyes wide as I tried to think what this might mean.

"He's a blue Omega," Joon said. "He has blue skin, his name is Blue, and he lives in a village no one knows about. Which means it probably hasn't been searched by the palace guard." He turned to Byriel. "Do you think he's the key to freeing your King?"

"I don't know, and I don't care," Byriel growled, his anger quickly growing. "What I do know is he's unmated and outside his village. I can't leave an innocent wandering around the forest. It's far too dangerous."

I shoved the parchment back into my pocket, unsure what

to do. I didn't think Byriel would hurt Blue, but there was something in the alpha's eye that made my wolf tense.

"There's no fucking way I'm letting you touch him," Joon growled, jabbing a finger at the dark alpha.

Byriel balled up his fists, his eyes glowing red. "What are you implying?"

"That you're a piece of shit intent on saving your precious King. You've murdered so many. What's one more to a monster like you?" Joon mocked.

Byriel tilted his head up, his jaw tight. "Your omega has repeatedly promised to kill our King, and I have done nothing but protect her when you couldn't." A slow growl pushed from Joon's chest. "While I doubt a single, small omega could manage to kill a King. If I was truly looking to murder innocents, she wouldn't be standing next to you."

I heard Joon's fist connect with Byriel's face before my mind registered what had happened. The alphas launched at each other, a blur of teeth, claws, and growls.

Sick of them, I turned away, not interested in watching the two wolves prove who was the mightier beast.

Blue's terrified eyes were fixed on the fighting alphas behind me as he burrowed hard into Lex's arms. The siren shook his head and blew out a frustrated sigh.

"Hopefully, this will calm them down," I said, kneeling on the other side of Blue and eyeing the satchel slung over his shoulder. "Would it be okay if I took my bag back?"

He nodded, shamefaced, and pulled the strap over his head. "Sorry," he mumbled, his eyes flickering between me and the fight in the distance. "I shouldn't have taken it."

"That's okay." I smiled, placing it in my lap. "Does your village have more wolves like you?"

I wanted to distract him from the display of dominance that was sure to distress the omega. I didn't know what kind of effect they might have on him, and I was thankful he hadn't slipped into his heat simply from their presence. Omegas always struggled when reincorporated into the pack after presenting. They had to be slowly exposed to a foreign alpha's scent. I could only assume Blue was a mix of some other creature that may be muted his omega instincts in that way. It would explain his odd coloring.

"No," he whispered, twisting his fingers together. "Well, not exactly like me, but there are other wolves." He turned to Lex. "I'm sorry, but I don't think the elders would be happy with me inviting an unknown siren within the borders either."

A vicious roar echoed through the trees behind me. Blue flinched. Then his eyes went wide, and his mouth slightly ajar as he sat up to get a better view.

"They shifted," he whispered in awe.

I glanced at the werewolves—one shaggy and brown, the other sleek and grey. They snarled, bit, and grappled—a tangle of two powerful beasts slamming into each other repeatedly. I narrowed my eyes, noticing how neither was going for the other's throat. They were simply brawling, and it infuriated me to no end.

"How about we make our way to your village while those two are distracted?" Lex asked Blue.

He nervously shook his head, pressing his lips together. "No," he whispered. "They already don't like me. They'll kill me if I bring in dangerous outsiders."

"How about just you and me?" I asked. "Surely, they wouldn't be upset with another omega visiting."

Blue's hypnotizing eyes moved slowly over my face before finally nodding. "I'm sorry," he mumbled to Lex.

"That's okay, sweetie." Lex smiled, releasing Blue's arm.

Slowly, with his attention repeatedly pulling back to the fight in the distance, Blue stood and grabbed my wrist to follow. He walked slowly, looking back a few times at the alphas and Lex.

Lex gave me a slight nod, and I returned the gesture in understanding; he'd follow us but keep his distance. I wasn't simple enough to wander into an unknown pack's den without some kind of protection.

The second we hopped down the side of a ridge, Blue's whole demeanor lightened. He smiled sweetly as the fighting faded into the background, his shoulders relaxed and breathing even.

"Alphas are really scary," he said with a nervous laugh. "I've heard lots of stories, but I never imagined them to be so true. And I've never seen one up close before. They're...big." His eyes widened as he described them.

"That's why it's important not to leave home," I scolded, feeling a little motherly. "I'm sure your parents will be very happy to have you back."

He shook his head. "I don't have parents."

"Oh." My chest tightened for him, and I grabbed his hand. "Grandparents?"

He shook his head again.

"Who takes care of you?"

He pressed his lips together, his eyes pulling down a bit at the corners. "No one." He forced a smile. "It's just me, but I'm used to it. It's okay."

I gave him a soft look, trying to hide my disbelief. Abandoned pups would never be left to fend for themselves in a proper village. If he belonged to a pack, he had a guardian.

"You really have no one?" His gaze dropped at my questioning. "Who feeds you? Clothes you? Where do you sleep?"

He nervously twisted his fingers together, struggling to meet my eyes. "I'm of age. I don't need anyone," he said almost defensively.

"Blue." I shot him a look, letting him know that he hadn't answered my question and wouldn't be getting off that easy.

"I have a room at the temple, across from the priest."

"So the priest takes care of you?"

"I guess," he mumbled. "But no one really cares if I come or go." He shrugged.

I kept my mouth shut, not wanting to argue with something that couldn't possibly be true. Omegas were highly coveted, and to let an unclaimed one wander about so freely was dangerous to everyone. Rogues would lose their mind around his scent, and possibly attack his village if they followed him home.

A chilly breeze filled the air, and the scent of a foreign flower tickled my nose. It was thickly sweet but still lovely. As we walked further, small, yellow buds with feathery petals came into view. The flowers hid deep within the tall stalks of dry grass all around us. They were so out of season. So vibrant and lush surrounded my dying grass. I had to fight the urge to lean down and smell them.

Turning to Blue, I opened my mouth to ask him what kind of flowers they were but stopped at the odd look on his face. He moved his eyes all around, acting as if we were being watched. Then he came to a complete stop, his body stiff and skin shimmering with an iridescent light.

"We can't go any further," he whispered.

"Why?"

He slowly moved his hypnotic gaze to a thick jut of trees in the distance. He eyed it like a beast might burst from it, ready to feast on our bones.

"Because if we do," he whispered, a shiver working through his shoulders, "I'll accidentally let them in."

The Fight

Joon

I LAUNCHED myself at Byriel's wolf, snarling and snapping at his grey pelt and legs. His jaws locked onto my scruff, and he bit down, puncturing my skin. I whipped around and shoved my back claws into his gut, flinging him away.

Snorting hard, I circled him. Byriel's wolf-form stayed still, watching my paws and the angle of my shoulders carefully. His skill and size matched mine meaning it wasn't possible to wound the alpha without killing him. Which was fine by me. But Tzidal was sure to have a few things to say if I gutted the fucker on the forest floor.

Byriel let out a sharp growl and shifted back into his human-form. I immediately followed.

"Are you relenting?" he asked, his tone almost bored.

"Fuck you!"

"You seemed done," he said calmly, stepping sideways to

track around me. "Or was staring me down your plan of attack?"

"If you think I'm that easy to best, you've got another thing coming," I snarled. "You'll have to kill me first. But I shouldn't mock you for that since we both know you'll fucking do it, then blame your perfect fucking father for making you so evil."

"I told you," his voice deepened, and the muscles in his neck strained, "I'm done killing. How the fuck can I make you understand that?"

"Forgive me," I rolled my shoulders, the bite on my back pinched as I moved, "I just find it hard to believe a wolf's lust for blood can dry up so easily."

"I never had bloodlust!" he yelled, his smug face finally showing some real emotion. "I did as I was commanded. I am a guard for his majesty and serve him well. I did my duty to protect my King."

Then he let out a deep rumbling breath. All emotion seemed to drain from him, but his lips were turned down just enough to display his rage. He told a decent bluff unless you knew the fucker.

"Were you never a guard?" he asked.

"You fucking know all alphas do their time in the guard," I said, crossing my arms. "I patroled my village like any other alpha."

"Were you so bold as to refuse your Pack Alpha's orders?"

Whatever point he was trying to make, it held no water with me.

"My Pack Alpha never ordered me to kill my brothers," I seethed. "You've killed too many to be trusted," I said, hoping he'd challenge me again.

Byriel shook out his fists, then rubbed the back of his neck hard. "It's time we go our separate ways," he said.

"I think that's a good idea."

Byriel moved to leave, then hesitated. "If you would be so kind, please give Omega Tzidal my thanks. She has a tender heart, and her caring has healed me in more ways than one."

His soft words about my mate knocked the anger out of me in one cold blow. I blinked a few times, not sure what to say.

My wolf was proud of Byriel's praise of our mate, and that fact made me jerk back. Byriel was my enemy, not my pack. His opinion didn't matter, but it pleased my beast that someone of such high standing would think so well of our omega.

"Byriel, I am..." I swallowed hard, trying to keep my pride intact. "I am aware that I am indebted to you." It hurt to say it aloud, but it was true.

Byriel cocked his head, confusion twisting between his brows.

"You kept Tzidal safe when I couldn't. I'm not blind to that." Holding my head high, I took a deep breath and steadied myself. "And since I'm not a complete asshole like you, I can admit when I need to show...when I need to say..." I cleared my throat roughly, then forced the words out. "Thank you."

He couldn't hide the shock in his eyes but quickly dropped his gaze, looking over the forest floor. He seemed to struggle to find his words. Finally, he looked up, meeting my eyes. "I—"He stopped talking, his gaze shifting just past my shoulder. "Siren?"

I turned to see Lex racing toward us. His eyes were wide, and his white hair bounced as he ran as fast as he could. Lex never ran unless he had to, and I immediately scanned the area for Tzidal. She and the youngling were gone.

"Lost them!" Lex yelled, breathing hard. "I..." he stumbled, smacking his hands on the hard ground. "I lost them!"

"Which way did they go?" Byriel demanded, stepping up next to me.

"Where!" I yelled, unable to stop the growl that burst from my chest.

"I was following them," he sucked in a deep breath, pulling himself to his feet, "I followed them toward Blue's village. Then I saw—"

I grabbed Lex's slight shoulders, pulling his feet clear off the ground. My voice distorted by my beast, I roared at the siren, "Where is my omega?"

My head spun, and I dropped Lex, trying to steady myself. My bond with Tzidal twisted and burned, her fear so strong it made it hard to breathe.

"You let them leave?" Byriel asked Lex as I tried to regain control. My wolf was in full distress, my insides shredding with my mate's fear.

"There's no *letting* Tzidal do anything," Lex snapped. "She decided to take him home while you two were acting like fucking animals!"

"Where?" Byriel snapped.

Lex turned and pointed to a ridge in the distance. I focused all my energy on the trees in the distance. A flock of starlings burst from the trees just as a battle horn split the air.

The Hidden Village Border

Tzidal

"WHO ARE you scared you'll let in?" I whispered to Blue, narrowing my eyes at the cluster of trees. It held his attention, his breath slow and hands trembling.

The hair on my arms raised as leaves shook and branches snapped. Leaves shook, then parted. A thunder of palace guards burst forth, marching straight toward us.

I grabbed Blue's arm and jerked him hard onto the forest floor. The tall grass hid us from the mass of alphas, but we couldn't stay here. I only prayed they hadn't already seen us.

Blue shivered hard, his scent flooding with terror. I needed to move downwind before the guards caught his sharp aroma. Balling up my fists, I forced my wolf to focus. Then I moved. Grabbing Blue by his collar, I dragged him toward a fat spruce, careful to keep our heads beneath the grass. I pressed Blue's body against the tree, his frail form swaying a bit. Once I was sure he wouldn't fall over, I peeked around the trunk.

The alphas moved in formation as if tracking prey. Several were in their wolf-form, and a few betas near the back held bows at the ready, their arrows itching to let loose. The danger around us made my whole body flash hot with fear, and I closed my eyes, hoping Joon would sense me quickly.

"What are they doing here?" Blue asked, tears glistening in his wide eyes.

I shook my head. I didn't know this area well enough to know if it was common to see patrols.

Blue pressed his lips together, his chin shaking hard as he sniffled. I cupped his cheeks and gave him an urgent look. "No sound," I whispered so softly I was scared he didn't hear me.

He nodded, then bit his bottom lip hard, squeezing his eyes shut tight.

Moving slowly, I peeked around the tree again. The guards stood awkwardly next to a dense cluster of yellow flowers. They strolled along the edge of the tall grass, scenting the air around them. A massive she-alpha with a thick, red braid leaned down and plucked one of the flowers. The feathery-looking petals released from the bud and caught in the wind, drifting away.

The fierce alpha nodded at her men. "We're close."

"I need to warn them," Blue whispered, tears dripping off his face.

"Who?" I asked, grabbing his arm as he jerked, trying to run. I squeezed his upper arms and shoved him back, keeping him in place.

"My p-pack," he whispered.

"Are we close?" I mouthed, so scared the alphas would hear us.

Blue moved his lips just next to my ear, "The entrance is just there. I have to warn them." He leaned back, pure desperation and fear consuming his soft features.

"Wait." I moved my hands down his arms, hoping to

soothe his fear. "Joon will—"

Blue bolted.

Without thinking, I raced after him. My short legs pumped hard, but he flew toward the alphas as if he had wings. He ran right past the guards, several yelling after the swift omega and a few giving chase. I managed to dodge the swipe of an alpha's clawed hand, then pumped my legs as hard as possible. Blue stumbled a bit, and I managed to snag the smallest section of his shirt between my thumb and finger.

The air crackled with thin, broken lines of light. My cheeks itched, and my ears tickled as we moved through something invisible that pushed slightly at my skin. Then the familiar autumn forest around us melted away, replaced by vibrant greenery only found in the Faelands. The whole area was filled with thick trees with twisting roots, lush down-fur grass, and fat flowers that swayed bright and heavy in the wind.

My eyes widened at the sight of several betas kneeling deep in the thick, green grass, all displaying looks of deep shock and fear. Blue slowed to a stop, then released a deep breath of relief.

"You fucking fool!" An angry beta yelled at Blue as he unsheathed his sword.

Confused, Blue turned around, and his eyes widened as they met mine. But then they shifted into complete terror as they focused just passed me.

Hot breath fanned across the back of my neck, and the deep familiar rumble of an alpha shook my bones. Slowly, I turned, looking carefully over my shoulder.

The red-haired she-wolf stood directly behind me, her face split into a vicious grin and her pointed teeth on display. Her excitement pulsed in the air, and she leaned down into my face, whispering,

"Found you."

The Ridge

Joon

"THERE!" Lex pointed at a small patch of yellow flowers. Tzidal's sweet scent lingered briefly before disappearing with the wind.

"Where?" Byriel barked.

"They were here," the siren panted, holding his side as he sucked in deep gusts of air. "They were right here," he motioned to the flowers. "I looked away for one moment, and they were gone. But there were others."

"Others?" I snarled. "What the fuck do you mean *others*?"

The air shifted, and my nerves stretched tighter. There was something about this land that made me want to back away and return the way we came. The wind didn't move right on my skin, and dread settled heavy in my gut.

Where was my mate?

"Do you feel that?" Byriel asked, walking through the

yellow flowers and tall, dry grass. A puff of feathery petals kicked up under his feet, hitting the air.

I angled my head, listening hard. The air moved as if something swift and thick moved around us, but there was no sound or creature to create such a feeling.

"Look," Byriel whispered.

He motioned to the petals on the wind. They swirled fast in the breeze, but as they edged further from us, their movements slowed in mid-air as if pushing through some kind of barrier. Then, just as quickly, whatever had slowed them lifted, and they moved freely once again.

Before any of us could speak, the space just beyond the flowers crackled and pulsed with vibrant light. Then a bloodied alpha materialized out of nowhere. My eyes widened as the space behind him revealed a tear into another world—a colorful one filled with fighting wolves, screaming pups, and my mate's vibrant scent.

I rushed forward, hitting the electric air before it could close up. I shoved through the tingly air, tipping forward into a whole new forest. Throwing a quick look over my shoulder, I could see a clear line between the trees where Byriel stood and this hidden, enchanted land.

The ground was littered with dead and wounded. A few of the dead wore palace uniforms, but most wore simple armor that suggested farmers or rural folk. An alpha not far from me walked over each dead villager, ripping at their clothes and exposing their skin. He looked over their flesh before moving on to the next body.

Byriel stepped up next to me. His lips curled in pure disgust at the carnage unfolding before us. Without a word, he shifted into his wolf, racing through the battle. I didn't wait for Lex, letting my wolf take control of my body to find my mate. Bone, tendons, and muscles slid into place, and fur burst from my skin.

I raced through the village, rushing past cabins and shops. The scream of a pup made my head snap around. A youngling, maybe three or four years of age, dangled from the roof's edge. His tiny omega mother was trying to pull him up. A guard landed easily onto the roof just behind her. He flexed his fingers as he moved to her, ready to grab the oblivious omega.

I changed direction and raced toward the pup. In one quick jump, I wrapped a paw around his middle just as his fingers slipped.

Grabbing the edge of the roof with my claws, I jerked both of us up, landing next to the pup's mother. She screamed in utter terror at the sight of me but quieted as I shoved her young into her arms.

Without another look, I raced past her to the stunned guard.

Angling my body down, I shoved my shoulder hard into the alpha, then sunk my teeth deep into his side. The fucker let out a guttural roar before falling off the roof. His flailing body just missed a young beta cowering behind a barrel. She screamed at the sight of the bloodied alpha, then raced off.

Sucking in as much air as I could, I caught another hint of my mate's sweet scent. It was muted over the rush of wolves, blood, and dirt, but she was close.

I jumped from the roof, landing not far from the guard's limp body. An arrow flew just next to my head, and I spun to see a rural beta reloading his bow, glaring at me hard. I ignored him. I was confident his shaking hands wouldn't hit their mark no matter how many arrows he let loose.

Closing my eyes, I let my mating bond guide me.

Then I saw her.

Lex had his arms wrapped tight around Tzidal's middle. She struggled in his hold, her arms outstretched as if trying to reach for someone.

I raced to her as fast as my body would allow. I ran past three betas shoving spears into a quickly dying guard and an alpha ripping a farmer's throat out. I barreled right into another alpha trying to light a storefront on fire, knocking the torch out of his hand.

Coming to an abrupt stop just in front of my mate, it took her eyes a moment before they focused, seeing me clearly.

"Joon!" Relief poured from her, but she didn't move into my arms. Instead, she pointed just behind me. "Blue!" she yelled again. "Help him!"

"No." I shook my head, unable to leave her in the middle of so much violence. She snarled at me, then struggled hard even though her strength was nothing to Lex, but she still tried. My little beast.

"Please, Joon!" she begged, her big eyes filled with fire and fear. "Help him!"

Unable to handle the desperation flowing off my mate, I turned and caught a glance at Blue. He was frantically racing through the village, two big alphas on his heels. The young omega's speed was impressive, giving the alphas a good chase.

"There's a river east of here," Lex said, pulling my attention. "I can smell it." I nodded quickly at his plan.

"Take Tzidal there." I angled my head down to look into my mate's eyes. "Go with Lex." She opened her mouth to protest, but I cut her off. "I'll get Blue. Then I'll follow the river and find you. Go!"

I didn't wait for her to respond but immediately ran at full speed to where I had just seen the small, blue omega. He was already gone, but he couldn't have gotten far.

Byriel appeared out of nowhere, cutting a quick path through the fighting wolves. He was on the trail of something, and I quickly followed. I prayed it was Blue. If I didn't return to Tzidal with that damn omega in tow, she'd have my head.

Racing around a storefront, I picked up speed as my eyes

fell on a guard looming over an elderly, sobbing beta. I cut straight to him, keeping Byriel in my periphery. Grabbing a splintered shovel off the ground, I leapt over the beta and shoved the broken handle deep into the alpha's chest. The wet gurgle behind me told me the elder was safe, but I didn't wait to make sure.

At the edge of the fight, Byriel crawled low and slow over a jut of rocks. Following his movements, I crept up next to him. He didn't move to look at me, but I was sure he could sense my familiar presence.

Blue was just in front of us, with three alphas in their human-form blocking our path. Byriel's muscles twitched with restless energy, and I grabbed his shoulder to keep him in place. If he rushed those guards, Blue would surely be hurt. He was too close to the alphas with no easy escape.

Hitching my thumb to the side, I motioned for Byriel to move around, closer to Blue. Pointing at the omega, I jerked my hand into a quick fist, indicating he needed to grab Blue while I fought the fuckers off. He nodded and slowly crawled back.

I watched him slip through the grass, circling wide to the other side.

The fight roared behind me. The smell of burnt wood and blood flooded the colorful space, followed by the sound of fire crackling and horrific screams—some alphas, mostly betas. But none of the voices were Tzidal, so I kept my eyes on Blue.

"Calm down there, little omega," a squat alpha with a shaved head inched closer to Blue.

Blue shivered and stuttered, his knees visibly shaking. His movements were so unsteady I half expected him to fall to the ground.

The other two alphas leered at him, stepping closer. None of the wolves I passed seemed to be claiming any of the omegas for their own. None had forced bonds or seemed to be abducting mates, but that didn't mean shit in war. Any one of these alphas might abandon their orders—whatever they were —at any moment to sink their teeth into Blue's neck.

An unclaimed omega was simply too tempting for most alphas to pass up. There was a reason omegas lived within the safety of villages. Order kept them safe.

"What, what do you want?" Blue stuttered, keeping his eyes down and arms wrapped tight around his chest.

"Calm down. This will be quick." A fierce, blond wolf smiled, but there was nothing friendly about his blood-stained teeth.

Blue squeezed his eyes shut and turned his head, exposing the side of his neck. "What, what do you want?" he asked louder as a stream of tears rolled down his cheeks. The smell of his distress was harsh and made me want to lurch forward, but I stayed put, waiting for Byriel to get a little closer.

"Come on," the third wolf whined. "He's a weak one. Just force him so we can move on."

The blond wolf stepped closer, his dominance pouring into every word. "Do you have a mark on your skin?"

"No!" The word burst out of Blue as he submitted to the commanding nature of the alphas around him.

"No?" the bald alpha snarled, baring his teeth.

A sob burst from Blue's throat as he struggled to speak again, shaking his head violently.

"Just do it," the third alpha yelled.

The blond alpha bared his teeth at his friend, then turned back to Blue. "Take off your clothes," he ordered.

Blue's lips trembled, and his eyes went wide as he reached for the hem of his shirt. He moved without wanting to, his wolf having no power against the dominant alpha. His hands shook hard as he struggled, trying to fight against the order to strip, but he had no real power to defy them.

I frantically cut my eyes around, looking for Byriel.

"Faster!" the bald wolf roared.

Blue's shirt slipped off his head, and a high-pitched wail left his throat. He sobbed, clutching the garment to his chest.

I pounced, not giving a fuck if Byriel was in position or not.

My wolf pushed forward as I landed softly between the wolves and Blue. I locked my powerful jaws around the bald wolf's throat, ending him with a snap of his spine. The blond alpha jumped to attention and landed a quick blow to my ribs, knocking me back and giving him a chance to shift into his wolf.

I edged around the white wolf as he snarled and growled deep and low. He was smaller than me, and I hoped he'd see the battle he was sure to lose.

Out of the corner of my eye, Blue stood up and tugged on his shirt, pulling my attention for a quick moment. It was just enough for the white wolf to attack.

His sharp teeth pushed into my neck, forcing me to the ground. I whipped around in his hold, trying to angle my body to keep him from being able to snap my spine or puncture a vein. Kicking my back legs out, I clawed at his gut and shoved my claws deep into his ribs, struggling to break free.

The white wolf let out a deep growl, tightening his jaws and piercing my flesh. I grunted and tried to flip our positions but found myself struggling to breathe. The wolf dug his claws into my back and turned, twisting my head with him. My eyes burned from lack of air.

I tried to move again, but I was stuck beneath his weight and suffocating. Narrowing my eyes, I tried to look at the fucker about to end my life, letting him know I didn't fear what was next.

My mind drifted to Tzidal, and I closed my eyes.

The heavy weight on my back disappeared as a horrific pain scraped along my neck. Sucking in as much air as I could,

I struggled to get my paws under me. I swayed for a moment as my eyes finally came into focus. Byriel's sleek, grey wolf stood over the blond alpha's dead body, his fangs dripping with blood.

Byriel's wolf-form stepped forward, butting his head into my side, checking on me. Blue was nowhere in sight. I had to trust Byriel got the omega to safety.

When I didn't move, Byriel shifted into his human form. "Are you okay?" he asked, his hand pushing through the fur on my back.

I let out a snort, letting him know I was fine. I just needed a minute.

Byriel nodded, then grabbed his discarded pants, pulling them on. He motioned me forward, sprinting through the trees.

I followed Byriel through the burning village. Chaos still ravaged the land, but we didn't stop to check on the wounded. The sound of rushing water hit my ears, and Tzidal's floral scent filled my lungs. My paws beat the ground as I forced my wolf to move faster and harder toward my mate.

I jumped over a massive fallen tree then my wolf let out a sharp whine as Tzidal came into focus.

She stood at a ledge, her arms locked around Blue. Lex stayed between the omegas and the mayhem erupting not far from them. The siren was still the young man but somehow bigger and more menacing. The dangerous energy that rolled off him was so thick it was impressive.

Seeing me approach, Lex bared his pointed teeth and flung out his razor-sharp claws. I immediately stopped and quickly shifted into my human, forcing the change so fast that my bones rubbed painfully across each other. Tzidal launched both herself and Blue into my arms, relief consuming her sweet face. I wrapped my arms around both of them, feeling

Blue's body shake with fear. Tzidal remained strong for him—not a single tremor or tear in sight.

"You'll need to jump," Byriel said, looking over the edge.

The drop to the black water below wasn't a dangerous height, but I didn't know if the omegas could swim.

Byriel jerked to run back into the village, but I gripped his arm, stopping him.

"We have to help them," he yelled, motioning to the screaming villagers. His eyes were wild with determination. I couldn't help but respect his desire, but I couldn't manage Tzidal, Blue, and Lex in the rushing waters on my own.

"There's nothing we can do," I yelled over the rush of the river and the roar of an out-of-control fire. He cut his eyes back at the fight, madness still consuming the small village.

"Byriel," I said, pulling his attention back to me. I glanced over the ledge. "I can't do this without you." He set his jaw tight, the look of an alpha not prepared to give up. "There's nothing we can do to help them. This fight is over."

Byriel's gaze moved over Lex and Tzidal. Then they fell to Blue. His eyes flashed red before quickly returning dark green. He took a deep breath then his features fell as defeat set in.

He nodded and grabbed Blue by the upper arm, securing the omega against his chest.

I tightened my hold on Tzidal, her worried expression hitting my gut hard as I prepared myself to fling both of us over the ledge. She nodded softly at me, her mouth tight with determination, then closed her eyes, trusting me.

Tipping sideways, we fell over the edge into the black water below.

The Black River

Byriel

I SWAM HARD, keeping one hand wrapped firmly around Blue's arm and using the other to pull myself toward the shore. Cold, black water sprayed into my face and up my nose as I struggled to keep Blue from sinking beneath the surface. The omega's body was tight and shook hard, his arms splashing everywhere as he tried to stay afloat.

Joon swam just behind us, Tzidal clinging to his back.

Lex was nowhere in sight.

Joon moved powerfully forward each time Blue seemed to falter in my grasp, helping me navigate him toward the shore. The omega's jerky movements made it impossible to secure him properly, and I wanted nothing more than to growl at him for making this so much more difficult than it should be.

The second we hit land, I heaved Blue up next to me, coughing and gasping, trying desperately to force the water from my lungs. My guts felt wet and weak with the awful black liquid.

Joon let out a deep grunt as he settled next to me. I released Blue to check on everyone. The second my fingers left his arm, the omega was on his feet and running. Moving on pure instinct, I launched myself off the ground, into the air, and on top of Blue's slight body. He hit the ground hard, and my wolf whimpered at being so rough with him, but I didn't have the patience right now.

Blue snarled and growled high in his throat, smacking my chest and stomach, trying desperately to wiggle out from under me. I straddled his small body and settled, letting my weight keep him in place.

Tipping my head back, I sucked in an exhausted breath, and my lungs filled with Blue's soft, fresh scent. It was so cool and soothing, making my wolf growl longingly. The omega smelled like nothing else in Havre. So delicately sweet and soft, like a gift to be savored.

Blue tried jerking away from me again, forcing his shirt to twist and rise. My cock hardened at the sight of his pale, soft skin beneath me...*where he belonged.*

"How far did we go?" Tzidal asked, pulling me from my shameful thoughts.

I turned away from Blue, trying like hell to force away the desire to lean into his neck and drag my teeth over his flesh. Given the horrors we had just witnessed, it was a disgusting impulse, and I shook my head to try to rid it.

My body's reaction to Blue was more than just fucked up. I knew of the pull omegas had over alphas, but one had never enticed my wolf like this before, and I was scared of what I wanted to do to him in the midst of his grief.

Joon moved onto his hands and knees and pulled Tzidal to him. He ran his nose over her neck, arms, and stomach, scenting for any deep injuries.

"I'm fine," she whispered, letting him continue his movements until he was satisfied.

I fought the urge to do the same to Blue, but I didn't trust myself to bring my canines so close to his sweet body. There was something about this omega that made me stupid and impulsive, two things I prided myself on never falling victim to.

Joon sat up and away from his mate, taking in our surroundings. "It doesn't look like we're still within the hidden village's borders."

He was right. The vibrant colors of the fae-like forest were gone. Shiny black bark covered the tall trees. Their leaves were varying shades of grey, similar to the crisp grass that grew all around us. It had been so long since I had been near the Black River I forgot how striking the forest was compared to the rest of the woodlands.

Leaves rustled, despite the lack of wind, making both Joon and me jerk around. My shoulders relaxed as Lex came into view. I remembered his dislike of deep, rushing water but was still shocked he chose to run instead of jumping in with us—it felt like the river had carried us miles. While I had only seen the siren run once, he didn't have the speed to cover such a distance so quickly.

"How did you get here so fast?" Tzidal asked, thinking the same as me.

Lex glanced around as if noticing the forest for the first time, opening his mouth in awe. "I'm not sure," he said, wiping a thin layer of sweat off his brow. A large grin slowly split his face, and he laughed. "This is just impressive. This magic is just too good."

"Why didn't you jump into the river?" Tzidal asked, peeking out from between her mate's arms. Joon held her as if his life depended on it. I swallowed hard, wanting nothing more than to wrap Blue up in my warm embrace.

I risked a quick look at him out of the corner of my eye. He was perfectly still, staring into the distance. Not a single sound came from his soft throat.

"I couldn't jump," Lex said. His tone had an edge of embarrassment, which surprised me. I didn't think sirens were capable of such an emotion.

"Dark water," he said to Tzidal, and she nodded in understanding. "I tried to keep up along the shore and ran as fast as I could, but..." he shook his head, "I don't really know. I remember being in the village, following the river, and then I was here."

"You don't remember coming here at all?" Joon asked. "You have no idea how far you came?"

Lex shook his head, giving the alpha a weak apology.

Blue's thin stomach moved beneath me as he inhaled deeply, then released a soft breath. The delicate movement made me feel like I was balancing on a blade's edge. The heat from his body was exhilarating, dangerous, and so fucking good. My entire being was alight with arousal I had never felt before. But I kept my eyes on the siren, too cowardly to look at Blue, scared of what I might do.

"Can you get us back to the village?" I asked, trying to distract myself.

"I'm sorry." Lex gestured all around us. "I'm not sure when I left the boundary or how far I've gone. It feels like it was far, but fast at the same time."

Tzidal nodded, assuring the siren it was okay.

"I thought magic doesn't affect you like us," I said. "Like with the witch's spell? It didn't sway you."

"This magic doesn't affect just me," Lex said, "it affects the land. It's different than something that flows through you. It's in the air and the ground. There's no pushing it away or stepping around it."

93

"So you can't get us back to the village?" Joon asked again, running his hands down Tzidal's arms.

The itch to run my hands all over Blue was all-consuming, so instead, I pushed my fingers through my hair. I jerked the roots hard, trying like hell to focus.

"No. I'm sorry." Lex's deep grey eyes conveyed just as much disappointment as mine.

"We're nowhere near Aberdeen," I said, noticing the cut of the mountains in the distance. They had been so far this morning.

"Where are we?" Joon turned to look at the horizon with me.

"We're near Ossory," I said, sure of it. "The palace is just on the other side of the black forest."

"Well," Tzidal shivered, "I guess that just saves us some time. We were headed that way anyway."

"Let me go," Blue mumbled.

I looked down, and his expression slammed into me. There was so much pain in his big, hypnotic eyes. I wanted to move away from him and give him space, but I couldn't. His soft grief poured into the air in waves, fusing me to him. I needed to keep him close and safe. My wolf demanded it.

"Get off me," he said louder, his eyes finally meeting mine. His cheeks were a deep pink, and his mouth was in a tight line. It was clear he was trying so damn hard to look fierce. He wiggled, small grunts and pants leaving his throat, but he didn't budge an inch.

"Byriel," Tzidal said with a motherly edge in her tone. She waved a hand through the air, urging me to move.

Slowly and with great effort, I stood, watching the omega carefully. The second Blue was on his feet, he jerked to run, but I grabbed his arm and slammed his little body to mine. He balled up his fists and pushed them into my chest, his nose scrunched with anger.

"I thought alphas were supposed to be mighty warriors, capable of anything. Meant to protect!" Blue snarled at me. The twist of color in his eyes seemed to swirl faster as his rage saturated the air. Fat tears dripped down his face, and his shoulders shook as he started to cry. I wanted to lick his cheeks and tuck him inside my chest, safe from all danger and torment.

He sucked in a harsh breath, then, just as quickly, the fight left his body, and he pressed his forehead to my chest, going limp in my arms. The poor creature was so distressed he couldn't even focus on a single emotion.

I wrapped my arms around his back, holding him to me. It took everything in me not to scent his hair.

"But you couldn't stop them," Blue sobbed. His voice was so small. Just like him. "Those alphas came into my home and killed everyone." He tipped his head back, looking right into my soul. "And it's all my fault."

"It's not your fault," Tzidal said, her voice cracking as she spoke.

Pulling in a slow breath, I tightened my hold on his trembling body, but I didn't speak. I knew if I did, I would promise the world to try to make this better. I wanted to promise him revenge and vow to take the life of whoever destroyed his pack, but there was no point. I heard the alphas while they ravaged Blue's village. They were looking for the marked wolf.

I couldn't admit that Haxa might be right, but it was still almost impossible to believe. I just couldn't imagine my father deciding that ripping through villages was a reasonable plan for finding a needle in a haystack.

Attacking, stripping, and killing villagers would only invite rage and revenge. And it wouldn't find that wolf. It would just drive them deeper into hiding.

My hold on Blue tightened as I thought of those guards forcing him to take off his shirt.

The fear that surrounded him.

The tears dripping down his face.

His velvety, unblemished skin.

"You're hurting me," Blue sniffled, trying to push a small space between us. "Let me go." I loosened my arms a bit but kept him pressed against me. He pushed his fists at me again, then quickly gave up.

"We need to take you home," Joon said, his voice holding too much authority given how upset Blue was.

Blue jerked, then shoved at me as hard as he could. "Let me go!" he yelled, his voice a little stronger. His anger took hold again, and he hit my chest with all his might. I let him hit me. I could have easily subdued him with a command, but he needed this.

Sometimes grief sits easier in your gut when your fists are sore.

"I am not going back," Blue snarled, his little, pointed teeth on display. I never found any amusement when an omega got worked up enough for their tiny fangs to engage. But on him, it looked enchanting.

"You're going back," Joon sighed, rubbing Tzidal's back and arms. Her face was buried in his chest, and the soft scent of tears pushed off her. Joon ran his hands through her hair, letting out a soft sigh. He looked like a mountain ready to crack, his mate's delicate emotions prying him apart, urging him to crumble. "We are taking you back to your home," he said again.

"Why do you care? Just let me go!" Blue's eyes flashed, and his skin seemed to let off a hazy pulse of light. But it was so dim it might have been a trick of the sun.

The sun.

I looked up, noticing it edge closer to the trees. It was well past noon.

It was early morning just a few moments ago, and now it was past midday.

"How much time has passed?" Lex gasped, looking at the sky as well. "How did we lose half the day? Did we really travel that far?" he asked Tzidal. The omega shook her head as she twisted around in Joon's arms. Her face flushed with emotion.

"This is very impressive magic." The siren shook his head in disbelief. "Unbelievable."

Tzidal took a step toward Blue, Joon reluctantly letting her go. Her hands were outstretched to hold him. I forced myself to release him, watching carefully in case he ran again.

"We'll camp for a few days," Joon said to Blue. "Then we'll take you home. Hopefully, the guards will have cleared out by then."

Blue took a deep, pained breath, letting Tzidal hug him. "I have no home," he whispered, his bottom lip quivering. "I can never go back. I did this. I let them in."

"You don't have a choice," Joon said. Tzidal cut him a glare, but she didn't rebuke him. At least not out loud.

Blue's jaw clenched, and he took a deep breath. He looked fierce, even with tears streaming down his face. "You have no idea where my village is or how to get back inside," he said, his voice quiet but still filled with a cutting, defiant edge. "I'm not going anywhere. You don't have a choice."

"Calm down," I ordered, unable to help it. If he didn't get his emotions under control, he was going to slip into complete distress, and we didn't have the resources to deal with catatonic omega. "You need to understand we are only trying to help you."

Blue's top lip curled slightly, flashing the tips of his fangs. My eyes went dark, and my fists clenched tight. My wolf didn't fucking care for his challenging glare, and the urge to spank his ass raw pulsed within me.

Oh, to see him bent over, flushed, and begging.

A rumbling growl pushed from my chest at the thought, and Blue slumped his shoulders as if trying to curl into himself.

"Byriel," Tzidal snipped softly. She smoothed her hands over Blue's shoulders and hair. "There's no need to be so angry. He's just upset. His village was just attacked. His pack is hurt."

I nodded, but I wasn't angry. The front of my pants were painfully tight, concealing my lengthening cock. Blue's defiant words and soft scent were fucking with my beast.

Blue needed to go home, I silently reminded myself. He needed to be comforted by his family and properly grieve for his pack. But my disgusting wolf just wanted to strip him naked and pin him beneath me, make him beg for my mercy and my cock.

What the fuck was wrong with me?

"Just leave me," Blue whispered, pain replacing the rage in his eyes as he stepped away from Tzidal. She looked wounded at his retreat. "I can find my own way. I'm not a pup."

Tzidal placed her hands on his cheeks, keeping him in place. "Please, let us take you back home. Once we get there, Joon and I—"

He jerked to run again, but I was ready, pulling him flush against my chest, his small body hitting me in all the right places.

"Don't move!" I roared, unable to control my temper as lust started to override all reason.

Blue's lips trembled, and he froze up, his body struggling between the urge to lash out and the deep need to obey me. Regret lanced my chest, and I moved to guide him onto the ground, gently taking his hand.

I loved how pliant he was to my will, and I fucking hated myself even more for relishing it.

The hidden village was right to hide from all alphas. We were monsters.

"Omega, please," I said softly, trying to refocus my mind and wolf. "It isn't safe outside of your village. Let me take you home." My wolf lashed out within me, refusing to let him go. He was ours. Mine. *Mate.*

I tried to hide my shock as my wolf settled in his decision. I could feel it deep in my bones and pulsing through my veins. *Blue was mine.*

"I can't go back," he whispered, his eyes filled with desperation. "This was my fault. I let those guards in. Everyone was killed because of me. Please, alpha." The swirl of blue and green in his eyes slowed with his breath.. "Let me stay. Keep me with you. Please."

Fuck.

I shut my eyes quickly, feeling them burn red, my wolf inching forward to claim the sweet omega. I sucked in a breath, then immediately regretted it. Blue was too close. He was all I could see, taste, and smell.

"Blue, sweetie," Lex said softly somewhere next to me.

"If you force me to go home," Blue whispered, "I'll refuse to tell you where to go, and we'll wander the forest forever."

I smelled Joon's rage before he spoke, his growl filling the skies. Opening my eyes, they landed on a cowering Blue.

"You will show us where you live. Now!" Joon commanded.

Blue clenched his jaw tight, a high-pitched whine pushing from his throat. Tzidal rushed to him, but he backed up, not letting her touch him.

Joon took a careful step forward, his eyes trained on the defiant omega. "Tell me," he seethed. Tzidal growled high in her throat at her mate, but Joon's eyes didn't leave Blue.

Quickly, I closed the space between Blue and me, creating a barrier between my omega and Joon. Confusion creased

Joon's brow at my movement, but he quickly turned his attention back to the omegas, his dominant energy pushing into the air.

Blue doubled over, and his body shook as his knees hit the dirt, gagging hard. The force he was using to defy Joon was making him sick.

A vicious growl burst from me at the sight of Blue's pain, and I immediately scooped him up in my arms.

Twin lines settled between Tzidal's brows, but she didn't protest as I held him. She just watched me. Her eyes narrowed ever so slightly. It was as if she could see through to my carnal intentions.

She saw through everyone.

"He's not going to tell us, and we're not going to make him," I said forcefully to Joon. Blue relaxed against my chest, thrilling my wolf. "We just need a different plan."

Joon cocked his head, moving his gaze over my face, then Blue. He shared a quick look with his mate, but neither pointed out my possessive behavior. I was thankful.

My pull to Blue was just too much, and I was sure the adrenaline of battle was making it much worse. I just needed to calm down. Then I'd be able to think properly. But the truth was, I already knew I'd never fucking let him go.

Blue was mine, whether he wanted it or not.

The Mountains

Tzidal

"ARE YOU HUNGRY?" Joon asked.

He was still tight with frustration at Blue's defiance, but, for the most part, he seemed to have let it go. I spent all day holding his hand and caressing his arm to settle him, and our bond was finally starting to ease.

My stomach rumbled in response, and I smiled, pushing into his side. He smelled so good. My wolf was itching for his touch. There was a reason newly mated wolves secluded themselves from their pack for a few weeks after bonding. Even after all the horrors we had witnessed, the lack of his attention was driving me insane, and I could sense he felt the same.

My wolf didn't care about grief or pain or prophecies. She just wanted to be claimed.

Joon smiled down at me with soft eyes. "How about you rest, and I'll hunt?" Not waiting for me to answer, he called Lex over.

Lex and Blue had been quietly chatting all day, lost in their own world. I was thankful for the siren. Blue needed love and affection, and, right now, I was struggling to pull away from Joon to give him what he needed. My need to be near my mate was overriding everything else.

"Will you stay with the omegas while Byriel and I hunt?" Joon asked.

Lex nodded, a curious look on his face. "I guess?" He shrugged.

It was an odd request. Joon never asked anyone to look after me when he'd leave our camp to hunt. I could only assume it had to do with Blue.

"Come on," Joon said to Byriel, pulling off his pants.

Byriel's eyes repeatedly flickered from Blue to Joon, and I pressed my lips together to hide my frown. Byriel was pulling hard to Blue. I thought I saw it at the river, but now there was no denying it, and it worried me. A possessive alpha was a dangerous thing, and this could quickly spiral into a very real problem—especially if Blue had no interest.

I held my breath, waiting for Byriel to refuse to leave Blue's side.

Joon rolled his shoulders, completely naked and ready to shift. He eyed Byriel, who was still staring at Blue. Thankfully, the omega was too busy collecting sticks with Lex to notice.

"Byriel." Joon shot, his muscles tense.

The dark wolf's eyes slowly moved away from Blue to Joon.

My mate jerked his head to indicate they needed to head out. "Come on."

Giving Blue one more glance, Byriel cleared his throat loudly. "Right."

Byriel reached for his belt as Blue turned to him. The omega's eyes moved slowly over the alpha's tall, muscular form. Byriel pulled his waistband down, and Blue spun, turning away. The youngling stared into the distance, a nervous energy pushing off him.

Blue had been so fidgety and quiet around Byriel all day. I couldn't tell if the alpha scared him senseless or if perhaps it was just a general fascination, having never been around alphas before.

"I'm going to race ahead and see if there are any paths or signs of a camp nearby," Byriel said, flinging his pants over a low-hanging branch. Blue cut a peek at Byriel's naked form, then shied away, his hands visibly shaking.

Both Joon and Byriel quickly shifted into their wolves. They each released deep snorts and rumbling growls as they raced off in opposite directions. The wildlife around us went quiet at their booming warnings to any predators that might be eyeing us as they left. Then the forest went completely silent as the two wolves slipped between the trees.

Blue pouted, mumbling about not getting to see them shift. His fascination with the alphas was kind of sweet. Growing up in a village full of them, I never thought of an alphas' ability to shift as anything but ordinary.

We collected sticks and rocks, quickly building a fire. Blue watched in awe as I sparked a flame with the two pieces of flint. He laughed, saying he simply went without the warmth of a fire when outside his village, or he'd find the remnants of a smoldering one and try to bring it back to life.

It was still hard to believe the omega wandered so freely around these woods by himself, but he was so relaxed in the vast space I was starting to believe him.

The flames danced as the three of us settled in, watching the late evening sun dip closer to the horizon. I could already tell it was going to be a lovely sunset.

"So, where are your parents?" Lex asked, his voice cutting through the serene atmosphere.

"Lex," I hissed, leaning forward to scold the siren with a stern look. Blue sat between us, smiling sweetly.

"It's okay," he said. "They passed away when I was young. I was sent to live with my grandmother in the hidden village, but she passed away before my coming of age." He shrugged his shoulders, wanting us to believe it didn't bother him, but I could scent his unease as he spoke.

"Are you more than just wolf?" Lex asked with a teasing lift to his voice. He snagged the purple strand in Blue's hair and gave it a playful tug. "Is there more than one creature swimming around in those interesting eyes?"

"That's very rude," I said. "You can't ask someone if they have more than one beast in them."

"It's okay." Blue laughed. His eyes were tired, but the sound was genuine. "I'm part fae. My grandmother was a fae, and while her pups were all normal wolves, I came out with bright blue hair. It's gotten really dark as I've grown," he moved his hand through it, "but that's why everyone calls me Blue. It's not my real name. But I like Blue better."

"What's your real name?" I asked.

"I'll tell you only if you promise never to repeat it." He was dead serious, and it intrigued me to no end.

I agreed, both Lex and I promising with blood if needed.

"Vihaan."

"That's a perfectly good name," I said, not understanding why he hated it.

"I think I'd go by Blue too," Lex snorted.

"Yeah," Blue smiled wide. "It's not great."

Lex and Blue talked about the omega's family. He smiled and laughed, occasionally looking away when too much attention was on him. It was clear he wasn't used to others being so interested in him, and I felt for the youngling. Blue had mentioned a few times that his village didn't want or like him, and I just couldn't understand why. He was so sweet.

Blue twisted a loose thread from his shirt around his finger, his voice dropping to a hushed whisper, "Why did those wolves hurt my pack?"

Lex and I exchanged a look, both our smiles falling.

I struggled for a moment, not wanting to talk about the prophecy or any of the awful things that led me so far from home. Today, I was sick of rage and grief, and I didn't want to torment Blue more than he already was.

I crossed my arms, wishing Joon was here to hold me.

"I think they were looking for someone," I said.

"Why did they force me to take off my shirt?" His big eyes were filled with fear as he spoke, but he kept it in control, speaking clear and soft.

"The wolf they're looking for has a mark. A red mark on their skin."

"Oh." He blinked in confusion, thinking it over for a moment. "How do you know that?"

I took a deep breath and reluctantly fell into the awful story, carefully skimming over the violent and scary parts. I told him about my mate, Korban, and Joon's mate, Fennah, and their deaths. I talked about how we found each other and tracked down the wolves in Stone City, then Vaesen.

It felt unfair not to tell him everything considering the horrors he saw inflicted on his pack. So I told him what I could.

Except for one thing.

Byriel.

I couldn't bring myself to tell him about Byriel's hand in all this.

Lex's eyes moved to me when I only mentioned finding Byriel injured by the river, but he didn't speak up.

I didn't know why I kept it a secret. Maybe I didn't want Blue terrified of the alpha; we were traveling together, and it could make things worse. Plus, I knew Byriel wouldn't hurt us. The alpha was a lot of things and had a lot left to atone for, but he wasn't the monster I first thought. He was just another victim of his father, broken like the rest of us.

Blue sat with all the information, nodding softly and thinking it over. His presence was so calm, and I hated that the alphas had worked him up so easily. He was an anxious mess around them, but in reality, everything about the omega was soothing. Even when his eyes teared up while he talked about his pack, his presence was gentle and his voice tender. It made my heart ease rather than burn with his pain.

I could only assume the attack on Blue's pack was happening all over Havre—innocent wolves being terrorized just to find one birthmark. It was unthinkable and evil, and there was no way it was going to work. After all, when looking for a needle in a haystack, the answer isn't to burn down the barn.

Blue tipped his head up, looking at the sky, and let out a gentle hum. "Do you know the mourning song of the Silver Moon?"

I smiled and nodded. "It's had been a long time since I heard it, but I do know it."

"What is it?" Lex asked.

"It's a very old song." I threaded my arm through Blue's, snuggling into his side. He traced the twisting purple mark on my arm with his fingertips. It tickled. "My grandmother sang it at every burial service we went to, but I don't think it's common anymore."

"Do you remember it?" Blue asked, his eyes wide with hope.

I smiled and hummed. Our voices blended together as we sang the melody I hadn't heard in so long.

The blue path to the silver Moon,
wrapped in love and light

Death to greet the weary wolf,
raging war with all his might
Hold them close and kiss their eyes,
a warrior's time to go
Feel his pride and keep his love,
giving strength to those below

The song ended, and I closed my eyes, feeling the love of those I once knew fill my chest. Blue was a gift of the Moon. His sweet presence and loving manner healed something deep within me that I hadn't realized was still in pain.

And for the first time since leaving home, I truly felt peace. I just wished my mate was here to share it with me.

The Camp

Tzidal

"THAT WAS LOVELY." Byriel's voice cut through the silence.

The three of us spun to see the alpha standing at the edge of our camp. His jaw was tight, and his eyes narrowed. He looked...off.

My gaze moved down Byriel's form, taking in his rigid stance. He was breathing hard, covered in sweat, and blood trickled down his chin and chest. A fierce punga bear lay at his feet. Pungas were smaller than most of their kind but feral and fast. It was a very impressive kill.

"Byriel," I said in awe, my mouth watering as I moved closer. "How did you manage him by yourself?"

It usually took two, if not three, alphas to maneuver such a kill.

"I wanted to make sure everyone got their fill," Byriel said, but his eyes were squarely on Blue. The alpha was showing off, and I was thankful. It had been a while since we had such a splendid meal.

Blue shied away from Byriel's intense stare, mumbling a quick thanks.

"You outdid yourself," Joon said, stepping up behind me and wrapping an arm around my waist. I hadn't heard him arrive. "I was pissed I hadn't found anything decent, but I guess we'll be eating well tonight after all."

Byriel nodded at the compliment, his usual stoic expression firmly in place, but his eyes sparkled every time he looked at Blue. I wanted to smile, but something made me feel uneasy about the idea of Byriel claiming Blue. Perhaps it was my prejudice against the alpha or the fact that I felt responsible for Blue, but I couldn't shake it.

BOTH MY STOMACH and wolf were very happy. In fact, the only thing that could make me happier was my alpha.

I stared at Joon longingly, wishing nothing more than to spend the night pinned beneath his powerful body. Everything in me ached with need, and now that my hunger was sated, my wolf's needs flared hard.

Joon added a few more logs to the fire, then turned to Lex. "Are you hunting tonight or staying here?"

"No hunting," he said, snuggling Blue. The omega looked sleepy. "I ate well last night. Why?"

Joon's eyes fell to mine. His expression held so much heat my breath hitched, and my heart fluttered.

"I need my mate," he said.

"Wait. What?" Lex squealed, sitting up. "Mate?" His eyes moved down to my neck, and his eyes went wide.

Jumping up, he grabbed me around the middle, pulling me into a crushing hug. "Oh, my stars! I can't believe you didn't tell me!" he gushed, squeezing me especially tight. Then just as quickly, he released me and turned on Joon with a stern tone. "You know, it's about damn time. If you took any longer, I was going to mate her myself."

"I thought you were already mated?" Byriel glanced between us.

"No," I blushed, watching Lex bounce giddily on his toes. It made Blue laugh.

Byriel arched his brow in surprise. "This whole time, she hasn't been your mate? Why on earth would you allow an omega that wasn't your mate to defy you so openly?"

I looked at Joon from under my eyelashes, giving him a playful smile. I bit my bottom lip, and his eyes flashed red.

"Just you wait," Joon said, keeping his eyes on my mouth. "You'll be amazed at the defiance your wolf will crave."

Byriel shook his head. "No sensible alpha craves defiance."

Joon snatched me up, flinging me over his shoulder.

"Where are they going?" Blue asked as Joon carried me away from the camp.

I heard Byriel's deep voice. "There is little more important to a newly mated alpha than taking their claim."

"Oh," Blue whispered. I could practically hear his cheeks blush.

JOON WALKED FOR A WHILE, moving quickly through the forest while I dangled over his unforgiving shoulder. I was growing restless and wanted to walk, but I knew there was no point in asking. He wasn't going to let me go.

"Joon?" He didn't respond, just kept walking. "I want to talk about Blue. About—"

"We can talk about the omega later."

"We need to find a village or encampment. We need to find someone to take care of him."

Joon grunted his agreement, clearly not listening to a word I said.

"I just can't leave him in the woods out here all alone, and I want—"

"Omega," he snapped, his tone telling me to be quiet. "We will figure out what to do with the youngling in the morning. Right now, I don't give a fuck." A soft rumble pushed out of his chest. "Now quiet down. You'll work yourself up."

I suppressed the urge to groan. He was the one worked up, but there was no point in provoking the beast. "Where are we going?" I asked.

He smacked my butt hard. "Quiet. We're almost there."

My bottom ached, but the sting made my nipples hard and my heart race. His aggression flowed freely, his scent thick with desire. And I couldn't wait to get him alone.

"Here we are." He placed me carefully on my feet.

We stood in front of a large, black spruce in front of a massive cut of lava rock. The bark was shiny, throwing off an iridescent glow in the light of the setting sun.

"I don't get it." I glanced up at my alpha. "Where are we?"

Smiling, he took my hand and led me around the tree. A break in the rocks revealed itself, and he pulled me through a cavernous tunnel. The air was cool, feeling so good against my flushed skin. Even in the crisp fall weather, I was heated.

A soft light appeared at the end of the tunnel, and I stepped out into the most beautiful pocket of nature I had ever seen. Everything was so green and lush, the chilly weather and black, sleek forest forgotten behind us. Smooth rock circled the little cove, caging in the little paradise. Looking up, I could see out of the top of the rockface. The last rays of the most beautiful sunset painted the sky pink and orange.

"This is amazing," I gasped. "How did you know about this?"

"I didn't go hunting," Joon smiled, his dimple gracing his cheek. "I scented the spring while trying to find somewhere to take you tonight, and I knew you'd love it."

A sweet mist curled around the trees and rocks, and bell-flowers swayed gently near a small hot spring of crystal clear water, steam rising from the top. Everything was so lush and beautiful. With a content sigh, I moved my hand over the smooth rock, loving how dark and shiny it was—like glass.

I turned to Joon, wanting to tease him a bit, but stopped before I could speak.

His tall, muscular form stood shirtless before me. His head was tilted back as he looked at the sky. I dragged my gaze down his firm chest, over the cut lines of his abs pointing deep into his waistband, to his large hands that hung at his sides. Those hands...

Sensing my growing arousal, Joon turned to me, and his eyes went hooded with desire.

He stalked toward me.

My heart pounded in my chest, and slick gathered between my thighs. With each step he took, I took one backward until my back touched the smooth rock wall. Joon braced his muscular arms just next to my head, caging me in place.

I felt so small and helpless under his hungry gaze.

And I loved it.

Slowly, Joon leaned in and licked into my mouth, twisting our tongues together at a slow, sensual pace. I moaned and moved to circle my hands around his neck, but he broke the kiss and took a small step back. A soft whine left my throat.

"Turn around." His voice was deep and sexy, with a hint of anger laced around the edges. It made me pant a little. "Hands on the wall."

I didn't move, feeling a little defiant.

Joon took my chin between his thumb and finger, tilting my head up a little more. "Don't make me force you into place, little omega," he whispered, his gravelly voice rippling across my skin.

Keeping my eyes on him for as long as possible, I slowly turned and pressed my palms flat against the cool stone. Joon channeled one hand through my hair and pulled at the front of my robes with the other, slipping it off my shoulders. I lowered my arms to let it fall, leaving only the necklace he gave me nestled between my breasts.

He jerked my pants down in one fierce movement, making me gasp. I swallowed hard, desperate for what he had planned next.

After a moment, his hands returned, moving over the curve of my waist, then squeezing my ass hard. One of his hands disappeared, then a sharp crack of his palm made me jerk and yip.

"That hurt!" I tried to spin around, but Joon wrapped a strong arm around my middle, pinning me in place.

He held me tight, pressing his chest to my back. Pushing his hips against my bottom, he moved his cock between my thighs. His length swayed, nestled right up against my clit.

"I told you that I didn't want you to bathe in the river where Byriel might see you," he growled in my ear. My wolf whimpered at his tone, rolling to display her belly, but I wasn't willing to yield just yet. "You need to learn to do what you're told."

"How are you still mad about that?" It felt like a lifetime ago.

Joon leaned away from me and landed another hard smack to my ass, making me grunt.

It hurt.

It hurt in all the right places.

Pressing his groin back against my warming cheeks, he

leaned into my ear again, his voice dangerously deep. "Want to try that again?"

"I just needed a bath," I whispered sweetly, looking at him from over my shoulder. "I didn't mean to defy you."

Another hard smack hit my cheek and my pussy clenched. The sting moved through my backside, straight to my nipples, and I struggled not to moan out loud.

"Don't lie to your alpha." He thrust his hips forward, pressing against my searing ass. I simpered at the sensation of his cool skin on my hot flesh.

"You are mine, Tzidal. This clever mind." A long finger flowed down the side of my face. "This heart." His big hand moved between my breasts. "This pussy." He cupped my sex, rubbing my swollen clit in slow, torturous circles. "But my biggest problem is with this mouth." He gripped my chin and turned my head to the side, placing a quick kiss on my lips from over my shoulder. "On your knees."

He released me and stepped back, leaving me cold and needy. I already missed the warmth of his big, muscular body.

I pushed myself away from the wall and turned to face him. My legs shook with excitement as I knelt directly in front of my mate. It was agony not to smile.

His fierce eyes flashed red at my willful submission, and I held my breath.

I loved him like this. An edge of fury with a very hard cock, swaying right in my face.

He gripped the base of his huge shaft and pressed the tip to my mouth, moving slowly over my top, then bottom lip.

"Open." His command was so deep and rough.

I did as I was told, and he slipped the tip of his cock into my mouth. He held the base firmly, then looked me hard in the eyes. "Suck."

Pressing my hands against his muscular thighs, I opened my mouth wide to accommodate his girth. I sealed my lips around his member, then dragged him in deep, swallowing him down. I moved, letting my tongue explore every inch, humming at his smokey, sweet taste.

"Faster," he grunted through clenched teeth.

Wrapping a hand firmly around his shaft, I sucked in a deep breath. Then I forced him down my throat as far as I could go. He pressed hard at the back of my throat, my eyes watering at the size of him.

He let out a strangled swear as I bobbed my head back and forth. Sucking hard and fast.

Joon gripped my hair and pushed into me, fucking my mouth like an animal. My eyes begged him for air, but I didn't move to pull away or struggle in his hold. I let him use me.

He let out a sharp gasp, then flooded my mouth with his wonderful, bittersweet fluid.

Slowly, I leaned back, leaving my mouth open so he could see his climax on my tongue.

Breathing hard, his eyes flashed, and he took several calming breaths. "Swallow."

And I did as I was told.

The Cove

Joon

IF THERE IS a creature in these lands that is sexier than my omega, I never want to meet them. It might kill me.

Taking in my mate's flushed cheeks and blown-out eyes as she swallowed my cum, almost ended me. I steadied myself while Tzidal sat on her little feet. She looked so sweet and angelic, like a good, submissive omega waiting for her alpha to tell her what to do.

It was a look I cherished. One I knew was only for me.

"Lay back," I ordered, pushing my alpha into my voice. It wasn't needed. She was far too excited for my game, but I couldn't help it. The need to dominate her was too strong. "Show me that sweet, perfect cunt."

Tzidal draped herself across the lush grass, her thick, dark hair fanning around her. Keeping her eyes on mine, she rested her hands just next to her face, then let her knees fall open—her soft body on display for me to lick, mark, and claim.

Fuck.

"Please," she whispered with a soft moan. It went right to my cock. I was already hard as stone and ready to fuck her senseless.

"Please, what?" I teased, my voice deeper than it had ever been.

"Punish me," she said in a breathy whisper, the glint in her eyes spurring me on.

I grabbed her hips and spun her onto her stomach in one fierce movement. She gasped as I pulled her ass into the air, fisted her hair, then slammed my cock into her tight pussy. Her sopping wet heat clenched around me as I set a brutal pace, fucking her with every ounce of strength within me.

Pushing between her shoulder blades, I forced her chest to the ground. "Don't you ever disobey me again," I growled, spanking her ass as I continued to pound into her sweet heat.

"Yes...nnngh...a-alpha," she moaned. Tilting her hips, she met my movements, pushing back into every thrust.

I brought my hand down, again and again, loving the jiggle of her flesh with each snap of my wrist. The clear outline of my palm and fingers stood out on her pale skin, and I growled low at the sight.

The color deepened as I punished her, changing from a soft blush to a molten red. It was fucking gorgeous.

Feeling my end near, I grabbed Tzidal's hips and jerked her back onto my expanding knot. She let out a broken moan as her cunt fluttered wildly around my cock, her thighs shaking and slick gushing over my hips. Her whole body shook as my knot took hold, and I rutted forward, coming long and hard inside her eager body.

My cock throbbed, and my head spun as her pussy sucked me in.

Closing my eyes, I gently pulled her abused ass back into

me. Her tight cunt pulled at my knot as I used her to milk my balls of every last drop.

Once my body stopped thrumming, I softened my hands and slowly parted her bright red cheeks. My wide knot was lodged deep inside her, cum and slick leaking out around the edges. I ran my thumb along the seal of her pussy around my cock, feeling how tight she was stretched around me.

She was so perfect.

Fuck, I loved her.

The Camp At Sunset

Byriel

BLUE'S CHEEKS blushed as Joon carried Tzidal deep into the woods.

"How long will Tzidal be gone?" Blue asked, his tone somewhat forlorn as he watched them disappear.

"I doubt we'll see them before morning," Lex said, his stomach growling.

"Why don't you eat?" Blue asked.

Lex glanced at the punga, his lips curling in disgust. We had stripped most of it clean, but Joon and I were careful not to finish it should the omegas get hungry again later.

"I don't do bear," Lex said with an edge of snark in his voice.

"I know." Blue laughed, bumping his shoulder into the siren. "I meant, why don't you go out and get something...*or someone*...to eat."

"You know?" The siren's eyes widened, and I had to agree.

Telling sensitive omegas about the beasts outside the villages wasn't something alphas or betas tended to share.

"Yes," Blue gave him a pointed look as if the hunting habits of sirens were common knowledge. "When I was a pup, we had a siren that occasionally came through our village. She was nice and never harmed any of our pack, but we were always warned about her...*diet*."

I leaned forward, capturing his attention. "You knew what his kind ate," I motioned to Lex, "and it still didn't scare you enough to keep your distance?" I also wanted to point out the ridiculousness of a village that banned alphas while welcoming a siren, but I kept that to myself.

Blue shrugged, biting the bottom of his lip to keep his smile from consuming his whole face. I laughed at the brazenness of the omegas in my company. I never thought of their kind as fearless, but between Blue and Tzidal, they were proving me very wrong.

Lex stretched out on the other side of Blue, tucking his hands behind his head and closing his eyes. A contented hum left the siren's lips as the sun started to set, the sky burning orange and pink.

Silence fell, and Blue grew restless, his scent laced with unease. He shuffled a bit as if having trouble getting comfortable. He needed a nest, not the hard ground to sleep on, but I didn't have anything that would provide that kind of comfort for an omega.

"What does your necklace mean?" Blue asked, his eyes fixed firmly on the charm.

"It's enchanted."

He reached out, touching the King's seal embossed on the front. His fingers grazed my chest, flipping it over to see the paw print on the back.

"What's it do?" he asked.

"Alphas can't shift when wolfsbane is near. The poisonous

plant keeps our wolves locked in place. This," I motioned at the silver charm in his hand, "makes it so I can shift no matter what."

"How does it work?" He leaned in, staring as if it might burst open and share its secrets. His breath fanned over my chest, making goosebumps flash up and down my arms.

I cleared my throat roughly. "It has bindweed in it and was enchanted by the witches."

"Oh," he leaned back, "witches. Not far?"

"Not fae." I frowned as he released the charm and leaned back, looking a little disappointed. "Not because I don't trust the fae."

His eyes widened. "You don't."

"Of course not. Wolves and fae might not always get along, but we're all one with this land. My father simply has a strong relationship with the witches that live in the mountains around the palace. It's nothing against the fae."

His expression softened, and a small smile lifted one side of his lips. Looking him over again, I could only guess he was part fae. His vibrant coloring, the way his skin seemed to flash white. It wasn't common for my kind and fae to mate, but it had been known to happen.

"Alpha," Blue whispered, running his fingers along the hem of his shirt. "Alpha Byriel?"

I leaned in, loving the way he said my name, and the fact that he addressed me formally thrilled my wolf to no end. My beast inched forward, desperate to hear his voice again.

"I'm sorry I refused to take you to my village," he whispered. "My pack is very strict about keeping alphas out. But you were so nice to me at the river," he swallowed hard, "not forcing me to tell you where my village was, and I just..." he shook his head, seeming to struggle to find the right words. "Thank you."

I wanted to touch him and scent him. "You were right not

121

to bring me to your village. It's smart to be cautious of unknown wolves. You shouldn't trust them. Even the nice ones." I smiled, and his pale skin warmed a soft pink.

"Does that mean I shouldn't trust you?" he asked playfully, scrunching the bridge of his nose.

I smiled wide, prepared to tell him I wouldn't hurt a pixie, but my expression fell just as quickly. It would be a fierce lie, and my tongue would surely slice itself open if I dared to tell someone so kind something so false.

"Are you okay?" Blue asked, inching closer.

He reached out, hesitating for a brief movement, before placing a small, pale hand on my arm. The feel of his velvety, white skin on mine sent an electric desire straight through me. My cock leapt to life, my heartbeat doubled, and my jaw tensed.

I looked over Blue's sweet expression, my eyes falling to the soft curve of his upper lip. His pout looked like a bow. Slowly, he captured his bottom lip between his teeth, and my wolf growled possessively. I squeezed my hands together to keep them in place.

Lex sat up and leaned all the way forward, giving me a wild, teasing smirk. His eyes were so wide with glee, making it clear he could taste my conflicted lust in the air.

Fucking sirens.

Ignoring the still smiling siren, I looked at Blue. "How did you get this?" I asked, motioning to the twist of purple that fell next to his ear.

He touched the lock, his fingers almost brushing mine. His delicate blue-ish cheeks dusted the softest shade of pink, and he bit that bottom lip again. The backdrop of thick black trees, and grey and white grass made his colors even more vivid. Pink, blue, purple, with big, green eyes. He was a tiny rainbow in a sea of black.

"I was born with it." He looked at his lap, his submissive

mannerisms calling to my beast.

The distant rumble of an unknown voice made me jump to my feet. Lex quickly followed.

"What—"

I held up a finger, silencing Blue. He immediately went quiet, his bright eyes moving all around the trees in the distance.

I scented the air. "It's an alpha."

Lex nodded, his playful energy doubling. "I think he's alone," he purred, his pointed teeth on display.

I didn't like the idea of someone stumbling upon our camp to find an unclaimed omega. Even though my wolf had already staked a claim on Blue, I wanted to take my time with him. I wanted to capture his affections before taking what was mine.

I had no interest in forcing a bond, even though so many alphas did. I needed Blue's approval of my wolf. His happiness was too important.

Cracking my knuckles, I reached for my belt, prepared to shift.

"By'," the siren smiled, gesturing for me to keep my clothes on. "Allow me."

He sauntered off, his form slowly changing with each step. He was almost out of sight by the time he finished phasing. A sweet female beta with wild red hair replaced the image of the young man.

"It's okay," I said, turning to Blue.

He gave me a sweet smile. He didn't look scared, and his scent didn't hold any fear. He just sat next to the fire, his bright eyes on me.

"You don't seem worried," I said, not understanding how he couldn't be. There were so many fierce predators in these woods, and he was defenseless and small. A smart omega would be terrified right now.

"I'm not worried," he said simply.

I shook my head, suddenly angry. The thought of him being unconcerned with a threat so close enraged me. "Do you not understand what rogues would want with an omega like you?" His eyes widened as my anger flared, but I couldn't calm down. He was too fragile. I needed him to take this seriously. "How can you not be frightened?"

"I'm with you," he said, confusion clouding his delicate features. "I know you...." he shifted nervously, his fingers twisting together, "... you'll save me...like you did before...in my village."

Pride burst from my wolf, and I instinctively puffed out my chest. The urge to snatch Blue up and mate him hard and proper pounded in my veins.

I couldn't wait until the moment I had him in safer lands.

I needed my sweet omega to be within the safety of a proper village, not a borderless patch of land surrounded by a flimsy invisible wall. Then I would have him without the fear of any threat.

My mind drifted as I looked at his sweet face. He was so serene right now, but on the shore of the Black River, he had been desperate and tortured. The carnage he was forced to witness, the way he sobbed afterward, and the deep shiver in his bones—all of it enraged and confused me.

What was my father thinking doing this to his own people? Was it possible he didn't order this?

I prayed the attack of Blue's village was that of an overly excited patrol. I wanted to believe the King's orders weren't so harsh. He was a stern ruler, but he would never torture his pack like that. At least, I hoped.

"Are you okay?" Blue asked.

My eyes focused on his curious expression, and I nodded, trying to shove down the storm clouding my mind. "My apologies for losing myself for a moment," I said.

"You're right. I'll protect you no matter what. You have my word."

Blue smiled and patted the spot next to him. My wolf was alight with renewed energy, and I struggled not to race to his side. Instead, I sat carefully, keeping a bit of space between us. He wasn't mine yet, and I wasn't an animal. I would court him properly like a civilized wolf.

"Why do you talk so funny?" he asked.

"Do I...*talk funny*?" I cocked my head, not understanding what he meant.

"Yes," he smiled. "You talk different from other wolves I've known. You speak very," he narrowed his eyes, thinking it through, "formal."

I suppressed a snort. "Yes. I suppose wolves from Ossory tend to speak in a formal manner. As a pup, my tutors encouraged this manner of speaking." I hesitated, feeling a little self-conscious. It was a foreign feeling and one I didn't care for. "Does it bother you?"

"No!" Blue grabbed my arm with both hands. His warm fingers curled over my dark skin. "I really like it," he said. "Please don't think I don't. It's interesting. It's like you're speaking in a poem sometimes."

"I've never heard it described that way." I stared at his hands. His touch felt so good and right.

And I wondered if he felt a pull to me too.

He had to. This was too strong, and if he didn't feel the same, I'd burn down all of Havre to sate my rage.

"Alpha Byriel?"

My eyes snapped up at Blue's uneasy tone, eager to hear him speak again. "Yes?"

"Can I ask you a question?"

"Of course." His eyes held mine, and my heart quickened.

"Um." He folded his hands in his lap, making my wolf whimper at the loss of his touch. Blue swallowed hard, smoothing his hands over the tops of his thighs and down his knees. "I was wondering if you could change yourself." His big eyes widened, brimming with restrained excitement. "I've never seen a wolf shift. The betas never shifted inside the village during the full Moon, and I've never seen someone change before."

I smiled at his sweet energy. His request was endearing.

I placed my hands on my knees, prepared to stand up. "Do you want to see my full wolf?" My beast preened within me, hoping to shift and put on a show for our omega.

Blue shook his head, making my beast whine. "You don't have to do that. Just something small, if that's okay."

Smiling, I beckoned him closer. He leaned forward, his soft scent filling my lungs. Opening my mouth slightly, I engaged my canines, letting them lengthen fully to a point.

"Wow." His voice was a breathy whisper. He moved his hand up, staring intensely at my mouth, then jerked back quickly. "Can I touch you?" He asked in such a bashful way I couldn't have said no if I wanted to.

"Be careful. They're sharp."

His lips lifted into a bright smile, and he leaned in, running a single finger down the length of my fang. Then he poked the bottom and jerked back, letting out a quick hiss.

Instinctively, I reached for his hand, pulling it to me. A tiny pin-prick of blood swelled in the center of his fingertip. I quickly licked it to clean and heal it faster. The second my tongue touched his soft skin, my whole body thrummed with a delicate sweetness that swirled within me, filling every pore.

It was intense and consuming, and it made me dizzy and hard.

Blue's breath hitched, and I glanced up into those hypnotizing eyes, my heart beating wildly in my chest.

My wolf licked his lips and edged forward, desperate to taste more.

The Next Morning

Joon

TZIDAL SIGHED as she eased herself into the hot spring. She moved slowly, her legs unsteady as she settled in the water.

"I was too hard on you," I said, pride and guilt clashing together at the sight of her red and slightly bruised ass. Deep love bites covered her shoulders, breasts, and the inside of her thighs. She looked claimed in every sense of the word.

Tzidal peeked up at me from under hooded lids. "Do you feel like you've been bad?" Her voice held a teasing, yet husky, lift to it. "Do I need to punish *you*?" She bit her bottom lip.

I moved into the hot water and pulled her back to my chest, caressing and cleaning her smooth skin. "How the hell am I supposed to control you if I can't punish you?"

"You just spent all night punishing me." She let out a breathy hum as I moved my fingers between her thighs, wiping at the mix of dried and wet fluids on her skin.

"Yes, but you aren't supposed to like it."

"I didn't," she said, twisting slightly in my lap. She placed her lips next to my ear and whispered, "I loved it."

I couldn't stop the smile that consumed my face. I should have been angry and frustrated, demanding she submit to me. But more than anything, I just wanted to ease into her sweet, soft body once more and lose myself in her throaty moans. I loved her defiant streak and looked forward to spanking her ass raw again. I was in no doubt that she'd give me a reason, hopefully soon.

"We should probably get back," she sighed. The mischief in her eyes dimmed. "And we need to talk about Blue." She rested her hands on my chest, teasing my skin with the tips of her nails.

"Tzidal." I braced myself for a fierce argument. "He's an adult. If Blue wants to roam the forest alone for the remainder of his days, we don't really have a say. We cannot force him to go home."

"Actually," she said, biting her bottom lip. She already knew I wouldn't like whatever she was about to say. "I want him to come with us."

"To Ossory?" I could only assume she meant the palace. She was still determined to see the King's end, but it surprised me to think she'd want the sensitive, male omega to come with us.

She nodded. "After what happened in Blue's village," she let out a pained sigh, "he needs someone to watch over him, but he also needs to know why his pack was attacked. If he doesn't want to go, I won't force him, but I think—"

I held up my hand, silencing her. Taking her chin between my thumb and finger, I forced her to look deep into my eyes. "If Blue wants to come with us, I'll gladly accept him. You tell me where you want to go, and I'll carve a fucking path." A small smile graced her sweet lips. "I will cut through a mountain if it'll make you happy."

She pressed her lips to mine in a quick, soft kiss. "Have I told you how much I love you?"

I hummed, kissing her properly, squeezing her tender thighs, and tasting her sweet breath. Breaking the kiss, I pressed my forehead to hers. "To Ossory?" I asked her.

She nodded, fire burning in her bright, brown eyes.

"WHERE IS LEX?" Tzidal scanned the area as we entered the camp.

Byriel leaned against a tree trunk with Blue curled up in a snug ball by his side, soft snores leaving the omega's lips. The fire at their feet smoldered with thick wisps of black smoke, making the morning mist smell smokey and charred.

"I'm here. I was hoping to be back before you returned," Lex said, moving through the trees. His hair receded into his skull, fading from a vibrant red to his usual stark white. "How was your night?" he asked Tzidal, raising his eyebrows in a suggestive manner.

Her eyes went wide as he approached. "How was yours?" she asked, poking a visible mating bite on his throat. "What does this mean?"

Lex clapped a hand over his neck, giving an exaggerated huff. "Sometimes, when I get an image too right, alpha's get a little feral and bite me."

"But this is a mating bite." Tzidal's mouth was open in shock. "Can you be...claimed?"

"No!" He let out a burst of laughter, causing Blue to jerk awake. "I'm pretty sure wolves can only claim wolves. This," he pointed at the clear indentation of fangs, "will fade in a few days. He just got excited and went a little...*hard*." His eyes flashed, a smirk firmly in place.

"It's still so shocking," Tzidal whispered as they both moved toward what was left of the fire.

We ate quickly, finishing off the punga. Tzidal stayed close to Blue during breakfast. Then, holding his hand, we set off north. The terrain got more uneven and the hills harder to navigate as we made our way through the mountains.

The sun felt good as the day wore on, warming both the earth and my skin. I could still scent a bit of grief surrounding Blue, but Tzidal's nurturing energy brightened the breeze as she soothed him without words.

"What is your plan?" Byriel asked quietly, keeping a cautious eye on the omegas in front of us.

"Tzidal hasn't wavered in what she wants. We're going to Ossory."

Byriel nodded, understanding my meaning. I didn't need to remind him that she wanted his father's head, just that our purpose hadn't changed.

"I've been thinking it over," he said. "And I think it might be good for you to search out Yasha."

"Why?" Tzidal stopped in her tracks, turning to us.

Byriel seemed a little taken aback but tucked his hands behind his back, a relaxed look about him. "She foretold the prophecy and can probably help you find that last wolf. If nothing else, she can at least tell you what it means." His expression seemed genuine.

"Do you no longer have an interest in that last wolf?" Tzidal asked carefully.

"I never had an interest in any of them. I just did as I was commanded. I—" He stopped talking, his eyes flickering to Blue. "I'm done."

Tzidal nodded at his words, a far-off look in her eyes as she worked something out in her head. "How do we find her?" she finally asked.

"I know someone along the edges of Ossory who might be

able to help you. He does well with those that wish to disappear, and witches don't tend to like company, especially after difficult readings."

Tzidal mumbled out a *'thank you'* and then walked on. Even from behind, I could see her mind working hard as she laid out a plan.

"The witch will be helpful," I said to Byriel, "but we need to know what the King is up to. He's clearly moved on from tracking down single wolves and is now terrorizing whole packs."

Byriel shook his head at my words. "I refuse to believe he sent guards into an ill-protected village and allowed them to search the way they did." He pulled me to a stop, placing a hand on my shoulder. "I've been thinking it over. They had to be a rogue group. There's no way—"

"Don't you dare fucking say your father didn't command this!" I roared.

Byriel's fists clenched, and his expression went stony at my outburst, but he didn't move to defend himself. "It's one thing for a King to defend the throne, but attacking packs across Havre?" He shook his head. "That makes no sense. He would never—"

"I know you aren't that stupid." I gave him a pointed glare. "Attacking his own people really makes no fucking sense to you?"

Thick emotion flashed in his eyes. Deep sadness followed by pain. It caught me off guard, and I took a step back.

"I'm tired of you two fighting," Tzidal said in a firm, soft voice. "I'm sick of the stench of alpha rage. You both need to calm down or take a separate path."

Blue's eyes widened, and he chewed on his bottom lip, waiting to see how we'd react. It pleased me that he didn't move away from us. He was growing more comfortable in our presence, which made me happy. If Tzidal wanted to keep him with us, it was important he settled with our group.

"Byriel," Tzidal turned to the dark wolf, "I assume you're headed back home to Ossory?"

He grunted out a quick *'yes.'*

"We are also heading to Ossory," she said, her tone as sharp as her scent.

"If you two can't get along," she crossed her arms, "I suggest you both go your own way, and we'll meet there." She gave me a pointed look. "Otherwise, we're not far off. Surely you both can get along for a few more days."

Byriel's eyes flickered to Blue, then back to Tzidal. He gave her a nod before turning his hard expression to me. "*I* am more than capable of controlling my temper."

"Me too," I growled at my mate. I meant to speak calmly, but I was too worked up, my wolf and adrenaline ready for a brawl.

Tzidal rolled her eyes, turning back to Lex and Blue.

I drew back my fist and punched Byriel in the chest as hard as I could. He stumbled, then jerked to rush me, but he instantly froze. His eyes fell to the omegas now watching us.

"Really?" Tzidal cut me a furious look.

I cleared my throat and moved past her, taking the lead.

"How does anyone live with an alpha?" Blue whispered, his voice laced with a bit of fear but mostly confusion.

Lex clicked his tongue. "This is why I eat them."

Through the Woods

Tzidal

BLUE and I sat beside a cluster of bushes, watching the alphas and Lex. They peered over the edge of a sharp drop in the land, eerily still like the predators they were. Moments like these reminded me how wildly different I was compared to them.

Joon and Byriel exchanged a few glances, seeming to have an entire conversation without saying a word.

Feeling uneasy, I looked up at the Moon. Despite being only a crescent, she was bright tonight, covering everything in soft white light. It should have brought me comfort, but the thick stench of dozens of unknown wolves consumed the air. Each shift in the wind made fear thread down my spine, and I pushed deeper into Blue's side.

I glanced at the rising mountains on both sides of us. The terrain didn't look promising, and with Ossory just in the distance—maybe a day or two away, at most—the quickest route would be down the ledge and through the encampment of unknown wolves below.

Byriel tapped Joon's shoulder, then hitched a thumb backward. All three inched back as Blue moved to stand. The second my feet touched the grass, Joon lifted me into his arms and carried me into the safety of the treeline. I pressed my cheek to his shoulder, absorbing his woodsy scent. My wolf settled a bit.

Once we were a good distance away, hidden in the shadows of several trees, Joon sat me down. Then turned to Byriel.

"What do you think? Do you know them?" he whispered as we sat in a tight circle.

"I recognize two," Byriel said. "Both good wolves. I want to say we can trust them, but, if I'm honest, I've been away from home for too long. I'm not sure what the air is like in Ossory anymore. It seems a lot has changed while I've been away."

His eyes pulled down as he spoke, and I couldn't help but feel bad for him. The alpha was full of so much conflict and fear, and when he thought no one was looking, you could scent the unease drifting off him.

"Then we need to avoid them," Joon groaned, clearly not liking Byriel's assessment.

"How?" I asked, pushing into Lex. Blue smashed into the siren's other side, both of us trying to leech the heat from his body. It was especially cold, the change in season cutting to my bones.

I missed that magical hot spring.

"We can't drop down," Joon said, pulling me away from Lex and tucking me under his arm. He was so warm. "It's too steep and will put us practically on top of them. You know this land," he said to Byriel. "Is there an easy way down?"

"I haven't been this close to the Black River in a few years. But, if my memory serves me, there should be a gradual decline in the land on the far west side of Ossory." He gave Joon a sympathetic look. "But there's a lot of mountain between here and there."

"Depending on how uneven the terrain is, that could easily add a month to our trip." My alpha groaned in frustration.

"Did you see the narrow path along the ledge?" Byriel asked.

Joon nodded, pressing his nose into my hair and inhaling deeply before answering. "Unfortunately, I think that's the fastest route. It'll put us on the other side of the camp and straight to Ossory. We just have to hope no one sees us."

"What path?" I asked.

Byriel leaned in, keeping his voice soft. "There was a ledge cut in the rock face. It looked wide enough to travel on."

"And the land on the other side appears to slope down," Joon said.

Byriel nodded. "It will be the most direct path, but we must be very quiet." He eyed me, then Blue. But my eyes cut straight to Lex, knowing damn well we wouldn't be the problem.

"No talking," Joon snapped, cutting Lex a stony glare. "Zero talking. Not even a whisper. They will hear it, and I don't know if they have bows."

Lex scoffed, then bared his pointy teeth. "How about I drop down and kill them all? Then we can stroll through as leisurely as we like."

"Can you do that?" Blue asked, eyes wide and mouth open.

"No," Joon said forcefully. "He can't."

Lex looked at my mate with big, offended eyes. A hand pressed to his chest. "How dare you." His tone was dramatic, making Blue smile wide.

"You are very powerful, siren," Byriel said. "I believe you could easily handle three or four alphas on your own. But a few dozen?" He paused, shaking his head. "I don't see that happening."

"Like hell," Lex snapped, leaning back as if to make room for his massive ego to fit between us. "Just because you can't handle yourself in a fight doesn't mean I'm useless."

Joon laughed, not the least bit interested in his challenge. "I hope to the Moon they all have bows, and they take out your shimmering, obnoxious ass first."

"I'm not against showing you how vicious I can be." Lex flashed his teeth at my mate, but Joon only chuckled.

"I've known you too long to be tempted by your flirty threats." Joon snorted.

"Can you really...kill...that many alphas at once?" Blue whispered, looking at Lex with so much awe.

"I am capable of many things, my little sweetie," Lex smirked, tickling under Blue's chin.

Joon groaned. "Just once, I'd love to see you humble."

"Truly fierce beings are beyond humble opinions of themselves." Lex winked. "We're too honest to be forced to submit to lowly thoughts."

Byriel let out a quiet, rumbling laugh, the corner of his mouth lifting a bit. "Well put, siren."

"Well," I said. "If we're all done being very impressed with ourselves, perhaps we should head that way. It would be best to do this before the sun comes up."

"I agree," Joon sighed, standing up. "But if Lex utters a single word, I'm pushing him down the mountain."

Lex smirked. "Don't think I won't take you with me, big boy."

The Narrow Path

Byriel

FROM A DISTANCE, the narrow path looked decent in size, wide enough to edge along if you laid flush with the rockface. But now that the trail was staring us down, barely illuminated by the waxing crescent Moon, it looked more like a sliver of cracked stone—unsteady and dangerous.

I glanced at Blue, nervous about having him cross but more uneasy about him traveling through the forest so close to Ossory. There would be numerous guards in these lands and even more lawless types.

The palace brought in all kinds of creatures across Havre, many of them unsavory. The thought of having Blue exposed to them made my wolf tense. I needed to get him inside the city where I could keep him safe. And, whether I like it or not, this was the fastest path.

We lined up, Joon taking the lead with Tzidal just behind him. He looked at his mate, and she nodded calmly, waiting for him to lead the way. Blue and Lex stood behind me, the three of us watching quietly as the pair crept across.

Tzidal's toes curled over the stoney lip as she moved, one hand in Joon's and the other pressed against the wall of rock behind her. She shuffled, Joon moving slowly to allow her to keep pace.

This was going to take forever.

Leaning forward, I glanced down at the camp, feeling just how exposed we were. Thankfully, the guards were distracted, busy eating, quietly chatting, and playing cards around little fires—completely unaware of our presence. The atmosphere was a little relaxed for an official patrol, and I struggled to see their purpose.

There was no repository of weapons, no barricade for prisoners, and no stockade of supplies. Their location didn't make any tactical sense either. Surrounded by the jutting mountain, the wolves below only had one way in or out. It made more sense for alphas looking to protect more vulnerable wolves or supplies—it kept enemies from sneaking into a camp from multiple angles.

I wondered if they were more rogue guards, like those at Blue's camp. My wolf growled, mocking my thoughts. He knew they weren't rogues, agreeing forcefully with Joon. I pushed my beast away and cleared my mind.

Joon and Tzidal approached the halfway mark, and I reached for Blue's hand. He startled when I touched him, pushing back into Lex. I took a calming breath, trying not to show my disappointment at his reaction.

Last night, after I cleaned his finger, he curled into himself, angling away from me. He wasn't asleep, but he pretended to be. It gutted me to know how much I scared him.

Slowly, I held my hand out to him, palm up, and waited.

Blinking rapidly, Blue swallowed hard, then slipped his

small, cold hand into mine. His enchanting eyes glowed in the moonlight, just like his skin. He looked covered in stardust, shimmering bright for all to see.

He was so lovely.

My stomach dropped.

Moving my attention to Lex, I swallowed hard. They were both pale and bright, a beacon in the dark night. They would be so easy to spot for anyone that might glance up.

I motioned the siren forward, and he leaned in so I could whisper in his ear, "Can you change yourself to be darker?"

"Darker?"

"You're as bright as Blue." I motioned to the omega by my side.

Lex looked at Blue's face, then down at his own hands. Slowly, he phased. Black seeped across the siren's skin, bleeding over his robes. His clothes, skin, and hair went a deep black, even deeper in color than mine. He still held a glowing sheen about him, but it wasn't silver anymore. Instead, he shimmered gold. He looked like a glimmering shadow.

I turned to Blue. His black pants covered him well enough, but his linen shirt and pale face were still a problem.

"Here." Lex pulled out a black guard's shirt from the satchel.

Joon and I hadn't worn anything outside our trousers since Vaesen, and we only wore them out of respect to Tzidal and now Blue. It was impolite to travel as beasts with omegas present.

I took a thankful breath and pulled the shirt over Blue's head, reaching behind him to pull his long hair out of the collar. It was so silky. Like down-feathers. His cheeks blushed as my fingers grazed his nape.

I prayed his reaction was out of affection and not fear.

But at this point, it was all probably just a frivolous dream. A monster like me didn't deserve such a heavenly creature.

"By'," Lex whispered, motioning behind me.

Joon and Tzidal were almost across the path, waving us over. I glanced back at Lex, ensuring he had Blue's hand firmly in his before moving across the ledge.

Blue's hand trembled in mine, and I squeezed it a little, trying to reassure him.

The wind kicked up a bit as we slowly inched across the ledge. A chilly breeze filled with misty droplets of water made goosebumps flash across my skin, and I carefully looked down.

At the very bottom of the ledge sat a rushing gush of water. Too small to be a waterfall but quick enough to make a decent amount of noise against the boulders. I let out a breath of relief. It was a welcome padding of sound should Lex get nervous and chatty.

I edged sideways, squeezing Blue's hand to pull him forward. My wolf remained completely silent within me, letting me fully concentrate on my feet and Blue's breathing.

As we moved, everything inside me screamed this was wrong. I was putting Blue in too much danger.

There was a crack of thunder, and I jerked, looking at the sky. There wasn't a cloud in sight. I widened my eyes over the camp below us, trying to figure out where the echoing sound came from and hoping no one below noticed it.

Tzidal squeaked, slapping a hand over her mouth. I followed her horrified gaze past me.

The stone under Blue's feet cracked again. Dirt and rock sprayed into the air in thick puffs as the small mountain groaned. Then it started to crumble beneath him. I squeezed Blue's hand hard and pulled him to keep moving, but he stayed still, frozen with fear.

His throat worked as he swallowed hard. He turned his eyes to the sky, tears clinging to his lashes. But to his credit, he didn't make a sound.

I looked around me, trying to figure out what the hell to

do. I couldn't jerk Blue to me—we both might fall. *Hell, we could all end up falling to our deaths.*

Deciding going back was the fastest option, I pointed past Lex, indicating we needed to retreat. The siren inched backward, trying to pull Blue with him. Blue moved one foot ever so slightly and more rock crumbled between his feet. He shook his head fiercely at the siren, going completely still again.

Making a quick and dangerous decision, I readied myself to grab Blue and fling both of us toward the other side. I met Joon's eyes, and he nodded, seeing my intentions.

Taking a deep breath, I turned back to Blue. A few tears fell down his face, and his scent was sharp with fear. I nodded slowly to try to reassure him.

Then just like that, his hand slipped out of mine.

And he was gone.

The Broken Path

Tzidal

I STARED at the cracked stone where Blue once stood. A cloud of dirt still hung in the air, drifting up with the cold breeze. I should have been screaming, crying, or trying to look for him, but I couldn't move. Fear and shock locked my mind and body.

The mountain groaned, angry and loud, snapping the night air once again.

Then Lex fell.

The ledge beneath him turned to dust as he disappeared into black shadows, his frightened eyes following Blue into the dark below.

I let out a horrified scream, and Joon clapped a firm hand over my mouth, pulling me against his side. The path suddenly felt like crumbled sand beneath my toes. My knees shook violently while I struggled not to slip into complete distress.

Lex and Blue could be hurt. *Or dead.*

Byriel's glowing red eyes looked past me at Joon. I felt my mate's body move slightly behind me. Then Byriel jumped.

I tried to yell around Joon's hand, but my mate refused to release me. Instead, he jerked me across the last of the path, flinging me toward the grass and trees. I hit the ground with a pained grunt, then rolled. Before I could push myself up, Joon was on top of me. His chest pressed firmly into my back, the cool, dry grass against my stomach.

It didn't help.

Every nerve in my body yearned to stand and scream into the valley. I needed to see Lex and Blue's bodies to see if they were really gone. I wanted to rip through the camp of alphas and scoop my friends up with my own two hands.

Sensing my spiraling distress, Joon settled even more weight on me, and my breathing slowed. His long fangs punctured the juncture of my shoulder, and my whole body eased. Joon purrs into my flesh, slipping his fangs in a little deeper.

The clarity and calm that settled over me allowed me to breathe. I filled my lungs with the cold night air, forcing my bones to stop shaking.

Once calm, Joon slowly lifted some of his weight off my back. I sucked in a deep breath, then reached my hands out in front of me. I dug my nails into the hard earth and inched forward. I was surprised when Joon didn't stop me but moved with me, looking into the encampment below.

At the bottom of the tiny waterfall, a soaking wet Blue and Lex sat next to a tuft of bushes. It was so hard to see Lex's dark form, but his glassy eyes gave him away. His flashing, grey eyes would have terrified me if I hadn't known it was the siren.

I blew out a slow breath of relief through my nose, thankful to see them alive and seemingly uninjured.

Movement caught my eye as a guard strolled through the tents toward them. His eyes were up at the ledge—where we just stood. He scanned the mountain, yet to notice Lex or Blue. I held my breath, wanting to scream out a warning, but, sensing my urge, Joon gripped my hand and shook his head.

My heart thundered as the guard brought his eyes down the rockface. Just before his gaze could settle on the waterfall, Byriel appeared from behind the brush, wrapped his arms around the middle of both siren and omega, and jerked them out of view.

The guard glanced over the area, snapping his head up as the rock cracked again. A few small pebbles beat down the side, splashing into the water. After waiting a beat, the guard finally turned back to his camp, quickly returning to sit by a fire.

Covering my face with my hands, I rolled onto my back and cried softly. It was all too much.

Joon lifted me into his strong arms, tucking me against his chest. I kept quiet as adrenaline, fear, and relief beat through my veins, making my whole body tremble uncontrollably. My wolf yowled with just as much distress.

I pushed into Joon's neck as he carried me away, sucking in as much of my mate's scent as I could. I didn't need to ask where we were going or what we were doing. It didn't matter. I was too overwhelmed to think of anything other than how terrified Blue must be.

Joon moved us under a thick canopy of trees, and the air dipped several degrees. The light from the Moon dimmed, but I kept my face hidden in Joon's neck even as he sat us down.

I was so raw.

My emotions, my heart, my wolf.

Everything was a twist of confusion and terror.

"It's okay, my omega," Joon purred. He stayed perched over me as he moved branches and sticks around us, keeping his body close to mine.

Finally, opening my eyes, I took in the sight of the tight

thicket of bushes. The long branches and cluster leaves kept us hidden, but it didn't give me the comfort of a proper nest. We were still out in the middle of nowhere. Open to anyone wanting to capture or hurt us.

I opened my mouth to speak, but all that escaped was a soft whine. I wanted so badly to be strong and steady, but I couldn't hold myself together anymore. So I cried.

Blue and Lex almost died.

They could still die.

They were trapped at the base of a mountain, pressed right up against those guards, and there was nothing I could do.

"I'm right here, my mate," Joon whispered, working quickly to hide us completely before turning his full attention to me. "It's going to be okay. Byriel is with them, and you know he won't let anything happen to them."

Joon's large body settled on top of me. His broad expanse of muscle held me safely against the soft earth. Gently, he purred and whispered comforting words, drifting his fingers through my hair and down the sides of my face. The weight and warmth of him made my wolf feel secure and grounded, and I wrapped my arms around his neck to bring him closer.

Letting out a long, shuddering breath, I allowed the love Joon pushed through our bond to ease me.

"I know, my sweet mate." His lips just next to my ear. "It scared me too. But they're okay. And we're okay. There is nothing to be scared of. I'm right here."

I let a few tears fall, then I inhaled deeply, filling my lungs with my alpha's smokey, sweet scent. Everything about him made me feel safe and calm. After all, he was right.

Byriel would keep Lex and Blue safe until morning. Then we'd figure out our next steps. I panicked when I should have been planning, but I couldn't help it.

"You're such a strong omega. You've been so brave and

strong," my mate whispered against my temple. "It's going to be okay. I promise."

"Joon?" My voice was barely a whisper.

"Yes?"

"I know this isn't...we shouldn't...but...." My breath hitched as I tried to speak. I felt stupid, selfish, and a little embarrassed, but I needed to connect with my mate. I needed to feel him, all of him. I needed to know we were both alive and safe. "Will you touch me?"

He smiled softly at my request, moving his thumb over my bottom lip. His voice was tender and husky at the same time, "Of course."

"I just need to feel something other than...I mean...I know it's not—"

"Tzidal," he cut me off, placing a soft kiss on my lips. "Wanting to feel something other than fear and sadness is not something you have to explain to me." He kissed the tip of my nose, then pressed his forehead to mine. "Never feel bad for asking me to make you feel good, my love. I am your mate, and you are my purpose."

Within The Bushes

Joon

GENTLY, I moved my mouth over my mate, feeling the tremble in her lips. I wanted to split myself open and pour her into me, cocoon her in my love and safety.

I could feel how raw her wolf was and hated that there was nothing I could do to soothe her deep fear. But this—holding her and loving her—this I could do.

Tzidal opened her mouth, letting me taste her sweet breath.

I tilted her head, kissing her deeper and pulling her closer. She moved easily, giving up all control to me. Giving up all her fiery power and strength. Letting me take her however I wanted. However she needed.

Not breaking our searing kiss, I pulled her pants down her slender legs. I worked quickly at the buttons of her shirt, lifting her slightly and pulling it off. I needed to see every soft curve of her perfect body.

I tugged my pants off, then quickly moved back over her.

Tzidal's puffy lips parted slightly, and her eyes were hooded with lust as she beaconed me closer. Her hands reached for me, her fingers curling into my shoulders.

I wanted to cover every inch of her in my scent.

I traced my thumb over her plump lower lip. "So pretty," I whispered.

She smiled, shying away from my gaze.

She was fiery and strong. Sensitive and sweet. Demanding and submissive. She was everything all at once.

My perfect omega.

I took hold of one of her knees and pulled it over my hip, opening her up for me. The delicious smell of slick filled our little nest of leaves, and my chest rumbled with pleasure. Tzidal's big, golden eyes dilated at the sound, and she gasped, allowing me to claim her mouth again. I thrust my tongue deep into her, searching and feeling every part of her wet mouth.

Her nipples hardened against my chest as I moved my hand between her legs. Her wet folds were so puffy and slick. Slowly, I moved my thumb just above her hard, little clit and circled it.

Tzidal let out a soft gasp and bit her bottom lip hard, trying to muffle her sounds. I hated it. I wanted to hear her sing out the wonderful sensations I was pulling from her, but she was right to stay quiet. We were still a bit too close to the camp of unknown wolves.

I sucked long and slow at my mating bite, then slipped a thick finger inside her heat. Her body clenched around my finger, making my cock so hard it hurt. I pistoned my finger, adding another and pressing the heel of my palm to her engorged clit. Her back arched, and slick gushed into my hand. Her pussy fluttered hard and fast against my fingers.

She held her breath, a soft squeak barely leaving her lips as pleasure rushed through her. I kept rubbing and thrusting, watching her face with rapt attention. Her cheeks went pink, and she bit her lip, leaving an indentation of her teeth. I leaned down and sucked her tongue out of her mouth, wanting to taste her moans.

Slowly, Tzidal's body softened beneath me. It was so hard not to let a vicious roar rip from my throat and to start fucking her senseless, but not now. She needed a gentle, loving touch. She needed to feel my safety, strength, and love.

Holding her gaze, I lined myself up with her slick entrance and slowly pushed into my mate. She opened her mouth slightly. Her beautiful eyes widened as I filled her completely. Then I moved, leaving soft kisses over her lips and neck. I rolled my hips, memorizing the velvety feel of her cunt wrapped tightly around me.

Her panting breaths and muted mewls were everything. She was so fucking beautiful in the soft light of the Moon, all tousled hair and flushed skin.

"You feel so good," I whispered against her lips, unable to stop myself from praising her. "So beautiful and perfect. So wet and sweet. My perfect mate."

Unable to form words, Tzidal nodded, then tilted her head back, exposing more of her throat to me. Her fingers curled into my shoulders as I thrust forward, letting myself lose a bit of control. My hips hammered against her small body. Her face flushed and scrunched with her building orgasm. Her pussy clenched, and her breath hitched.

Sooner than I wanted, my knot expanded, and I pushed hard inside my mate, sealing us together as she came hard on my cock. Her body convulsed, and a moan spilled out of her throat. I leaned down to drink it down quickly, rocking my hips against her wet heat through my pulses.

"So...ugh...so big," Tzidal whispered against my tongue and shuddered.

"Such a good, omega." I pushed deeper into her. Her sweet cunt soaked up every last drop of my climax. "So perfect."

We stayed like that, connected and quiet, for a long time. Just kissing, caressing, and scenting each other. I kissed her lips, cheeks, and chin, making her feel my love for her.

Sinking my weight onto her lithe body, I buried my face in her neck and nuzzled softly over my mark. I needed her to feel my calm and comfort and to know there was nothing to fear.

I meant what I said to Tzidal; Byriel would keep Lex and Blue safe. I might still have a lot of anger for the alpha, but Byriel wasn't evil. Just stupid.

And his attachment to the small, male omega was clear. I was confident if Byriel sensed any threat among the camp of wolves, he'd keep them hidden. I had no worries for them tonight.

I just had to figure out how the hell to get them out of there come morning.

The Base of the Mountain

Byriel

I PEERED around the edge of the boulder and through the misty from the small waterfall. A guard I didn't recognize looked up the mountain. He watched a few pebbles and dirt slide down, splashing not far from me. Scenting Blue's fear and Lex's unease behind me, I held my breath, not moving until the guard finally left, disappearing back into his camp.

Relieved, I turned and stepped down into the cove where I had shoved the omega and siren. Inside a jut of rocks, the small space was hidden in the dark by a few massive boulders and hanging vines. The top of the encircled rocks was open to the night sky, making me uneasy; all someone had to do was step around the boulders to find us.

Sitting deep within the shadows, I was confident we were safe for now but come morning, I couldn't guarantee we wouldn't be found.

Tipping my head back, I looked at the Moon's light

breaking through the branches above, saying a quick, silent prayer to her. Her gentle light illuminated the small space, making it feel almost cozy. I was hopeful Blue would be able to sleep comfortably here while I fashioned a plan to sneak us out before daybreak.

Blue and Lex huddled together, both soaking wet and shivering. We were fortunate they had slid down the rockface and not fallen. From that distance, both could have been seriously injured, if not killed. My claws pushed out at the idea of Blue getting hurt, and I shook my head, trying to shove the thought away.

"Are you okay?" I whispered, my wolf begging me to lean in and scent Blue properly. He could have unseen injuries like cracked ribs or deep bruises. Not knowing for sure made my wolf restless, but I kept my distance, not trusting myself to touch the omega.

Blue nodded as he tucked his fists under his chin, a tremor working hard through his shoulders. I instantly reached for the satchel around Lex's neck. The siren hissed out an angry protest as I ripped it off his shoulder. I pulled out the last shirt we had. It was surprisingly dry, considering how wet the bag and siren were.

I quickly held it out to Blue. "But you..." he mumbled, his chin trembling as he tried to refuse it.

"I'm fine," I said firmly, setting the garment next to him. My pants were soaked, but it was nothing I couldn't handle. Omegas, on the other hand, were far too fragile to shiver all night.

I turned my back to give him some privacy. The wet smack of fabric was followed quickly by Blue's soft scent. I closed my eyes and inhaled deeply, my mouth watering at the delicate perfume that settled on my tongue. I wasn't sure if anyone had ever thanked the stars for the presence of a siren, but right now, Lex was my saving grace. He was keeping my wolf's desires at bay.

If left alone, I was sure my rational mind would slip away, and I'd be tempted to claim my sweet omega.

My wolf desperately wanted to slip into a fierce rut of lust and need, and I finally understood why alphas took unclaimed omegas without courting or even consent. Blue's delicious scent was testing every fiber of my willpower.

But I wasn't an animal.

I was civilized and would do this properly and with his permission.

While it was clear I still scared the delicate omega, I was determined to win him over. But I needed more time before I could pursue him properly. I needed to build his wolf's trust before taking him as my own.

"Okay," Blue whispered.

I faced him and instantly shut my eyes, cursing my painfully hard erection.

Blue's wet hair fell into his eyes, the dark shirt fell to his knees, and he twisted his fingers together while averting his gaze. He looked so submissive and enchanting. Everything about him begged to be handled and dominated.

It was more than my wolf could manage at the moment, and I prayed to the Moon for strength.

"Are you okay?" Lex asked me a little too loudly.

I opened my eyes, then motioned with my hand for him to keep it down. While the waterfall might muffle a lot of sound, someone might still hear us.

Lex shrugged, then snuggled next to Blue. The siren's clothes suddenly looked dry, but his hair was still wet. I simply didn't understand his magic.

"Are you sure you're okay?" Lex asked me again, not having the decency to let it be. Given my urges and his ability to feel emotions, I was sure he knew exactly what my problem was.

"Yes," I cleared my throat, "I'm fine. How about you two?" I moved my eyes up Blue's soft, pale legs. His skin held a hazy blue hue in the dim light, making him look even more alluring. Like a soft, glowing treasure begging to be discovered.

"Just a scratch, but I'm okay," Blue said softly, looking at his hand.

I was instantly next to him, causing the omega to startle at my swift movement. "You're hurt? Where?" I ghosted my hands over his arms, enraged that I hadn't immediately caught the slight tinge of blood in the air.

Blue took a calming breath, then pushed his sleeve up to reveal more of his velvety skin to my hungry eyes. The heel of his hand, up the side of his forearm, was scraped. A small amount of blood seeped out in a few spots. Nothing dangerous or life-threatening, but still more pain than my omega deserved.

"Can I?" I asked, holding his arm gently in my hands. It was agony to ask and not just tend to him.

Blue swallowed hard, then nodded, his lips pressed tight.

My tongue touched his warm skin, and I fell into absolute bliss. I lapped then sucked gently, really tasting him for the first time. A burst of sweet energy poured through me. My wolf was alive—truly alive—for the first time in my life. Every moment and purpose within me zeroed down to this one omega—this one enchanting creature.

He was my wolf's claim.

My heart's desire.

He was mine.

I moved over his scratches, cleaning them thoroughly and allowing myself to pull in all of his beautiful flavor. Blue's scent was so delicate and clean, but it somehow still filled my whole body with a flood of sugar that made my teeth hurt. It was electrifying and soothing at the same time.

My body thrummed with sensation, and I squeezed my eyes shut tight as my fangs lengthened involuntarily. I needed to stop, but I couldn't.

"Does that really heal wounds faster?" Lex scrunched up his nose, watching me work. "Or do alphas just have a blood-sucker fetish?"

I narrowed my eyes at the siren, wishing the fall had killed him.

Blue kept his hypnotic eyes on the ground, frozen as I continued. His wounds were clean, but the urge to continue touching him was too fierce. My tongue flicked over the side of his little finger, and he leaned away from me. He pressed his nose into Lex's arm as a slip of a whimper left his lips. I instantly forced myself to stop, removing my hands from his body.

He was scared, and I was making it worse.

As carefully as I could, I pulled the sleeve back down his arm, then sat as far away from the omega as the small space would allow, my feet resting just next to his.

I needed to stop being so reckless. I hated feeling so out of control, but the feelings Blue pulled from me felt too good.

Blue kept his face hidden behind Lex's arm, unable to see my internal struggle. The siren's big, grey eyes moved over my face, and he cocked his head to the side. Inhaling the air around him, he glanced at Blue, then back to me.

My eyes pulsed red, and Lex smirked.

"I think I'm going to head up and check out the camp." The siren stood up, smoothing down the front of his robes. "I should eat."

Blue's scent lingered on my tongue, and my wolf thrilled at the idea of being alone with the defenseless omega, but my mind was still fully intact.

I couldn't be alone with him.

I would hurt him.

I just knew it.

"You just ate," I snarled, jumping to my feet. The second the words left my mouth, I froze and listened carefully for any sound of movement. I hadn't meant to be so loud.

Lex dragged his hand down through the air—just like I had done to him—motioning for me to be quiet. I closed the space between us, wanting to grab the siren and force him to sit back down.

"You just ate," I whispered harshly, leaning down a bit to look him hard in the eyes. "Coming and going from here is a bad idea. They might see you. Attack you. Follow you to Blue. It's not smart." I tried to sound calm and rational, but judging from the smile pulling hard at one side of Lex's mouth, my desperation was far too clear.

"Nah," Lex shook his head, his eyes flickering to Blue, "I think I'm in the mood for a midnight snack, and these mutts just smell too damn good."

The siren swished around me, and I spun, grabbing his arm and jerking him to me. "Stay," I whispered low, forcing every bit of angry alpha into my voice. I knew it wouldn't affect him, not like an omega, but I was desperate.

Lex laughed, then jerked his arm free. "Have fun," he winked.

Then he was gone.

He was fucking gone, moving quickly up and out, away from us. I stared at the dark boulders and deep shadows, willing him to return.

Blue shifted behind me, and my wolf let out a slow, hungry growl. My claws were jagged and heavy, and my fangs slipped into painful points.

"Alpha Byriel?"

I tipped my chin up and said a quick, silent prayer,

begging the Moon to give me control. I wasn't a mindless beast. I wouldn't force myself on an unmated omega.

I was civilized.

I had self-control.

I had a raging hard-on that made it so fucking hard to think straight.

"Yes?" I said, my voice hoarse. I sucked in a deep breath and forced my fangs to push back up. The movement was slow, and my gums ached as my wolf tried like hell to take over.

Once steady, I turned around to face him.

Blue's hypnotic eyes met mine. The soft purple strand in his hair looked almost grey in poor light. His knees were pulled under his chin, and his arms wrapped firmly around his legs. I took another breath and sat back down, fists clenched, keeping my distance.

"What's wrong?" I asked when Blue didn't say anything else.

He shook his head, mumbling out a soft *nothing*.

I hated seeing him like this, so uneasy and small. I wanted him to find comfort and strength in my presence, but I only scared him.

"Don't worry, omega. I'll protect you," I said, pretending his fear had more to do with the encampment than me, but I knew better.

Blue looked up at me, a sweet smile brightening his face. "I know." His features looked relaxed despite the smell of distress swirling around him. "But in case you're worried," he continued, "I'll protect you too."

I straightened my back and cocked my head. Was he teasing me? He still smelled of fear, but he looked almost playful. The contradiction was a bit confusing to my wolf, making me want to lean in to scent him.

I stayed put.

"That's very kind," I said, letting out a small laugh, "I'm sure I will sleep very well tonight, knowing you're on guard."

Blue's voice was soft but somehow a little challenging despite the sweet glint in his eyes. "I know you're teasing me, but I've lived my whole life without an alpha protecting me. I know a few things about escaping your kind." He looked so proud of that fact.

My wolf snarled, and I crossed my arms. I didn't like him implying he didn't need me.

"Don't be mad, alpha," he whispered, resting his chin on his knees. "I've decided I'll let you protect me. Just this once."

My shoulders relaxed, and I returned his smile. I wasn't used to being teased, and I wasn't sure what to say. "That's very kind of you. And I promise I will do my best to keep you safe."

He bit his bottom lip. "I know."

The air felt a little calmer, letting my wolf settle. Blue's scent edged softer, not as fearful. I stretched my legs out, my feet resting just next to his. He had big feet for his size but still much smaller than mine. They almost looked like he'd be clumsy, but he was far from it. Fast and graceful. An impressive omega.

"Can I ask you a question?" His eyes met mine, and I nodded immediately. "The King of Wolves is your father?" I nodded again, slower this time. Blue was already aware of this, having heard Joon and I argue about it. "Omega Tzidal said you don't want him to die, but if that's true, then why are you helping her?"

Every muscle in my body went tight, and my mouth flooded with a bitter panic. I wondered what else Tzidal had told him—not that she owed me any secrets. But I didn't want Blue to hate me for killing innocents...just like his pack.

"He is my father," I forced out. Admitting it felt like a confession of all my sins.

I opened my mouth to say more, but I wasn't sure what. And I was terrified that Blue would ask questions, and I couldn't lie to him. No matter how badly I wanted to, my tongue wouldn't allow it.

Blue crossed his legs under him and leaned forward a bit, his eyes big and curious as he patiently waited for me to continue.

"I'm helping Tzidal because I owe her my life," I said simply. It was true. She saved me when she should have killed me. Hell, I even begged her to kill me. But she was endlessly kind and gave me the chance to try to mend my soul.

"But Alpha Joon and Tzidal want the King to die. And he's your father. Are you...do you want him....?" Blue struggled to find the words, clearly wanting to ask if I wanted my father dead as well.

"My father is not a kind King," I said. "He does things that are cruel. Even before the marked wolves." I shook my head, finding it all so damn hard to talk about, but Blue deserved the truth. Especially after what happened to his pack.

"The King has been known to frequently order the guard to round up wolves that live outside of the villages and force them within boundaries he can control. He attacks peaceful colonies of non-weres because he doesn't like sharing our land with other species—even if they have been here as long as we have. He's...not kind."

It was all true. It didn't answer his question, but I couldn't bring myself to tell him that I wouldn't condemn the King to death because if he deserved to die, so did I. My father told me to kill, and I did. Commanded by my King or not, it wasn't an excuse.

"The King has done horrible things, but so have I," I said. "We're the same in that regard. So I don't wish him death, but I understand Omega Tzidal's desire. I won't help her kill him, but I won't stop her either. I owe her that."

Blue's eyes held so much pity for me. I hated it.

"I'm so sorry," he whispered, placing a hand over his heart. "I never knew my parents, they died before I could talk, but I think I'd prefer no memories over awful ones. It must be so hard to know a horrible parent."

His face flushed, and his eyes suddenly widened with fear. "I'm so sorry, alpha!" He held up his hands as if I were going to launch myself across the small space and attack him. His fear confused me for a moment. "I didn't mean to say the King was horrible. I just meant—"

"Blue," I whispered, trying to push my calm voice into him. "It's okay. I understand what you meant, and I agree. The lack of memories of those that loved us is sometimes kinder than being forced to know them."

Nodding, Blue let out a thankful breath. His skin seemed to brighten slightly for a moment. His dark eyes moved over my face, and he twisted his fingers together. "I'm just so sorry," he whispered.

I inched closer, wanting so badly to touch him. It was fucking agony not to. "Can I ask," I said, feeling that as long as we were talking my wolf would be too distracted to act on his instincts. "Your skin. You seem to glow. You appear to get brighter sometimes."

Blue fidgeted, looking very uncomfortable. It wasn't the reaction I had expected. "Yeah." He pressed his lips together, looking as if he might cry.

"You don't have to talk about it," I said. It had not been my intention to make him feel bad.

"I can't always control it." His voice was so soft I had to lean in to hear him. "My grandma used to call it pulsing. It's a fae thing. A few of the full-blooded fairies that lived in my village tried to teach me how to control it, but I don't have the same power they do. I'm not strong enough to own it."

Giving in to the intense need to feel his skin, I reached out.

Blue's eyes widened at my outstretched hand, and his whole body trembled. He looked up at me, and I could feel my eyes glow red at the soft, frightened look on his face.

Snapping myself out of it, I leaned back, hating that I terrified him. I was failing miserably at trying to court him. It only made sense. I failed at most things.

"Blue?"

"Yes," he whispered, keeping his eyes on the stone at his feet.

"I'm sorry I scare you. Please, know I would never hurt you."

He chewed on his bottom lip, moving his eyes to his hands, then slowly, he nodded. "You do scare me."

I let out a shuddering breath, trying not to display my heartache, then stood. My wolf was a violent mess within me, begging me to stay put and claim our omega. Take him by force.

"I'm sorry," I whispered, keeping my eyes on the entrance of the little cove. "I'll sit outside near the water. I'll keep my distance."

Placing my foot on the smooth stone, I moved to step up when a small hand touched my back.

"No," Blue said. The single word was somehow so jittery and filled with...*something*. I couldn't place the emotion.

I turned slowly, trying not to frighten him further with any sudden movements. His hypnotic eyes glowed in the moonlight, and his velvety cheeks were wet from his damp hair.

"You," he nervously licked his lips, "don't scare me like that."

I didn't know how to speak. The way his eyes roamed over my face and his little bow of a pout struggling to speak. His gentle nature made me stupid.

"What do you mean?" I sounded so weak, but I didn't care.

Moving slowly, Blue carefully pressed his hands to my chest. His fingers were so cold, and the chill felt good on my hot skin. I lost myself for a moment in his beautiful scent.

Then my wolf purred.

I couldn't remember a single moment in my life when my beast had ever purred.

My whole life, I was simply an extension of my father's right arm, sent out to fulfill his most violent whims. I never had lovers or indulged in frivolous activities. I was just a weapon. I had no reason to purr.

But right now, with this soft, sweet omega looking up at me like I was mighty and wonderful, I felt a little more human. My heart thundered for him, and my head spun. He was kind and calm, and curious. He was perfect, and he was looking at me with something beautiful dancing in his eyes.

"You do scare me," he said again. "But it's not...I mean..."

He glanced away quickly as if gathering his courage before looking back up with a sudden fire in his eyes.

Blue pushed himself onto the balls of his feet and placed a small, soft kiss on my lips. I felt his bottom lip tremble ever so slightly, and my wolf stretched out in euphoric bliss. Then very slowly, Blue settled back onto the ground.

He swallowed thickly, waiting for my reaction. I was scared to move. Worried I'd consume him if I lifted even a finger.

His eyes dimmed and he bit his bottom lip, removing his hands from my chest. "Um, I—"

I grabbed his shoulders and pulled him to me, beating back the urge to lay claim to his tempting body. *He was mine.*

His breath hitched, but he didn't fight me off or protest. He just let me pull him closer and tighter, willing me to control him.

"Blue." His name pushed out of me like a violent prayer to the Moon. I was desperate for control over my beast. I didn't want to claim him right now. Not with the encampment so close. But I was losing myself to my wolf, the urge to mark him pounded hard in my veins.

Blue's pale cheeks darkened, and I could practically taste his blush in the air. Slowly, losing my grip on what little willpower I had left, I leaned down, inhaling his sweet breath. He released a delicate, little gasp against my lips, and I crashed our mouths together, taking him rough and hard.

Slipping my tongue inside his mouth, I growled deep and slow, feeling the nervous movements of his tongue against mine. His inexperience was so endearing and tempting, making me want to ruin everything about his sweet, soft body.

Needing more of him, I fisted his hair and tilted his head slightly so I could bring us closer. I needed to feel more of him: his lips, his mouth, his breath, his taste.

His fucking taste.

It was like nothing I had ever experienced before. Light, sweet, and powerful. He was a summer breeze swimming in my veins. Soothing, comforting, electrifying. He lit me on fire.

Is this what it felt like to truly be alive?

Unable to help myself, I moved hungrily into my omega. Wrapping an arm around his back, I pressed my heavy erection against his hip and his trembling body against my chest. He gasped into my mouth, shaking a little, and my wolf let out a deep, possessive growl.

Breaking the kiss, I looked at his lovely face—his puffy lips, blushed cheeks, and gorgeous, hooded eyes focused entirely on me. *Fuck*, he was breathtaking.

And tonight, he would be mine.

"Wolf!" Lex's voice rang out just beyond the boulders. "You are never going to believe this!"

Blue immediately pushed away from me and hurried to the other side of the cove, curling into a dark corner. I swallowed hard to suppress a growl and curled my hands into fists to hide my lengthening claws.

I wanted to rip the fucking siren in two and bathe in his fucking blood.

Lex pushed past me and stood with his hands on his hips, bursting with energy. He looked elated, like he was begging to share a wonderfully awful secret.

I didn't give a shit what he had to say. I just wanted him gone.

"Why is it," I growled, my fists aching to be used, "you're either gone all fucking night or you're back in two seconds?"

"Depends on if I'm in the mood to play with my food," Lex smirked. "But seriously," his face dropped, all amusement gone, "you'll want to hear this."

The Makeshift Nest

Tzdial

I WOKE to the feel of a wolf's soft fur pressed against my back. It was so thick and warm. Inhaling deeply, I wiggled back into Joon's wolf-form, letting his warm scent envelop me. He stirred, and firm muscle and soft skin replaced fur.

A strong arm wrapped around my middle. "It's just past dawn," he whispered, his voice rough in my ear. "We should go. I'm sure Byriel has gotten them to safety and is looking for us."

I peeked my eyes open and took note of the green foliage, relieved that we had passed the stark black trees at some point in the night. The lack of color was draining. My wolf craved the color green.

I rolled onto my back. Joon's black hair hung into his eyes, and his lips looked far too inviting.

Looking down at my naked body, he brought one big hand up my belly and squeezed my breast firmly, puckering my nipple up to him. He lowered his head and gently sucked. His hot, wet mouth, in contrast with the chilly air, made me gasp, and my legs fell open for him.

Joon pressed my pert bud between his lips in a lingering kiss. Then he released me and rolled away, crawling out of the nest of leaves and brush.

I sat up quickly, confused and a little angry. "Joon," I hissed, trying not to be too loud.

He stretched his arms out. "Yes, my mate?" His tone was light and playful as he pulled his snug leather pants over his thick thighs. My eyes moved over his firm physique in the early morning light. I loved how good he looked and hated that he wasn't buried deep inside me.

"What are you doing?" I sat firmly in the bushes, wishing more than anything he'd come back.

"We need to go." Joon looked at me as if the answer was obvious. Letting out a pained huff, I grabbed my clothes and stepped into the cool morning air. It felt like winter was pushing at my back, making goosebumps rise across my exposed flesh.

The hazy morning fog clung to the base of the trees. The sun wasn't high enough yet to burn it off, giving the forest an enchanted feel. It was a lovely patch of land, soft and inviting, but I was too annoyed to enjoy it.

Pulling on Joon's oversized shirt and my pants, I glared at my mate. He flashed me a cocky grin, and my wolf snarled at him. Leaving me needy wasn't funny in the least.

"Don't think you can play with me like that and then just leave me in this state without consequences," I warned, hating how hard it was to talk with my clit swollen and my nipple still tingling from his tongue.

"It's important to leave your mate wanting more." The smug look on his face made me want to poke him in the eye. Hard.

I walked up to him and tipped my head back to look him in the eye. "I will remember this," I warned, moving a hand slowly down his chest, over his abs, and right to the front of his pants. His rigid cock pressed tight against the material, and he hummed as I gripped it through the fabric.

"This is mine," I said, my voice soft and husky. "And if you insist on playing with me...." I paused, letting my words sink in. He smiled wide, loving every second. "Then I will *not* be playing with you." I gave his balls a soft tap with my other hand. He grunted, his big hands suddenly gripping my ass hard.

He leaned in to kiss me, and I turned my head. "Nope. I was just told we needed to go." I spun, buttoning my shirt.

"Come here," Joon growled. His voice dropped, so deep and sexy.

I gave him a coy smile over my shoulder. "Make me."

The corner of his lips twitched, and I ran.

I raced through the trees, pushing down the urge to laugh and squeal. He was just behind me, letting me keep a slight lead. I could hear his playful growls as his long legs carried him quickly through the brush. Rushing toward a downed tree, I moved to jump over it, but Joon's muscular arms wrapped around me and pulled me to him.

I let out the softest giggle I could muster, wanting desperately to laugh long and loud. Joon spun me, pressed my body to his chest, then kissed me hard. His long fingers channeled through my hair while his tongue twisted skillfully with mine, tasting, feeling, and loving me.

I didn't want the moment to end.

Joon jerked back, breaking the kiss. He stood to full height as his eyes darted over the trees around us, sensing something I couldn't. My wolf sat at attention at his alarming movements. I was ready to run or hide.

Joon's dark eyes narrowed, and he sniffed the air. I pressed into him, looking around the best I could, but I couldn't see the threat he so clearly felt.

"Come," he said.

He grabbed me by the waist to lift me over the downed tree, then hopped over in one swift motion. We walked quickly down the steep hill, my legs struggling to keep up. I stumbled, and Joon scooped me up. He ran at full speed, not stopping until the ground leveled out.

"What is it?" I whispered as he placed me back on my feet.

He gave a jerk of his head, and I went quiet. The line between his brows deepened as we crept through the trees. The land next to us grew, jutting upward into a massive wall of boulders and dirt, finally looming thirty feet above us.

Keeping my hand firmly in my mate's, I moved toward what looked like a little meadow. Joon pulled me to a stop, and I followed his eyes, seeing tents and smoldering fires within a pocket in a mountain. It was the guards' camp from last night. We had made it down and around, the ground sloping just as Byriel said it would.

Joon sniffed the air. The ease in his muscles was notice-able, but my wolf found no comfort in it. We were too close to the encampment of palace guards, and we were walking straight toward them.

Joon pulled me along, right into the camp. I wanted to run and hide, but I shoved down my fear, trying like hell to absorb my mate's confidence. I just wished I understood how he knew these wolves weren't a threat.

Then I heard it.

Lex was chatting and laughing somewhere within the camp. He was in the middle of a tall tale. The siren's voice was loud and animated, and I could practically envision his hands moving through the air as he talked.

A palace guard stepped out of a tent and eyed us, but he didn't stop us or demand to know what we were doing. Joon didn't give him a second glance, still pulling me along. More wolves appeared, but no one said anything about our presence. It was so odd I almost forgot my fear.

We cut around a large tent to find Lex and Blue smiling and eating next to a few other wolves, a dying fire at their feet. The flames were gone, but deep grey smoke swirled up from the black logs making the cold air smell of warm cedar and hot embers.

Lex's face lit up. "Good morning, puppies! We've been waiting forever for you to get here." He pretended to be cross, patting the ground next to him.

I glanced at Joon, and he released my hand, looking at the tents around us.

"Alpha Byriel is talking to the important wolves over there," Blue said, pointing to a tight group of pine trees in the distance. Byriel and three other wolves, two alphas, and a beta talked at the edge of the camp. All four held intense expressions, leaning close so no one could hear what they were saying.

Without looking back at me, Joon stalked off. His stride was full of dominance, and I could practically smell his wolf begging for a fight.

"Are you hungry, dear?" A middle-aged beta with dirty blonde hair asked as she held out a bowl of something steaming. It smelled wonderful.

"Yes, please." I eagerly took a sip of the deep broth. It reminded me of the winter root stew my mother made when I was a pup.

"Isn't it wonderful?" Blue asked, bringing his bowl to his lips. "This is my third helping."

"Growing pups need food," the beta cooed, tickling under his chin. "Eat!"

Blue smiled brightly at her before turning his attention back to his breakfast. My eyes moved over his clothes. He was wearing his usual dark pants, cuffed just above his ankles, but his black shirt matched mine and reeked of Byriel. A sense of unease settled in my bones, and I quickly sat next to Blue, trying to hide it.

While Blue was of age, he was far too innocent to be taken advantage of by an aggressive alpha. Byriel didn't seem to be the kind of wolf to push himself on an unclaimed omega, but you never know.

Determined wolves rarely mimicked their humans when instinct was involved.

"How was last night?" I asked Lex, trying to sound casual.

"Pretty, good," he smiled. "I went out hunting. I couldn't find anything good to eat, but sometimes it's fun just to see what's on the menu. That's when I overheard that lot," he pointed at the huddle of *'important wolves'*—as Blue called them.

I turned to Blue, worry rising in my chest. "So it was just you and Byriel?"

He gave me a quick nod, and his cheeks went a deep shade of red. He bowed his head, pouring all his attention into his food.

"Did anything happen?" I asked. I sounded like a nosey parent, trying to catch a pup in a lie, but I just wanted to make sure no one hurt him. "Was Byriel...nice?"

He paused mid-bite. A puzzled look pulled his brows together as he turned to me. "Why don't you address him formally? You never call him Alpha Byriel. Why?"

I hesitated, not knowing if he was trying to change the subject or if he was just curious. "He and I...have an understanding," I said, not wanting to have this conversation. Especially while surrounded by palace guards. What would they do if they knew I was once mated to a marked wolf Byriel had killed? I wasn't sure if it mattered, but I wasn't eager to find out.

"But he calls you Omega Tzidal." Blue tilted his head, not letting it go.

"Some wolves just behave differently around each other," Lex said, squeezing Blue's hand.

"Is it because she grew up in a village with borders?" Blue whispered to Lex.

Lex stared at him for a moment before nodding. "Yes," he said firmly. "Her village is filled with mouthy, defiant omegas."

Blue's eyes went wide, and I turned away from them to hide my smile.

A young pup toddled past us, his alpha father on his heels. The pair smiled at the beta serving breakfast. She handed the youngling a bowl, and he squealed. His father—wearing a palace uniform—picked his youngling up, chatting happily with the beta.

Why were there pups here?

"What is this place?" I asked Lex.

"Oh, puppy." Lex let out a long, dramatic sigh. "You will not believe the shit we've stepped into."

The Guarded Camp

⚬⚬

Joon

I released Tzidal's hand and marched straight to Byriel. It was clear there was more going on here than just a camp of palace guards, but I didn't trust Byriel to be straight with me while surrounded by his own people. He was too blind when it came to the King, and I didn't need him making light of whatever was going on.

Byriel's fists curled tight, and his eyes flashed red. Whatever they were talking about enraged the usually collected alpha.

"This is complete bullshit," Byriel snarled as I stepped up next to him.

He looked like he wanted to rip into the she-alpha in front of him. She was pale and just as tall as me, with muscular arms and spiky black hair. She kept her expression blank, but her eyes held too much fire for her to be considered calm.

I crossed my arms over my chest, each wolf turning to look

at me. Byriel gave me a quick nod, and no one challenged me for intruding on their conversation. Byriel was clearly the highest-ranking alpha here.

"The time has come," the female said, her tone respectful but still commanding. "This is your birthright. And your people demand it."

Byriel shook his head. "This is my sister's birthright, and you damn well know it, Jonelle. Not mine."

"We understand, Sir," a familiar alpha said. He had a thick scar down one side of his face, and long, brown hair fell over his eyes. He placed a hand on Jonelle's shoulder, silently urging her to submit to Byriel. She relented, lowering her gaze to the ground.

I stared at the scarred alpha, realizing how I knew him. He was the cocky guard from the Vaesen gates. I remembered how he leered at my mate as if she were a decadent meal at the end of a long journey. Now he looked aged and worn. His mouth turned down at the corners, and dark circles made his eyes appear sunken. Life had apparently been unkind to him in the few months since I last saw him. But then again, it hadn't been kind to any of us.

"Change is coming, Sir," the scarred alpha said. His voice matched his appearance. Rough. "A transition to a nobleman, whose royal blood could easily take the throne, will keep the stewards in line and will keep the peace. No one would dare to challenge your claim and destined purpose." He met Byriel's red eyes and leaned in, talking softer. "To leave the throne empty will start a war among the village Pack Alphas to claim it. So many more will die."

"I don't fucking believe this, Dane," Byriel growled in a harsh whisper. The tendons in his neck flexed with his restrained fury." You cannot seriously be talking about over-throwing the throne. It's treason. Hell. This entire conversation is treason."

"Haven't you been committing treason since the moment we met?" I asked Byriel, smiling wide at the anger in his eyes. The she-wolf jerked her blazing glare to me and then to Byriel, gauging his reaction. Dane squinted, a hint of recognition in his eyes.

"Shut the fuck up, Joon," Byriel snarled before turning back to the shocked alphas.

"Alpha Byriel," a dark-haired female beta whispered. She had a nervous, submissive edge to her voice. The alphas around her dwarfed her tiny form to the point that I forgot she was here. Judging by her uniform, she was a palace service-beta, probably a valet or caretaker for the royal family. "The mood within the palace has shifted. The King's actions cannot be ignored anymore. It's only a matter of time before the people demand his blood."

Jonelle stepped closer to Byriel, clearly struggling to keep her tone and expression polite. "The King's reign is over. It's time for new blood in Ossory." Her voice dropped to an urgent whisper, "Do you really want your sister to lead these lands? Strayton is completely—"

"It doesn't matter what I want," Byriel snapped. He looked to be on the verge of shifting into his wolf, his hands shaking and the tensions in his neck pulling tight. "This is simply the order of things. When the King passes, Strayton will inherit the throne, and there is nothing I can do to fucking change it." He turned, pacing. He was so wound up, it was hard not to feel it too. The thick, angry energy pouring off him made my wolf itch to run.

"And not to mention," Byriel spun on the scared alpha, Dane, his teeth flashing as he spoke, "you are talking about killing my fucking family!" His voice dropped as he closed the space between them. "You took a fucking oath."

"So did he," Dane said quietly, looking Byriel right in the eye. "He took the oath that all Kings pledge: to protect the packs of Havre and lead his people. Not to kill them without mercy or thought."

"Are you meaning to challenge me, Dane?" Byriel squared his shoulders, and Dane immediately broke eye contact, bowing his head.

"No, Sir."

A slow growl pushed from Byriel's chest as he moved his gaze over each wolf.

The beta shivered and immediately showed the back of her neck in submission, but Jonelle took a few more glaring breaths before finally bowing her head. Byriel didn't even bother looking at me, knowing full well I wouldn't submit to him.

"I understand your concern about Strayton," Byriel said, his words more controlled but still filled with authority. "But there is no helping the way of things."

"Sir," Dane whispered, keeping his eyes averted. "The King has ordered the guard to kill all wolves with anything resembling a red birthmark. It's happening all over Havre. Even in the villages you and Hida already searched."

My mouth fell open. My arms heavy at my sides.

I couldn't have heard the alpha correctly.

Even after seeing what had happened with Blue's pack, I didn't want to believe him. My mind immediately drifted to my village, my parents, my brother, and his mate.

Thick silence pulsed in the air while we all waited for Byriel to react. His scent edged into a mixture of grief, distress, and violent rage. It was so fucking sharp I had to turn my head and beg my wolf to settle. My beast's desire to whimper at the intense emotions made me want to curse out loud, but I remained quiet and still.

I didn't bow to Byriel's status and wouldn't cower to his rage either.

When Byriel finally did speak, his words were controlled

and deep, filled with so much fury. "I have spent the last year murdering innocents to protect my King," he said, taking a slow breath before continuing. "I have destroyed our people and killed my soul. I have killed myself repeatedly for my family and my pack. But it's still not enough. Is it?"

No one spoke.

They all kept their eyes down as wave after wave of restrained violence and grief poured off Byriel's dark skin.

A sharp growl burst from his chest before he spoke again. "The horrors I have been forced to inflict. The pain I've pushed into the earth." He shook his head. "I am sick and fucking tired of innocent wolves dying!" His eyes darkened with a jarring sadness. Almost as if the words he spoke physically hurt. "And now you plan to kill my family, and you expect me to rejoice and join you!"

Dane swallowed hard, keeping his eyes down, and his shoulders curled inward.

"You're scaring the omegas." Lex stepped up next to me. His tone had an annoyed chirp to it, and his eyes were exactly what you'd expect from the deadly creature: completely unaffected by the dominant anger saturating the air.

I looked past Lex to see several frightened eyes watching us within the camp. Omegas, betas, and a few pups. Some clung to alphas, and others ducked quickly into tents. Tzidal and Blue held hands, both watching us with big eyes. Even if they couldn't hear our words, it was clear they could all scent Byriel's emotions even from a distance.

"If you don't help us, these wolves," Dane motioned to the camp, "will eventually be found and killed."

"Why?" I asked, eager to finally know their purpose. This was no guard encampment. "What makes these wolves a target?"

"They all carry birthmarks," Jonelle said. "Every wolf here either has a circular birthmark, a red one, or an odd mark in general. Or a loved one does," she added, her eyes briefly flickering to Dane. "The King isn't looking for anything specific anymore. He's killing everyone."

I looked around the encampment at the mix of wolves. Some were guards, others well-dressed in posh robes with straight backs, and a few looked to be rural wolves, with handmade clothes and worn feet. It was an odd mix of classes, but their connection was clear. They all carried the same fear.

Jonelle narrowed her eyes at Byriel, but she didn't raise her chin to issue a real challenge. "Some are here because they're sick of killing their own kind. And if the King isn't put in the ground soon, he'll find them and kill them all."

"Yari works in the palace," Dane said to me, motioning to the timid beta. "She has heard reports that they've already found the last marked wolf, but the killings haven't stopped." He turned to Byriel. "I'm not convinced he'll ever stop. Not until every wolf the King deems a threat is dead."

"It's true," Yari whispered, shying away from Byriel's intense gaze. "According to what the witches believe, the King's reign is safe, but he's still spilling blood. It's like he's lost his mi—"

"Enough!" Byriel roared so loud it made me cringe. He leaned into Dane, his fangs on full display. "You want me to lead our people because my veins carry my father's blood? But you also stand here asking me to kill him and spill the very blood you claim is divine and sacred. You can't have it both ways. You can't praise me for my breeding and then proclaim my blood unworthy of the dais."

"Alpha—"the young beta tried to speak, but Byriel's hard, red glare cut her off.

"Death to any wolf that threatens the King," Byriel said, glaring at Dane, then Jonelle. "That is what we're taught and how we live. If I can so easily dismiss my father's claim to the throne and steal it out from under him, then anyone can do the same to me. Your plan is shit."

The she-alpha let out a soft growl. "You can't possibly—"

"Jonelle," Dane held up a hand, silencing her. He turned back to Byriel, desperation in his voice. "You won't help us? That's your final word?"

Byriel took a few steps back, looking over each wolf in front of him. His eyes met mine, and I held his stare. His rage eased the longer he looked at me, and his fists uncurled. He let out a heavy breath. Then he looked past me, red disappearing in his usually green eyes.

I followed his gaze, seeing Blue sitting next to my mate. The omega's large, sad eyes watched Byriel. Then slowly, Blue gave him a small smile filled with so much sorrow.

"I'm sorry, Dane," Byriel said, holding his head high despite the defeat in his eyes. "I have enough blood to atone for, and I will not be forced to answer to the Moon for killing my King as well."

Lex snorted loudly, placing his hands on his hips. "Well, since you're so intent on being a coward," he snipped, "will you be heading over to tell Blue that you just don't give a shit that his entire pack was murdered on your father's orders? Or should I?"

Byriel snapped.

His clawed hands flew around Lex's throat, slamming the siren hard against the nearest tree. The beta ran off, and Dane and Jonelle took several steps back, not eager to get caught between the siren and wolf.

I let out a heavy sigh.

I swore Lex did this kind of shit just to kill his boredom.

Lex hummed, and his eyes flashed with excitement as he dragged his pointed fingernails over Byriel's arms, blood blooming in their wake.

"I will not be submitting to you, *alpha.*," Lex whispered in a mocking tone. "So kill me if you must, but this is your only chance. After this, I will slice you open if you ever touch me again." A teasing smile played on his lips.

Byriel's fangs punched out as he squeezed Lex's throat. The siren's smile dropped, the pain in his eyes startling me.

"Stop!" Blue's voice cracked as he screamed, running toward us. "Alpha! Stop!"

As if breaking from a trance, Byriel immediately dropped Lex, backing up quickly. He shook his head, then turned to face me. He looked dazed, visibly shaken, almost like he was going to be sick.

Then without a word, he turned and vanished into the trees.

The Edge Of Camp

Tzidal

I RAN AFTER BLUE, scared he'd follow Byriel into the trees. Thankfully the swift omega didn't. Instead, he flung his arms around Lex, scenting his neck. Lex patted Blue's back and whispered that he was okay, but I wasn't so sure. I saw the look in Lex's eyes. Byriel bested him.

I had never seen anyone gain the upper hand on Lex. I didn't think it was possible. And to see Byriel be the one to put the siren down was shocking. While I wouldn't say Byriel's presence was calming, he was always slow to anger.

Lex rubbed his throat and swallowed several times, letting Blue check him over.

"Where is Byriel going?" I said to Joon, looking into the trees but seeing no trace of the alpha.

"I don't know," he said, shaking his head. He looked a little shocked at what just happened. "He didn't say. Maybe home?"

My eyes widened as I took in his words. Disbelieving, I whispered, "He's leaving us?"

Joon circled an arm around me, kissing the top of my head.

Confusion, anger, and sadness pounded in my chest. Byriel might not have been a friend—our alliances were firmly on very different sides—but we had been through so much together. We fought our way through Vaesen and across mountains, he helped keep Joon safe when I had no idea what to do, and he got us help and medicine.

We were tied together in battle and survival.

That meant something.

I always knew we'd part in Ossory, but this felt personal.

He abandoned us.

Pushing myself into Joon's side, I couldn't help feeling a little lost. I didn't know how we'd find Yasha without Byriel, but I needed to see this through. Too many had died. Too much blood was owed.

"I knew he was full of shit." Joon's words were harsh, but there was no real fight in them. His arm tightened around me, and I leaned into him, needing my mate's comfort. "His people are desperate, so he's running away. Fucking coward."

"Wait. Byriel is leaving us?" Blue said, turning away from Lex. His skin shimmered, and his eyes went wide as he stood, looking frantically into the woods.

"Byriel is a good leader," a scarred alpha sighed, stepping forward to introduce himself and the she-alpha, Jonelle. "I knew it would be hard for him to hear, and he wouldn't be easy to convince to abandon everything he was raised to believe. But I had hoped he'd stand with us. There's nothing we can do except hope he changes his mind. The plan still moves forward."

Jonelle nodded fiercely in agreement.

"No!" Blue yelled into the trees, his fist clenched. His eyes met mine, and his skin flashed a brilliant white. I flinched, moving to shield my eyes. When I finally lowered my hands, I caught the brief flash of Blue's shiny, dark hair as he disappeared into the trees.

I immediately jerked to run after him, but Joon grabbed my arm, pulling me to him.

"He's not ours," he said softly, his dark eyes filled with so much sadness. "I'm so sorry, Tzidal, but Blue gets to decide which path he wants to take. We'll still find our way, but not with Byriel."

All the fight in me whooshed out in one quick breath. I was so exhausted.

"I'll go make sure Blue finds Byriel safely," Lex said, smoothing a hand over my hair. "If he doesn't go with By', I'll bring him back."

"If you end up eating Byriel, be careful not to hurt Blue," Joon said, giving Lex a weak smile.

Lex grinned, but his expression wasn't nearly as animated as usual.

I kept my eyes on Lex, watching him disappear into the trees. I didn't want Blue to go with Byriel, but Joon was right. The omega was an adult. He was allowed to make his own decisions, but it just felt wrong to let him go.

Everything that was happening felt wrong.

"Do you really want to help us?" Dane looked at Joon.

"Yes," my mate answered immediately, his posture tight and eyes alert.

"How do we know we can trust them?" Jonelle asked Dane. Her lips curled up as she spoke, displaying the tips of her pointed teeth. "We don't know them, and there are a lot of sides to this war."

"I trust Byriel," Dane said, "and they're his friends."

Joon stiffened next to me but didn't say anything.

Jonelle narrowed her eyes at my mate, speaking with a

clear challenge in her tone. "Byriel is struggling with his allegiance, and I have to wonder, as his friend, if you are too? Do you follow the King, wolf? Who's side are you on?"

"I'm on her side," Joon snarled, hitching a thumb at me. "But let me make myself clear, so there's no confusion." He pulled in a slow breath and stepped closer to the she-wolf. "I have never, and will never, have any alliance to the King. Even if he crosses the stars, ascends to the Moon, and consumes her whole, I would rather die an empty vessel with no wolf and no light than be forced to bend at his feet and thank him for his existence. He's a murderous fuck, and I look forward to ripping his unholy head from his body."

I held my breath, waiting for someone to speak or move.

Every muscle in Joon's big body was so tight. He looked ready to lash out at the first person that dared to breathe.

"Well, shit," the she-wolf snorted, breaking the silence. "Tell him what we need, Dane."

The scarred alpha turned to Joon, smiling wide at my mate. "It's good to have more help. Our numbers aren't as strong as they used to be. We have too many that require alphas to keep watch over them, making our allies in the palace scarce. We can use you."

"My mate too." Joon motioned to me.

Dane and Jonelle looked me over with wide eyes before turning back to Joon.

"Really?" Disbelief marred Jonelle's tone. "This could be very dangerous, and dragging an omega with you—"

"She's got more balls than half the alphas in Havre," Joon snarled. "She has trekked the faelands and deserts and even pushed through the cursed lands without any help. It was her blade that killed Hida in Vaesen, and it will be her that kills the King. So show a little respect."

Both alphas turned to me, and I had to resist the urge to hide behind Joon. I appreciated his praise, but it wasn't completely honest. I had received a lot of help and relied on a lot of luck to get here. But I wasn't about to say that out loud.

"Actually," Jonelle said, looking me over as if seeing me for the first time, "having an omega might be useful."

Dane glanced into the trees, then turned to Joon. "If Byriel returns, maybe you can speak to him. Help him see that—"

"We aren't friends," Joon cut him off. I was shocked to feel unease in our bond. My own emotions had washed out his, but now that I was calmer, I could feel how upset Joon was about Byriel leaving. "We were just traveling together," he said.

Dane nodded, his lips pressing tight. "Well," he sighed, "maybe Byriel will see the light on his own."

"You truly believe he would best for Havre?" Joon asked, taking my hand in his.

"Byriel is a good wolf," Dane said, "and what we're asking from him cannot be easy. But he's precise, careful, and compassionate. I've known him for years. Battled beside him, been commanded by him, drank with him. He would be a good King."

Joon turned his head, snarling at Dane's words. "The Byriel I know doesn't deserve that much respect."

The young female beta glared at my mate from under her eyelashes, and Jonelle's fists went tight. The wolves here had put a lot of hope into Byriel's hands, and, even though Byriel had no interest in helping them, it was clear they weren't going to let their loyalties die so quickly.

I stepped around Joon and cleared my throat, feeling the need to soothe the harsh energy pulsing in the air. "Byriel has been kind and helpful, but our...." I paused, trying to think of the best way to word it, "...first impression of him wasn't good."

"We've all done things we aren't proud of," Jonelle said flatly. Judging from the scars on her knuckles, she had done plenty. "But I never saw Byriel act out in an unprovoked rage.

I've only seen him bare his teeth when directly challenged or commanded by his King. Are you saying he has no honor?" She glared at me as if trying to decide exactly where to sink her teeth.

Joon growled low and long, pulling me behind him. The rumble from his throat pushed through my bones, and my heart fluttered. His possessive wolf licked at my skin in a primal way, making me press my knees together. I turned away from the group, suddenly embarrassed.

What a horrible moment to be turned on.

Joon took a careful step forward, challenging the she-wolf. "Do not look at my mate like that ever again."

He stood so rigid, every muscle tense as if the tiniest thing could set him off, and he'd completely unravel.

Dane, ignoring the thick air between the two, leaned down to look me in the eye. "Can you take a letter to Ossory? We need to make our allies aware of what's developed and that we're moving the camp. I don't think Byriel will give our location away, but I'm not willing to stake so many lives on it."

I nodded, a little bit of hope warming my chest. Joon and I suddenly weren't alone in our fight against the King. We had allies.

The Woods

Byriel

I COULDN'T THINK STRAIGHT.

There was so much pounding in my head, I didn't know what to focus on first: the rushing sound of my blood in my ears, the frantic beat of my heart, or the ache in my bones from my wolf wanting to shift.

I wanted to fall to my knees and pound my fists into the dirt. I wanted to scream at the sky until my voice broke.

The King had finally gone too far. All his backhanded deeds and questionable decisions had caught up with him. I never thought this day would actually come, but I also dreaded that it might. And up until this moment, I always knew I'd die defending him.

But how could I?

Guilt squeezed my chest as I thought of the wolves in Blue's village. They all fought with so much honor. Just like the marked wolves I had killed.

Maybe I could have stopped all this, but I had been blinded by duty. I was a coward, too willing to turn a blind eye out of loyalty. I should have been stronger.

My mind drifted to Blue, and I stopped walking, letting the sun warm my face.

My wolf had already imprinted the feel of the delicate omega's lips and the sweet scent of his skin deep within me, ruining my heart for any other, but I couldn't risk taking him to Ossory. The King's stewards and my sister's followers would try to hurt me any way they saw fit. And that now included Blue.

As much as it gutted me, I needed to let him go. It was too dangerous to keep him with me, and I loved him too much to risk it.

I'd simply have to find a way to live the rest of my days surviving on the memory of a single kiss we shared in the dark.

The leaves overhead shifted with the cool breeze, and their shadows danced over the withering grass at my feet. I closed my eyes and pictured Blue. His heart-shaped face and velvety skin. His big, curious eyes and soothing nature.

I loved everything about him.

I inhaled deeply, and my wolf purred. I could still smell the omega. For a blissful moment, my chest warmed at the thought of him. Then my heart cracked at the realization that I could never actually have him.

Whatever I chose to do next, it couldn't include Blue. I wasn't sure how I'd tell him, but I had enough respect to say it in person.

I let out a defeated sigh and opened my eyes.

"Blue." His name jumped from my lips as I took a quick step back.

The omega stood just before me, fists clenched and eyes narrowed. If his gaze had been a dagger, I'd be dead.

A deep pink hue colored the apples of his cheeks, and his

dark hair framed his face like a wild mane, but the fire in his eyes was like nothing I had ever seen from him. It actually made my breath catch.

"You left me," he snarled, his little fangs pointed and sharp.

His rage was thick and fear nonexistent. His bravery at facing an alpha like me with such emotion made me want him more.

"I couldn't stay. I was going to kill Lex," I said simply, not fully understanding his anger. I only needed a moment, a breath of fresh air, but he was acting as if I had abandoned him. "I completely lost myself and needed to calm my wolf."

A slip of a growl jumped from his lips. "You left me," he said again. Louder this time.

"Blue," I sighed, hoping to calm him.

"You left me!" he screamed. His fists were so tight I wouldn't have been surprised if his nails drew blood. "You kept me with you. You made my wolf fall for you. You took my first kiss. Then you left me!"

All the breath in me flew out in one painful gust.

"You fell for me?" I whispered, hopeful. It was the wrong thing to focus on, especially given how fucked everything was. But, dammit, it was all I could hear.

"You left me!"

Blue swiped a hand through the air, his palm landing on my cheek. He had no strength in him, and I barely felt it on my skin, but it carried the weight of a rolling boulder to the gut.

He drew his hand back again as a sob ripped from his throat. I caught his wrist and spun him hard, forcing his back to my chest. His whole body went limp, and he crumpled in my arms. He sobbed and coughed and sputtered onto the forest floor as I eased us both onto the grass. I softened my hold and rocked him gently, his whole body wracking with horrific sobs.

"Everyone leaves me," he wept. "No one wants me, and everyone leaves."

"Blue, I didn't leave you," I whispered against the back of his neck. "I just needed a moment."

It wasn't a lie. I had every intention of returning to the camp, then explaining to Blue why we needed to go our separate ways. But right now, with his distress filling my lungs and his heart breaking in my arms, I no longer cared what was right or what was smart. I just wanted to keep him.

"Everyone hates me," he mumbled, his chest heaving.

"I don't hate you," I said firmly, hugging him tighter. "No one could ever hate you."

He glanced at me over his shoulder, his wet eyes narrowing and his mouth tight. "I killed my mother when she birthed me, so my father forced me on my grandmother. Then when I was a pup, I pulsed and, and I accidentally k-killed her." His lips trembled as tears poured down his soft cheeks. "My pack encourages me to leave our boundaries because I'm too dangerous. And I *am* dangerous." He gulped down a big breath of air. "I let those guards through our borders, and they killed my pack. *I* killed my pack."

He inhaled a deep, angry breath, then screamed, "And then you left me!"

"I want you." I spun him hard, forcing him to meet my eyes. I looked at him with so much intensity and honesty I hoped it scared him. "I want you!" I yelled, my eyes flashing red.

Blue's fire dimmed, his eyes going soft and mouth slightly open.

"You are mine!" I roared. The force of my voice made him flinch, but he kept his eyes on me.

I felt unhinged and possessive. I wanted to strip him naked, lick every inch of his soft skin, then sink my teeth into his warm, wet throat. I wanted him more than anything else in this world. More than my father's acceptance, or my pack's safety, or my own fucking sanity.

I just wanted him.

Blue swallowed hard, his breath starting to even out. "Don't go," he said in a breathy whisper. "I'm so scared of the things you make me feel," he pressed a hand to his chest, "but it scares me even more to think I'll never feel this way again. Please, keep me."

My heart swelled, and my skin warmed. Without stopping to think, I nodded, leaning in to scent his sweet breath, "Will you keep me as well?"

He smiled at my words, a silent promise passing between us. I couldn't help but smile too. It felt so good to look happy and mean it.

Cupping my omega's cheeks, I held him in place as I moved my nose over his chin and mouth. I dragged my lips over one cheek, then slowly licked the tears off his beautiful face. He let out a breathy laugh, and I moaned, making a shiver work through his thin body.

My perfect mate.

Fuck, this was a stupid decision.

Perhaps life in Ossory wasn't meant for either one of us. Perhaps I could abandon all of this. Death, pain, treason, vengeance. I could leave all of it.

Blue and I could live in the faelands or near the sea. *Hell*, I'd take him all the way to Myphic if it meant his happiness. But wherever we ended up, I would keep him safe, even if it killed me.

"Who's there?" A familiar voice cut through the trees, and I crushed Blue to my chest, desperate to hide him in my arms.

I forced my attention away from my omega and concentrated on the forest around us. On the other side of a few pine trees, Kenji, a palace guard I had known for years, walked straight toward us. His eyes lit up as he recognized me, and he picked up his pace, moving quickly through the trees.

He took in the sight of the distressed omega in my arms, and his smile fell. "Sir, are you okay?" he asked, his eyes moving between Blue and me.

"I'm fine," I said, standing. I picked Blue up, not giving him the option to walk. He wrapped his legs around my waist and hid his face in my neck, too scared to look at the unknown alpha.

"We all thought you were dead." Kenji took a disbelieving breath, standing back a bit to look me over.

"I'm very much alive." I gave him a quick nod, fighting the urge to run away with Blue tucked firmly against my body.

I turned slightly, looking toward the camp, then back at Kenji. I couldn't go back the way I had come. I couldn't risk all the wolves Dane had worked so hard to protect. They just wanted to keep their lives, something the King was determined to rip from them.

But I also couldn't go back to Ossory. Not with Blue.

"Sir," Kenji said, running his nails through his short, black hair. "His Majesty has taken up camp just past the vast ridge," he pointed east, "close to the Black River. He will be so happy to see you're alive. Everyone was ready to give up hope."

I hesitated.

I didn't want to see my father. Maybe ever again. But I couldn't think of a good reason not to go, and refusing would look too suspicious. I had been away from home for well over a year, maybe even two—it was so hard to know for sure—and anything short of returning home would be questionable. My father would send out scouts to drag me back to him. They might hurt Blue.

There was no option that wouldn't put a target on me, Blue, or Dane's camp, so I tightened my hold on my omega and cleared my throat.

"Lead the way."

The Walk To Ossory

Joon

"WE NEED TO HEAD OUT," Jonelle said, strapping a long, curved kukri blade to her hip. Her palace uniform was immaculate, pressed, clean, the definition of professional. She was clearly a high-ranking official within the guard.

Tzidal turned away from the spot where Lex had disappeared this morning, her eyes brimming with worry. "I feel like we should go looking for them," she said softly.

Jonelle flung her hands up in silent annoyance. The she-wolf had been trying to leave for Ossory all afternoon, but Tzidal was apprehensive, wanting to wait for Lex and Blue to return. But, at this point, it was pretty clear they both had decided to stay with Byriel.

While I could feel how upset Tzidal was at Byriel leaving us, I was enraged. No amount of good deeds could right the wrongs he set against Tzidal and me, but I wasn't too proud to admit his help had been a blessing. We had so much left to do, things that would be easier with Byriel at our side, especially in this part of Havre. We still needed to find Yasha and gain access to the family quarters of the palace. We still needed to know for sure if the last wolf had been killed. But without Byriel, I wasn't sure if any of it was possible.

Tzidal looked anxiously into the forest, then back at Jonelle. I closed the space between us and whispered in my mate's ear. "If you want to look for them, just say the word." I placed a finger under her chin and tipped her head up to look into her eyes. "We don't have to go to Ossory right now. Just tell me what you want."

She let out a resolved sigh, then shook her head. "No," she said confidently, but her eyes still held a lot of unease. "They obviously went with Byriel." She pressed her lips together, our bond thrumming with her sorrow at our friends taking another path.

"We'll meet up with Lex and Blue in the city," she said. It wasn't a question, but the way she looked at me told me she needed assurances.

"I promise we'll find Lex and Blue in Ossory. It's safe to assume that's where Byriel was headed, and we'll easily find them. Don't worry, mate." I kissed her temple and then turned, giving Jonelle a quick nod. The she-wolf released a thankful huff and slung a black satchel across her body.

Tzidal knelt and cuffed her fitted black trousers so they fell above her ankles. The ally camp had some palace uniforms in stow, and Dane was kind enough to give us both new clothes. The uniforms would be easier to move through the city and gain entry to the palace.

Tzidal was dressed as a member of the prim-staff. The all-black uniform complimented her tempting figure well. The fitted robes were held together by a gold-embroidered sash, the flowing material falling softly at her knees. Small ribbons ran the length of her forearms, creating a snug fit before the looser material at her upper arms. She looked so laced and fancy.

"What?" Tzdial asked, catching me staring as we followed Jonelle and a beta, Arian, out of the camp.

"You look like a proper lady." I smiled. She gave me a bashful laugh and looked down, smiling at her feet. She was too fucking cute. "Anyone that sees you won't have a clue the little monster you actually are."

"Hey!" She smacked my arm, then took my hand. She moved her eyes up and down my body. "You know," she bit her bottom lip, letting it slowly slip from her teeth, "you don't look too bad, yourself."

I smiled, fighting the urge to carry her off into the trees and fuck her proper. "I'm wearing the same palace uniform I had on before."

"Yes, but this one is clean. That changes everything." Her eyes fell to a small patch stitched over my right pec, and she poked it. "And it's not exactly the same. This is different."

I looked down at the patch. It held the King's initials in one corner and an ax and sword in the other bound together with a crown. I had never seen a patch like it before.

"What kind of uniform is this?" I asked Jonelle.

"It means you're a skilled worker for the King," she said, seemingly disinterested. Her eyes stayed firmly in front of her, marching like the warrior she was.

"What kind of skill?" Tzidal asked, running a finger of the bright red and gold thread.

"A skill not taught by the palace or by joining the guard," Arian answered, "but instead, it's something you mastered and now provide that service to the King for special favors and prestige."

The muscular beta secured the fastens along the shoulders of his leather breastplate, and he carried the same heavy knife as Jonelle. It was clear he was more than a simple guard.

He nodded at my patch. "It's a good uniform to have as skilled wolves rarely spend any time inside Ossory, so it will make sense for no one to recognize you."

"What kind of skills?" Tzidal asked again, but this time her voice held a bit of worry. "Is there something they'll expect Joon to know? Or expect him to do?"

"It varies," Arian said. "Could be fae tracking, mineral hunting, crystal mining, distilling whiskey. There are so many kinds of skilled workers in the service of the King, but it doesn't really matter. The important thing is that you won't seem out of place."

"Whiskey?" I raised a brow. A few in my pack brewed whiskey, and no one had ever seen it as a special skill.

Jonelle looked over her shoulder at me. "Elvish whiskey."

Tzidal turned her wide eyes to me, confused.

"They infuse magic into their spirits," I said, impressed that a wolf could learn to make something so difficult. "Making their drink isn't easy."

"Omega Tzidal." Jonelle held out a small envelope. It had a deep green seal along the seam with a waxy image of a Centaurea flower in the center. "This is the letter for our people in the palace. It'll be best for you to carry it." Her gaze moved over my mate, assessing her. "I've never seen an omega outside a village before, so your presence might be noted. But no one will suspect an omega of this kind of thing. That's all that matters."

Tzidal placed the envelope in her pants pocket, giving me a teasing grin. "It's because my kind are so pure."

I snorted. "So fucking pure."

WE TRAVELED QUIETLY. The task before us weighed both heavy and exciting. It wasn't every day you got to help overthrow a monarchy, and the electric energy pushing through my bond with Tzidal had me hard.

Her lust for justice was so pure and impressive.

Within a few hours, the peaks of the Ossory palace came into view. The heavy black stone of the enormous structure looked carved out of lava glass.

"Have you ever been to Ossory?" Tzidal asked, her eyes moving over the massive towers in the distance.

"No," I squeezed her hand. "I've never been in this part of Havre before. My time in the guard was mostly in Stone City and The Furthermore."

The clouds parted, and the whole city shimmered, creating a magical yet eerie sight; dark, glittering stone set against the pale blue sky. It was a testament to my people and our successes in battle. We were the dominant creatures in this land for a reason, and the magnificent city in front of me was proof of our power.

"How will we get past security?" I asked, hoping someone had a plan.

Jonelle let out an amused snort. "Getting past security won't be a problem. Half the wolves at the palace want the King dead, and the other half want Strayton dead, and I'm sure a few indecisive ones want Byriel dead. With the palace crumbling and allegiances shifting, security is shit. No one cares anymore. This house is fractured, and as long as you look like you belong, you will."

"What about me?" Tzidal asked, looking down at her uniform. "I might have to interact with the family. Right?"

Jonelle gave her a friendly smile. "I selected this uniform for you on purpose. This is an easy job with very little expected of you. Prim-staff mostly cleanup during garden parties and other ridiculous events. It's a safe position. But if you get nervous, just tidy up and don't make eye contact. However," Jonelle stopped, stepping closer to my mate, "you're an omega, and your kind rarely hold palace positions. So don't make yourself known. I doubt anyone will notice since you're mated, and your scent is muted, but you still need to be careful."

I leaned into Tzidal's ear. "I'll scent you before we arrive." My wolf growled, looking forward to nuzzling and tasting her. We might be separated once in Ossory, and I'd need a bit of my mate's sweet lips before parting. My wolf raged at the idea of leaving her, but I trusted my fierce, little omega to keep herself safe for me. If separated, we'd find each other quickly. I hoped.

Tzidal ran her fingers over the sash tied at her middle, her nerves thrumming through our bond.

"Remember what Haxa said?" I squeezed Tzidal's hand. "Change is coming. And we'll be the ones to bring it." The witch hadn't said that last part, but that didn't stop me from believing it.

"It's true," Jonelle said. "Change is fast approaching within Havre, and the fairy-folk are restless. *The vengeful wrath of the marked wolves' love will end the King.*" She said the last sentence as if it were a fact she had read in a scholar's book.

"The witches are seeing things," Arian whispered. We were completely alone in the middle of the woods, but he shared the information carefully, making all of us walk a little closer together to hear him. "Their visions are becoming clearer now that the prophecy is unfolding."

Tzidal reached for his arm, pulling the beta closer. "A witch foresaw us killing the King? That's not just a rumor, but something true?" she paused, but neither answered. "Who? Was it Yasha? We need to speak with them."

"Commander Arian?" A young beta, dressed in a scout's uniform, raced toward us. He held an urgent expression, not bothering to move out of the way of the branches that smacked into his face as he ran.

Tzidal eased behind me, keeping her distance from the unknown wolf.

"What are you doing out here?" he asked as he came to a stop. He moved his gaze over Tzidal, then myself, his eyes widening as they landed on the patch on my chest.

"It's not your place to question me or my whereabouts, Beta Fallin," Arian growled.

The young scout instantly jerked to attention, the curious expression draining from his face. "Yes, sir!"

"Where did you come from?" Arian asked, his voice booming with an authority I had never heard from a beta before. It made me respect him a bit more.

The young scout turned and pointed a timid finger toward the river. "His Majesty is encamped not far from here. Lady Strayton is with him."

"She left the palace without her guard?" Arian's whole body went rigid, his eyes wide and angry.

"Yes, sir," the scout's voice trembled as he spoke. The more nervous he got, the younger he looked. I expected him to mewl for his mother at any moment.

"Why the fuck would she do that?" Arian demanded, baring his teeth. Being a beta, his fangs didn't lengthen, and his claws didn't engage, but they might as well have for all the terror pouring out of the scout's eyes.

"Byriel, son of the King, has returned."

The King's Camp

Joon

WE WALKED QUICKLY toward the King's encampment and right towards Byriel. I simply could not get away from the fucker. It was as if the Moon was determined to punish me.

I wished Tzidal and I could break away from the ally wolves and head to Ossory without them. But being unfamiliar with this part of Havre, the lay of the city, and unaware of the best entrance to the palace, it was reckless to travel there without Jonelle and Arian. It was best we go with them, for now.

The tents that came into view were nothing like the small guard encampments I was used to. This camp was enormous with roaring fires and huge tents—twenty alphas could easily camp in one. The thick, blue fabric looked like it might kill the occupant should a good wind knock it over.

My eyes fell to the unusual comforts no traveling wolf got

to enjoy. Tzidal nudged my side, making me aware of my expression, and I quickly closed my mouth.

A massive bonfire sat near the far edge of the camp, with spits of both fresh and roasted meats, and a few betas sat at two large wooden tables. One was serving meals while the others sharpened swords and daggers. Ale, food, and rowdy wolves mingled everywhere, making the atmosphere seem more like a village than a temporary base.

Rather than walk straight through the smaller servants' tents along the perimeter, Jonelle motioned for us to follow her around. Arian cut away from us toward a chatty group of alphas. Most of them immediately snapped to attention as he approached, but one looked at the beta with sour disgust at being forced to obey a lower-statused wolf. I couldn't blame him. It was unnatural for my kind to follow anyone other than an Alpha.

"I have to give my report to his Majesty," Jonelle said as we marched past a bustle of service-Betas and valets. The busy wolves cooked, cleaned cauldrons and pots, and scrubbed dirty uniforms, dunking them repeatedly into wooden buckets of soapy water.

I immediately felt in the way.

"Stay here and try to look busy," Jonelle said in a hushed tone. "Don't make yourself noticeable. Hopefully, this will be quick. I just need to report on my mission, and we can go."

"What was your mission?" Tzidal asked, stepping out of the way of a very huffy-looking scullery maid.

"To look for ally camps." The she-alpha winked at my mate before marching off.

The flurry of activity seemed to swell around us as we stood awkwardly next to the laundry. Tzidal tripped forward into my arms to avoid several servants carrying firewood, and a stern elder snapped at me to get to my post before she put me to work. Tzidal mumbled a few apologies as I pulled her to the other side of the clothesline.

Soft, white sheets fluttered in the breeze, hiding us from the chaos. The crisp fabric soaked up the last rays of the setting sun and caught wayward pollen from a nearby patch of lavender. It gave off the most comforting aroma. I was reminded of my old pack and the omegas that did their wash by the river.

As a pup, I loved playing with my friends in the maze of linen while our parents worked. We were always scolded and walloped when we inevitably spattered mud on the clean laundry, but the memories were still good.

"What are you thinking?" Tzidal asked, looking around to make sure we were alone. She looked a bit on edge, rubbing her hands together as she cut her eyes all around us.

"I'm thinking that you are very beautiful." I cupped her face, moving my thumbs in gentle circles over her rosy cheeks.

She smiled sweetly, but then her expression shifted as her voice dropped to a whisper. "I can't believe we're here, with the King so near. How did this happen?" She was distressed but focused, determination edging out her fear.

"Well," I kissed her nose, "A vicious predator attacked me in the woods, and the most enchanting omega came to my aid. Every moment since then has been destiny. So it only makes sense that we'd find ourselves exactly where we need to be."

She gave me a teasing scowl. "I am a nervous wreck right now, and the fact that you are happy is unnerving. I swear you enjoy getting into trouble."

"I'm with you, so how can I be anything but happy?" I said, feeling her tension melt through our bond. She loved being teased.

"You are just determined to distract me," she smiled, biting her bottom lip.

I hummed in response, then pulled at the collar of her robes, placing a lingering kiss to my mating bite. Tzidal's throat worked as she swallowed, and I slowly pushed my fangs into her exposed shoulder to soothe her. She settled her hands on my chest, her whole body softening against me.

Leaning back, I took in my mate's much calmer expression, those golden eyes filled with so much love and fire.

"Joon," she whispered my name like a secret, soft longing and sweet desire pouring off of her.

The things I would do for her.

I captured her pink lips, taking her mouth with rough and needy movements. Now wasn't the time to tease. I didn't know how long we'd be alone together, and I wanted to feel her soft body pressed against mine before we left for Ossory. It might be a while before I could taste my mate again, assuming we made it through all this madness alive.

We hadn't discussed what would happen if we got separated or if one of us was hurt or killed—there was no point. We both knew the odds of what we were trying to do. And while the thought of anything happening to my Tzidal made my heart squeeze and wolf wail, I'd be damned if I took my mate's most burning desire away from her.

Tzidal let out a sweet moan and clutched my shoulders for support as I sucked the tongue out of her mouth. Then I crashed into her again. I wanted her never to doubt my love or desire for her.

Pushing herself onto her toes, Tzidal channeled her fingers through my hair and tugged at the roots, making a gravelly moan rumble from my chest. She swayed, and I moved slightly with her, stumbling into the clean clothes. I wanted nothing more than to throw her soft body on the ground and bury myself in her delicious slick.

I let out a hard groan of pleasure and leaned back to look at my mate's gorgeous face. Puffy lips, hooded lids, and flushed cheeks. My cock was stuffed tight in my pants and pressed right against her belly. The sweet scent of slick bloomed around us, and I growled, ready to claim my mate.

"Yah!" An elderly beta yelled at us, her hands on her hips and a scowl firmly in place. She marched past the long line of sheets, looking ready to tear us to pieces. "I know you aren't knocking down my laundry!"

Tzidal stepped away from me, hiding her face behind her long, dark hair. I stooped and grabbed a few shirts and a formal-looking cloak off the ground.

"I apologize." I bowed quickly, trying to place the clean items back over the clothesline. They hung awkwardly, bunched up. The cloak fell again, and I scooped it up as the beta let out an annoyed huff.

She snatched the garment out of my hands and waved me off. "Go do something useful," she snapped. "Sneaking kisses doesn't get all these wolves fed!"

The second we were around the sheets and out of the angry elder's sight, Tzidal turned to me and smiled wide. "I thought she was going to take a switch to the bottom of your feet," she laughed.

"Ossory does not breed weak Betas, that's for sure," I snorted, shaking my head. "We should probably find somewhere less busy to wait for Jonelle."

"Theo?" A young alpha with rounded cheeks and a snub nose stopped directly in front of me. He looked at my chest, and relief poured off him. He smiled as if gifted an incredible treasure. "I can't believe you're here. Lady Strayton has been waiting days for your arrival, and her patience is wearing very thin."

I glanced at Tzidal, unsure of what to say to the youngling. He clearly had me confused with someone else, and the last thing I wanted was to cause a scene. Tzidal's eyes moved to my chest, and I followed her gaze to the patch stitched over my pec. I met her eyes, not sure what to do. I didn't want to leave her.

"Pup!" The elderly beta snapped at Tzidal, waving her over. "Get your rear over here!"

Tzidal gave me a nervous glance and a tight smile before slowly moving toward the grouchy female. Our bond thrummed with her resolve. She was a little scared, but more than anything, she was determined—my fierce warrior.

The young alpha in front of me shifted nervously for a moment, pulling my attention. "I don't mean to be pushy, but Lady Strayton is waiting, and...um..." he glanced around as if making sure no one could hear him, "she's been very... unhappy today. Seeing you will surely lift her spirits."

I nodded at the alpha, not really listening.

I caught one last look at my mate's back as she followed the elderly beta through the camp. I prayed this wouldn't be the last time I'd see her. It made my chest tighten and blood pound, but I took a long breath, reminding myself she would be okay. After all, she was dressed as a glorified maid. At worst, she would collect dirty plates and work a dusting rag.

She was also mated. Twice. The risk of her being snatched by a wildling or drunkard was incredibly low.

"Theo?"

My attention snapped to the young alpha. He stood quietly, watching me with expectant eyes.

"Lead the way." I gave the guard a stiff nod, figuring I might as well get a look at Byriel's sister. She'd take one look at me, then scold the youngling for bringing the wrong wolf to her. But at least I could get a good feel of her—see if she really held the scent of a deranged wolf.

The young guard released an audible sigh of relief, then turned on his heel. I pushed my head back, kept my shoulders squared, and my chest puffed. The fiercer I looked, the less likely anyone would look too hard at me. I just prayed no one realized I had no business wearing the patch on my chest.

We stepped up to a big, blue tent. It wasn't the largest in the camp, but it was pretty damn close. Two guards flanked both sides of the entrance. The one closest to me moved his eyes over my face and down to the patch on my chest. I flashed my teeth and gave him a pointed glare, forcing his eyes to the ground.

"Lady Strayton!" the young alpha bellowed at the entrance. "Theo has arrived, My Lady."

There was a long pause, then a soft, feminine voice drifted through the thick fabric, "Enter."

The youngling, keeping his eyes down, pulled at the edge of the flap, revealing a ridiculously decorated room. A full-sized bed sat on one side of the room covered in cushions and blankets, out-of-season flowers and herbs sat in vases all along the edge of the room, and a heavy table with a few ornate chairs was situated in the back. Scrolls, maps, and loose parchment covered the top.

I hesitated, eyeing the plush red carpet. My bare feet were dirty, and I didn't want a posh noblewoman scolding me for dirtying a rug set in the middle of the forest—even if it was inside an overdone tent.

"I said 'enter'." Strayton cocked a dark eyebrow at me, her gaze moving slowly up and down my body. She was like nothing I had expected. She was definitely an alpha—her scent unmistakable—but her features and build more closely resembled that of a beta, or maybe even an omega, except taller.

There was a delicate curve to her lips, a softness in her cheeks, and her eyes held a false innocence that made my wolf nervous. Her face was lovely, and her hair was a cascade of wild, black curls. Her simple robes exposed her collarbone and arms, and a long slit showed one toned leg. She had the same complexion as her brother, very dark, but unlike Byriel, her skin was smooth and free of any scars or marks.

While not as tempting as my Tzidal, I could see how the she-wolf would be an object of desire for many.

"Are you hard of hearing?" she snapped, annoyance rolling off her.

I walked toward the impressive female, my feet melting into the plush carpet. I expected her to say she had no idea who I was. But based on the look in her eyes, she was greeting a stranger.

"Wine?" Strayton asked, sweeping her long, shiny hair over her shoulder. She didn't wait for me to answer, taking long strides across the makeshift room to a drink cart.

"It took you long enough to get here." She gave me a tight smile before showing me her back and slowly pouring two cups of amber-colored wine. "I thought you were dead." She narrowed her eyes over her shoulder. "Next time, take the gate. I don't like waiting months on end because you're too nervous to step through a shimmer."

I nodded, pretending I understood what she was saying.

Grabbing both goblets, she turned to me, but she didn't move any closer. Her gaze dragged over my face and down my body again, but this time she seemed to be enjoying, rather than assessing, what she saw.

Taking two careful steps forward, she bit her bottom lip as her expression melted from hard dominance into a flirty smirk. "I guess I should just be thankful you arrived at all. I had hoped and prayed you'd show up for weeks now, and," she licked her lips, "I must say you are such a delicious sight to my hungry eyes."

I stiffened as her focus lingered just beneath my belt buckle. I glanced around the room, trying to hide my nerves, when I suddenly realized we were alone. A member of the royal family was never without their guard.

What service was I here to provide?

Standing so close to the she-wolf, this suddenly didn't seem like a very good idea. I needed to leave.

"How was your journey?" she asked, handing me a glass.

I took it, giving her a quick nod. The less I said, the better.

She took a slow sip, her eyes staying fixed on my face. "Did you like it?"

I glanced at the wine, then immediately sat the glass on the table. I never drank from an enemy's cup, no matter how friendly the gesture or beautiful the face. "I'm sure the wine is fine."

"No, silly," she closed the space between us, inhaling the air around me. "My gift. Did you like it?"

"Yes," I said simply, keeping my voice official and clipped.

"It was my way of saying thank you," she smiled, placing a warm hand on my chest. My heart pounded hard against my ribs. My wolf didn't care for the female acting so familiar with me. She wasn't Tzidal, and it infuriated my beast that I was allowing this woman to touch me in such a way.

"I know mining the Cristal Terre isn't easy," she whispered, "but you and your men have made me very happy. I cannot wait..." her eyes fell to my mouth, "...for you to deliver on your promises."

Staring over the top of her head at the only exit in the room, I nodded.

"Tell me. Do you have it on you?" Her voice sat on the edge of desire and rage, the thick scent of arousal pushing off her.

"No." My blood rushed in my ears, and my wolf grew nervous. I was used to a good brawl and welcomed any challenge, but this was different. This was a woman that wanted to bed me, and all I wanted to do was run for the hills.

"What do you mean 'no'? Where is it?" she snapped, taking several steps back.

"Somewhere safe." I arched my brow, smiling slowly. I didn't want to flirt or fill her with any more desire than was already pouring off her, but having her angry was a far worse fate. She was rumored to be unpredictable, and I wasn't in the mood to find out if that was true.

"But you do have it?" Her voice rose, each word punctuated hard.

I nodded again.

"Prove it!" Her teeth lengthened and a growl pushed from her chest—a chest that heaved with far too much cleavage.

I smirked and narrowed my eyes at the devilish woman. "Paranoid?"

Strayton held my narrowed gaze for a moment before finally letting out a melodic laugh. She swished her hair as she turned away from me and crossed the room to the table at the back. "I'm not interested in whatever little game you're playing here, Theo. I know you think you're cute, but I have too much riding on this." She drained her wine and set the glass on the table before turning to me again. "And I have every fucking right to be paranoid. My father is out of control. He's convinced I'm out of control, and no one can find Byriel. Paranoia is the very heartbeat of my father's house."

"Byriel has returned," I said. I was a little surprised she didn't already know since it was rumored he was here.

Her eyes widened with either shock or rage. I couldn't tell. "How do you know?" she growled, baring her teeth.

It was definitely rage.

"I have my sources, My Lady," I smiled and winked, trying to ease her temper. When Lex crossed a line with his pointed attitude, he always winked, and the ridiculousness of his words would feel much less offensive. I just hoped it worked on this she-wolf.

"You'll forgive me if I don't believe you," she snapped, placing her hands on her hips. "Although it would make me very happy if it were true. To have Byriel back...." She looked down as if deep in thought, then whispered, "I need my brother. Now more than ever."

Silence hung in the air as she stared at the carpet. I inhaled deeply, trying to figure out what was happening in her head. Her perfume was still sharp and angry, and I couldn't pull any sadness or relief off her.

Everything about this she-wolf felt wrong.

"I heard there were issues in Cristal Terre. What happened?" Strayton's voice caught me off guard, and I snapped my eyes to her. Her expression was set, all business.

I shook my head, trying like hell to be as vague as possible. "Nothing to worry yourself with, My Lady."

"Why did it take you so long to arrive?" She narrowed her eyes as if seeing me for the first time.

I gave the room a sweeping glance. "I don't think we should talk here," I whispered, looking at the tent's entrance. Thankfully the bustle of dozens of wolves could be heard just outside, giving my words a little more weight.

"Paranoid?" she smirked.

I smiled wide and nodded at her turn in my words. Strayton bit her glossy, red bottom lip.

My wolf whimpered, begging me to cut and run, find our mate and fuck her wild to prove our devotion.

"You know," Strayton let out a breathy sigh. Her eyes moved over my chest, then lower. "You aren't what I expected."

"What did you expect?" I had no fucking clue what to say anymore. I just needed to kill time until she dismissed me.

"I guess I expected you to be old and ugly. You are much younger than I expected." She tilted her head as if thinking. "And you were much more forward in your letters than you are in person. How can someone be so flirty and dirty on paper yet so stiff in person?" She leaned forward a bit, a gleam in her eye. "I think you need something to take your mind off that long journey."

She slid her bottom over the edge of the table, gripped the slit in her dress, and slowly pulled it to the side. I swallowed hard, my eyes pulling to her lap against my will. Soft, dark curls at the apex of her thighs dripped with slick. Every muscle in my body locked up, fear and uncertainty flooding my veins.

"My Lady." The voice of the young alpha that brought me here cut through the tent's entrance.

Strayton jerked her dress back in place, smoothing the fabric over her thighs. "What?" she snapped, her eyes flashing red.

"Alpha Byriel is here to see you, ma'am."

Fiery excitement filled her eyes, and she quickly hopped off the table. Closing the space between us, she quickly kissed my lips, catching me off guard. My wolf snarled long and low at me.

"It's really happening, Theo." A quiet giggle lept from her throat, her voice a breathy whisper, "If I'm careful, I might end up getting everything I've worked so hard for."

I forced a smile and nodded.

Her nose scrunched with excitement before she fixed her face and spoke in a dignified manner. "Get behind my dressing screen," she pointed to a partition covered in black silk. "I don't need Byriel asking any questions."

I settled behind the screen, crouching at an odd angle to keep the top of my head hidden.

"Enter," Strayton commanded.

I prayed Byriel wouldn't scent the room. If he did, he'd know I was here. I just hoped the mix of so many guards and servants, coupled with the stress of being around his family, was enough to keep his wolf distracted from finding me out. I didn't think he'd give me away, but I wasn't willing to bet my life on it.

"As I live and breathe," Strayton said as if in awe.

I could practically see Byriel's tight expression, and I had to fight the urge to peek over the screen to see if I was right.

"What are you up to?" Byriel demanded.

"That's not a friendly greeting," she said with fake offense. "You've been gone so long, and the moment you come home, you instantly snap at me?"

"I'm serious, Stray. What the fuck are you doing?"

"I have no idea what you—"

"This!"

A moment of silence made me straighten my back ever so slightly. Byriel held out a small piece of paper. Strayton narrowed her eyes at it.

"Why would I know about the trash in your pockets?" the she-wolf snapped, all fake emotion replaced by pure annoyance.

"I know what you're doing, and you will fail," Byriel growled long and hard. "Where is the rest of the prophecy?"

"You are un-fucking-believable." Strayton swished to the other side of the room, stopping at the drink cart.

Byriel followed, shoving the paper back at his sister. She swatted his hand away and growled low in her throat.

"You don't get to act like this after failing the most important task of your life!" Strayton yelled. The chatter of wolves outside the tent dimmed a bit. She cleared her throat and continued, speaking softer this time. "You were sent to save our father's life. And you failed so spectacularly. You actually managed to lose the witch's son and left Hida and Byna to be murdered by rouges. Father has always loved you so much more, but the satisfaction I've had in knowing how much he has hated you for this..." she hummed with satisfaction, "...it was almost worth all the chaos you've created."

"Eight wolves," Byriel said.

"What?"

"Eight wolves," he repeated. "I was sent to kill eight wolves marked with the blushing Moon. That morning, when I set off on my journey to find the marked wolves, you told me eight."

"So?" She glared at him.

"So this," he held up the paper, "is what Father had Haxa read for him. It doesn't mention the number eight at all."

Strayton's eyes flickered between the paper and her brother. While she didn't fidget or sway, there was an unease in her posture that gave away her nerves.

"Where is the rest?" Byriel demanded in a dangerous growl. It had my wolf raising his hackles, ready to strike if needed. But I wasn't sure who my beast wanted to protect, Byriel or Strayton.

Strayton opened her mouth, the look in her eyes making it clear she was about to argue. Not giving her a chance, Byriel shoved the paper into his sister's hand. The she-alpha quickly unfolded the parchment, and her expression fell.

Her eyes widened as she read. "How—"

"I know you can't kill our father and expect to take the throne without major upset. The stewards might even be emboldened enough by our people's outrage to take your head for such a crime. So tell me," Byriel leaned down into her face. "Who are you hoping will kill him for you?"

Strayton pulled in a deep breath, taking in Byriel's rage. "I have no idea why you're going on about killing Father. I would never do anything to hurt him." She crossed her arms. "I think living in the woods has made you crazed. At least you and Father have that in common now."

"It can't be a guard or a maid," Byriel said, ignoring her insult. "Everyone will think it was on your orders. You need it to be an outsider, so you aren't suspected. You need a rogue or drifter."

Her voice rose, anger making her tone pitch high. "What the hell makes you think I want him dead?"

"That," Byriel tapped the parchment in her hand. "The blue path. Like the song? Killing the marked wolves doesn't save our father. It kills him. *'The blue path to the silver moon, wrapped in love and light.'* That's how it goes, right?"

I shook my head, trying to shove down my anger. He knew what it meant this whole fucking time.

"You mean to kill the wolves and the King, but why?" A soft growl pushed from Byriel's chest. "What do you get out of this, Stray? Where's the rest of the prophecy? How did you know it was eight wolves?"

She refused to answer, her shoulders tight with determination.

"Tell me." Byriel's tone eased a little softer, breaking his sister's resolve. I could see it in her eyes even from here. She wanted to tell him. "Who is going to kill the King? I know you have a plan. You're too brilliant not to have every moment planned. Who are you hoping will put you on the throne?"

Strayton pressed her lips together, her eyes flickering to me briefly. I nodded at her, hoping she'd see my encouragement as support and not desperate curiosity.

She turned back to her brother, then whispered, "You."

The air in the room seemed to still and heat. Thick anger and confusion flooded the tight space. Byriel took several steps back—Strayton meeting his movements. She placed a hand on his arm, her expression clearly trying to calm him.

"He's crazed, Byriel. He's convinced war will break out with the Fae. He means to kill all of them," Strayton said in a rush of words. "No one will touch you for saving Havre from his bloodlust. And, as Queen, I'll be able to protect you. The people of Ossory have always loved you, and they'd see your actions as a love letter to them. And since you can't take the throne and have always been so devoted to Havre, no one could accuse you of trying to gain anything."

"Are you fucking kidding me?"

I couldn't turn away. I stood and watched, unable to believe this ridiculous female could actually think Byriel would kill the fucker. He didn't have the balls.

"I've always tried to take care of you," she said, cupping his cheeks. He pressed his lips together as his clawed fists went tight. Blood slipped out from between his fingers. "I sent Hida and Byna to protect you. I asked Heath to help. I wanted you done and home as quickly as possible.."

Byriel jerked out of her hold. "Fucking liar. You wanted me watched. You wanted me killed when it was over," he snarled.

She shook her head fiercely.

"Did you realize too late that you had no one else to do the old man in?" Byriel spat. "Did you think one of the stewards or a lover would kill the King of Wolves for you?"

"No!" A few tears slipped down her cheeks, but they smelled fake.

"I'm done." Byriel moved to the tent entrance, but Strayton grabbed his arm, keeping him from leaving.

"If you did this for me," she said, desperation flowing off her in waves. "The things we would gain go far beyond sitting on a throne. Oh, Byriel, the things we could do for Havre. But I can't kill our father and keep the throne. The marked wolves set everything into motion, and if they're all dead like it's rumored, all that's left is our father's head, then..." She let out a restrained breath.

"Then what?" Byriel narrowed his eyes, watching his sister's reaction carefully. "None of this makes any sense. You're destined for the throne anyway. Why is carrying out this prophecy so important? What is it you get out of killing so many?"

"We have everything to gain, my sweet brother." She placed a hand on his shoulder. "All the magic that the witches, elves, and fae hide and hoard. It would belong to us. I'll share it with you. I just need your help."

Byriel took several steps back, his lips curled in disgust. "Father isn't killing the wolves of Havre. You are."

"I have no power to command the King's guard," Strayton tipped her head back, looking offended at such a thought.

"But you've encouraged him, haven't you?"

The she-alpha narrowed her eyes at her brother. I could see it in her face. She knew he wouldn't do it. She was fucked.

Byriel grabbed her upper arms and pulled her to him. "Where's the rest of the prophecy, Stray. Tell me."

Her face hardened, and she twisted, pulling herself free. She smoothed down the front of her dress and tipped her head back. "That's it. There's no more." Byriel bared his teeth, and Strayton smirked before speaking again, "I will remember this. When I am Queen, I will remember how you failed me."

"You've failed all of Havre by not stopping any of this. Have you seen how our people suffer? Can you not feel the pain seeping into the earth? You are poisoning the land with your greed."

"I haven't stopped him because I can't, and you know it. No one tells him what to do." She crossed her arms. "If nothing else, his actions will make his death a relief to our people. A transition of power will be welcome."

Byriel took a step back, shaking his head with disgust. "So that's your plan? A crazed king, killed by his son, and the lands are so relieved no one will challenge you for the crown?"

"You make me sound evil." Strayton's pretty face pinched with restrained anger.

"Because you are," he spat. "If Father's continued reign means saving Havre from you, I'd weather his worst days willingly. Find someone else to do your bidding. I'm done washing blood off my hands."

Strayton opened her mouth, but before she could speak, Byriel ripped open the tent flap and disappeared.

The air in the room cooled considerably as Strayton stared at where her brother had just disappeared.

"Tell me," she said. She slowly turned to me, her eyes pulsing red. "Do you have it?" Her glare narrowed, rage flowing off her in waves. "Right now!" she yelled. "I'm sick of this game. Do you fucking have it?"

"No."

Honesty felt best at the moment as I didn't think she'd let me live if she strip-searched me and came up empty-handed.

"Is it still in Cristal Terre?" she asked, her expression hard.

"Yes." It seemed the safest thing to say. Cristal Terre was so far away, it would take her months to confirm, and I just needed a quick moment to sneak away.

Her features seemed to soften a bit as annoyance replaced rage. "Very well," she groaned. She moved directly in front of me. "We'll discuss it tonight?" She phrased it like a question, but it was clearly an order. One I had no intention of following.

"Yes, My Lady," I said quickly.

"I have so much to figure out now that I know I can't rely on Byriel. Don't disappoint me."

"Never," I promised, then turned to leave the tent as quickly as I could.

I sucked in the cold air as I stepped outside the tent. The hair on the back of my neck prickled as if the she-alpha might snatch me back inside at any moment.

Feeling restless and needing to find my mate, I rushed toward a rowdy crowd of alphas. Wolves were all cheering and roaring out encouragement for a beating that was unfolding not far from me. Wet, smacking punches and pained grunts filled the air as I walked closer, hoping to blend into the chaos.

The wolves moved and flowed, a break in the crowd giving me a quick glimpse of the punishment taking place.

Lex.

The siren was weak and broken, lying in the center of a ring of alphas. He was covered in bruises and black, sticky blood. His eyes met mine briefly before a swift kick to the face forced his head to jerk back and away from me.

I left out a vicious roar and raced to him.

Into The Tent

Tzidal

"IT'S ABOUT FUCKING TIME," a commanding voice barked as I entered the spacious tent.

It took my eyes far too long to adjust to the dim light, but finally, a large figure came into focus.

Ares, the King of Wolves, was not what I had expected.

He sat in a big, wooden chair with a high back, the table in front of him covered in letters and maps. A smattering of lanterns around the room made his eyes appear deeply set in the dim light.

I saw him many years ago during a visit to my village. I was just a pup, but I still remembered him clearly. He was fierce and muscular, with a thick head of black hair and a powerful smile. Now he looked tired, with deep lines around his mouth and eyes. His short salt and pepper hair was very thin on top, revealing a shiny circle of dark skin along the crown, and his beard was almost entirely grey.

Joon was right about one thing: the King might have been buying himself more time in this life, but how much more could he possibly have?

"Whiskey," he said lazily, waving his hand at a drink cart.

I moved quickly to the other side of the room, careful not to give the King a wide berth. Grabbing what was needed off the cart, I returned and poured his drink. His eyes settled on my trembling fingers, and sweat trickled down my back. His scent was so powerful and cutting. My wolf begged me to run and hide. But I couldn't. I had wanted this for so long, and now that the old wolf sat in front of me, I wouldn't let my fear steal it from me.

I bowed low, then carefully took a step back, waiting for his next command. He grabbed his glass, taking the slightest sip. His throat worked as he swallowed, his eyes never leaving my face.

The belt that held my dagger seemed to tighten and pulse with an energy that reminded me it was ready for its true purpose.

"Are you an omega?" The King tilted his head slightly, watching me carefully from the corner of his eye.

"Yes, my King." I stared at his profile. I didn't give a shit how inappropriate it might be for someone as lowly as me to look at him. He had killed so many, and while my wolf begged me to bow to his intense power and overwhelming scent, I held firm.

I wanted to see the white of his eyes before I took his last breath.

Slowly, his expression lifted into a broad smile at my boldness.

"Come around so I can properly see you."

My knees shook as I moved around the table, stopping so he could look at me head-on. His gaze lingered over my mating bite, and the excitement in his eyes dimmed a bit. He looked away with a sour expression.

"I didn't know we were in the habit of allowing omegas to work." He took another long drink. "Shouldn't you be at home, tending to your pups?"

I lowered my gaze, fighting the urge to snarl and tell the King I never had the chance to have any pups; he killed my mate before he could give me any.

A few rowdy wolves outside the tent bellowed and laughed, their presence making my spine tingle with awareness. Fear settled in my gut as I realized there was no escape once this was done, but there was nothing for it. I still had every intention of ending this wolf's life.

"My mate doesn't mind me working," I said quietly.

"That seems...careless." His eyes moved over the length of my body. It wasn't violent or sexual, but it still made me shiver. "Back to your station," he ordered.

My fingers twitched to grab my blade, but the time didn't feel right. I needed him distracted. Right now, he was too aware and far too strong for me to risk it.

Standing next to the drink cart, I tucked my hands behind my back, hoping this was where I was meant to be. The King didn't give me a second glance, and I let out a slow breath, thankful I seemed to be in the right spot.

"Father." Byriel's deep voice hit me like an open-handed slap to the cheek.

The tent flap moved, and I quickly angled my head away, trying to hide behind my hair. A thousand questions burst through my mind as I tried to calm my wolf. If he saw me, would he turn me in? Order me to leave? Have me killed?

And where was Blue? Or Lex? Did he bring them here too?

Byriel gave his father a low bow, then sat across from the

King at the table. I stared at Byriel's back, my body locked with fear and curiosity.

"Where have you been?" the King steepled his hands under his chin. He looked down at Byriel with a silent rage that made me want to curl into myself.

"I apologize, your Majesty. I was—"

"Strayton is telling everyone you were kidnapped," the King cut in, narrowing his red eyes. The old wolf's rage pulsed in the air, and I stifled a gag from its force. "Is that what happened, boy? Were you kidnapped?" His voice was a dangerous growl. Byriel didn't move to speak, letting his father continue. "I am the King of the fiercest beasts in all of Havre. I command and control everything that walks this land. Is my son so weak that he actually let a few rogues steal him away without a fight?"

Silence hung in the air as the two alphas stared at each other. I wished I could see Byriel's face.

The King curled his lip in disgust. "How fucking weak are you?"

"I was not kidnapped." Byriel kept his head up and his tone respectful. I knew his face would be blank of all emotion. His ability to control and hide anything outside of dominance was impressive sometimes. Rage, fear, sorrow; he hid them all well—except when Joon pushed his buttons.

"Did you desert your people to fuck that little, blue-haired omega? Is that what you've been doing? Are you the kind of alpha that abandons your post for the first harlot that throws themselves at you?"

Byriel's posture tightened, and the muscles in his jaw ticked, but he didn't say a word. I couldn't help but wonder if his father's words hurt him as much as they hurt me. Blue wasn't a harlot, and Byriel, from what I could tell, had been respectful of the unclaimed omega.

If I was honest, not many alphas would have had the

strength to keep their distance from Blue. There was a reason omegas lived within the safety of villages: family members could keep a watchful eye until they were mated.

"Don't you fucking glare at me, boy." The King slammed his fist on the table, making me jump. "You were meant to be a force to other nations. A leader to my warriors and a reminder of my strength!" His voice dropped, the harsh baritone making my wolf whimper. "We are on the cusp of war, and you are out there getting your cock sucked."

Byriel tilted his head. "War?"

"Yes! You have no idea what I have sacrificed trying to protect our people."

"Protect them?" Byriel's voice was so soft I almost didn't hear him. "You are killing them. Father, please—"

The King's fist connected hard with the table again, cracking the air. "I have done everything I can to mold you. To make you a true commander of wolves, but you have continuously failed me!" He let out a vicious roar and threw his glass across the room. It shattered against the side of a cabinet, covering the ground in jagged shards.

I hadn't even noticed the ridiculous furniture filling the tent. An imposing bed, heavy chairs, and several bookshelves made me feel as if I were sitting on top of the enraged wolves.

Eager to disappear into the shadows, I grabbed a hand towel off the cart and hurried to the mess. My hands shook from the rage pulsing in the tight space, and I needed a moment to steady myself.

"I cannot trust my throne to your sister," the King growled at Byriel as if it were his fault. Then like the release of an arrow, his voice came out so quiet, but his authority was still just as sharp. "Her anger..." he sighed, scrubbing his face with his big hands.

"Perhaps you shouldn't have killed her lover," Byriel snapped.

I froze—a shard of glass pressed between my fingers—and waited for the King to react. He stood and leaned far over the table. Byriel tipped his head back and looked his father in the eye. From where I sat, I could see his face. He kept his expression under control, but his eyes looked murderous.

"Fae and shifters don't mate," the King growled. The air crackled in my ears as his anger grew. "The result of such a union is dangerous. I saved your sister a lifetime of pain. We stick to our own kind."

Byriel dropped his gaze, and so did I. Was he thinking of Blue?

The King placed his palms flat on the table, leaning toward his son. "I did what had to be done. I understand Strayton's anger as young love is always the hardest to lose. But fucking the enemy is unforgivable. How she couldn't see how he was using her. Bending her to his will." The King straightened his back. "I fear she has completely lost her way."

"She's not the only one," Byriel whispered, his eyes glowing red.

Silence crackled in my ears, making my jaw ache. My wolf whimpered, and I circled my fingers around the hilt of my dagger to both calm her and remind myself of my purpose.

A deep rumble pushed from the King's chest as he spoke. "Watch your fucking tone. I have done what any good King would have to protect my people. It was them or all of fucking Havre!"

Byriel's eyes snapped to his father's face. "You aren't making any sense! Killing pups—"

"You are so fucking weak!"

The King gripped the edge of the table, flinging the massive piece of furniture to the other side of the room. The lanterns flew and broke. The table landed hard on its side, crashing into the side of the tent. The top spoke swayed a bit, and I held my breath, terrified the whole thing would crumble. Neither alpha seemed to notice or care.

I stayed fixed in my spot, not daring to move an inch. But with all the light gone, except for a small lantern next to the drink cart, the whole space was dim. I doubt either would notice me.

Very slowly, the old wolf walked toward Byriel, his breath leaving him in harsh pants. "I will not let our era end with me. The prophecy is clear."

Byriel rose from his chair, holding his head high. The wounded look in his eyes was gutting. I frequently forgot this crazed man was his father.

"This!" The King motioned to Byriel's pained expression. "This is why I had to kill my people. Your weak heart and lack of strength left me with no other fucking choice! And with what the witches have seen," he let out a harsh breath, "I can't let Havre fall to war."

"What war?" Byriel's voice rose. He held his hands out, and for a moment, I thought he might grab the old wolf. "There's no war, Father! There's no reason—"

"If you had read the prophecy, you'd know."

"I have read it." Byriel let out a pained sigh, shaking his head. "It says nothing about war. And having a green witch read it—"

"The dawn of a new era!" the King yelled out one of the lines from the prophecy. "The era of wolves is over, my boy. My kingdom is in danger with those poor, blessed marked wolves still alive. I didn't want to kill them, but I had to."

"*I* had to kill them!" Byriel roared. His rage finally burst out of him like a damn, making me flinch. "Not you! Me! I sunk my blade into that pup's belly! I listened to their dying prayers and their pleas for mercy. I watched their mates grieve and fight. *I* did! Not you!"

I held my breath, expecting the King to lash out and rip

Byriel limb from limb. But instead, he crossed his arms, a self-satisfied grin stretching across his face.

"I hate how right I am about you," he said. "I wanted to leave the throne to you, but you can't finish anything. You "couldn't even find all the wolves. You just didn't give a shit and gave up." He paused, waiting for Byriel to respond, but he remained silent, glaring at his father.

"You have consistently," the King continued, "since the day you were born, found any excuse to run from a fight."

"I have done every fucking thing you have ever asked of me," Byriel gritted out, his eyes glossy with tears. "Mother always said wielding peace is the first and most important step in a fight."

"Your mother had no fucking clue—"

Byriel cut him off with a vicious snarl that made my chest tighten. My wolf was on the verge of a full-on panic, and I squeezed my fists repeatedly, trying to calm myself. There was simply too much rage in this room, and my eyes stung from the force of it.

"Careful," the King warned, his voice like gravel, "or I'll give you the last fight you'll ever have." I could hear the hope in his words. He sounded like nothing would thrill him more than to rip into his only son.

Byriel swallowed hard, his breath jerky. He took a moment, his fists uncurling, before finally bowing his head in submission to his father.

"I apologize," Byriel finally said. His eyes were just as flat and lifeless as his words. It made my heart break for him.

The old wolf's face split into a satisfied smirk. "No backbone at all."

Byriel nodded once, "May I go?"

"No." The King settled back into his chair. The wood creaked beneath his weight. "I'm waiting to meet this omega that was so important you were willing to abandon my orders and throw away your whole life."

Byriel took a slow breath but showed no other reaction to his father's words. "He's simply a wounded pup I found in the woods. He's not of any importance to me. I barely know him. I was planning to take him to the temple and see if they could help him find his parents. If nothing else, maybe settle him with a new family."

"How charitable of you," he shot, his eyes moving slowly up and down Byriel's stiff form. "Omega!"

I hesitated, not sure if he was speaking to me. When the King didn't move, I slowly stood up, leaving the mess of broken glass at my feet.

Byriel spared me a quick glance. Then his head snapped fully to me. His eyes went wide, and his mouth slightly opened as he watched me move into the light directly in front of the King. Byriel stared at me, then he spun, checking all the corners of the tent as if expecting Joon to jump out of the shadows.

"Yes, Sir?" Blue's voice made me spin to the tent's entrance.

The look of absolute terror that filled Byriel's face made my bones shake.

Within The Camp

Joon

I BARRELED straight through the crowd of burly wolves, shoving and punching my way to Lex. Almost all the young alphas quickly wandered off, not interested in challenging an older, more skilled wolf. But a few seasoned alphas stayed put, stepping up, ready for a brawl.

Pushing my way passed the alphas that refused to back down, I balled up my fists and set my stance. Ready.

"What the fuck?" A tall alpha with a chipped front tooth puffed up to me.

"You will not fucking touch him again," I growled, knowing damn well that defending Lex was putting an unnecessary target on my head, but I couldn't just let them kill him.

"You cannot honestly mean to defend this piece of shit!" The alpha's eyes burned red. It was clear whatever enraged the alpha was personal. Perhaps a loved one was consumed by a siren. Hell, maybe it was Lex that did it, but I still wasn't going to give the asshole a chance to exact his revenge.

"Is there a problem here?" Jonelle eyed the group as she strolled past them, glaring at each, forcing them to submit to her higher rank.

"My apologies, Warrant," the alpha took a careful step back. "We were just trying to dispose of this deadly creature, but this," he snarled at me, "this alpha stopped us."

"He was right to," Jonelle snapped. "Sirens tend to have lots of secrets. Capturing one is next to impossible, and killing one is just stupid. He could know where allies are hiding or the location of unusual camps. Hell, he might even be working with an allied group for all we know."

"My apologies," the alpha lowered his eyes, and I smirked.

Jonelle didn't move, just glaring at the wolves in front of her. Once she had her fill of their unease, she barked out their dismissal, and they hurried away.

My shoulders relaxed a bit as they disappeared, leaving Jonelle and me on the edge of the camp. I glanced back at Lex, fighting the urge to tend to him, but anything that might come off as caring for a siren would not be well received. I noted his bruised and bloody face and the cuts along his hands and arms. He'd need to feed and rest, but from what I could see, he'd live. Hopefully, it wouldn't take too long for him to heal.

"What the fuck is a Warrant?" I asked, needing something to distract me. I itched to find Tzidal but had no idea where to look, and I needed to help Lex, but I couldn't with so many eyes on me. So instead, I stood, fists ready and wolf on edge.

"It's my rank," Jonelle said. Her sharp tone conveyed her insult.

"I fucking know that," I said in a harsh whisper. "I've never heard of it. What is it?"

"It means I'm an expert." She tipped her head back,

surveying the camp around us. She looked fierce in the light of the roaring bonfire not far from us.

"Expert in what?"

"I'm a combat leader and a tracker." She sighed as if annoyed she had to explain it to me. "I mostly teach my men how to fight, but lately, I've been tracking down allies for the King."

"Are you looking for the last marked wolf?" I was curious if she was the one that had found and killed whoever it was.

She shook her head. "No. The King has others doing that. His last tracker was killed in an inn in Stone City. He's not eager to have me far from Ossory and instead has me searching the mountains around here for allies. He feels the wolves staying close to the palace might have an interest in his head." She gave me a knowing smirk. "I guess we'll never know."

"Any chance you can help me find Tzidal?" I asked, hopeful.

"She's with the King."

I jerked at her words. "How do you know?"

"I saw her enter his tent not long ago." She motioned to the large structure at the center of camp. The entrance was just visible through the crowd, and my wolf begged to race to her. I searched out Tzidal through our bond, needing to make sure she was still okay and that that fucker wasn't touching or abusing her.

Just like always, my mate was steady and calm. She was nervous, but her determination thrummed through my veins. It should have calmed me, but it just made me want to get to her faster.

"Calm down, friend." Jonelle placed a hand on my shoulder. I didn't realize I was growling. "You can't race into the King's quarters, or you'll give us all away. Your omega is serving him whiskey. That's all."

"You don't fucking know that," I snapped. I wanted to be calm, but I simply couldn't. My wolf wouldn't allow it.

"His Majesty is known for running off the service staff. It makes sense the first prim-staff was grabbed and shoved in there to serve him."

"What the fuck do you mean '*serve*'?" I snarled, my meaning clear.

Jonelle laughed, and I resisted the urge to punch her in her smug face. "The King has no interest in mated omegas." She shook her head as if the joke was more than obvious. "He has a whole harem to tend to his needs."

Jonelle motioned to a small tent with a slight, posh omega standing in the entryway. The small female wore pink and red robes covered in delicate roses. She seemed to be enjoying the way all the alphas shied away from her. I imagined speaking to one of the King's consorts would mean an immediate and very unpleasant punishment.

"Trust me," Jonelle said. "The King has no carnal interest in your omega. He likes his partners to be only touched by him and never mated. He's very particular in that."

Her words should have soothed me, but they had the opposite effect. The King was unhinged, bloodthirsty, and surrounded by wolves desperate to see Byriel on the throne.

And Tzidal was sitting in his den.

The King's Tent

Byriel

THE KING SAT in his chair, leaning lazily to one side. "Come here," he commanded Blue, motioning the young omega forward.

Tzidal looked nervous, stepping back and allowing Blue to take her spot next to me. Blue's eyes widened at the sight of her, but thankfully he didn't say anything.

My sweet omega had been cleaned up—his hair brushed out, bathed, and he wore formal, dark green robes.

It was as if he had been prepared for the slaughter.

Blue's hypnotic eyes met mine, and he gave me a small smile. He had no idea the danger he was in, and it took everything in me to look away from him, not returning his smile or offering any kind of comfort. I didn't want my father to know he meant anything to me.

Tzidal inched backward, tucking herself into the shadows just behind us. Her hand slipped within her robes, and I knew she was reaching for her dagger. It made me feel better knowing she was here to watch over Blue and get him out quickly should my father choose to act like the animal he was.

"My son must think very highly of you," the King said, dragging his eyes up and down Blue's body. My omega bowed his head and clasped his hands in front of him, not saying a word. "He abandoned his people for you, so you must be important."

Barely raising his head, Blue's eyes flickered to me, then immediately back to my father.

"I did not abandon my people for this pup," I said, trying like hell to sound both respectful to my father and disinterested in Blue. "I was simply trying to be kind to a lost omega. I was tracking the wolves that killed Byna and Hida. I lost them, then my direction. I headed for Ossory the second I found my way and stumbled across this youngling in the woods."

A confused pain flooded Blue's eyes, but he kept quiet. It gutted me to know my words had sliced him, but it was better my lies hurt him than the King's fury. It was clear my father was itching to lash out. What he chose to do next just depended on how bored he was.

My father turned a stern glare to Blue. "Is that true, omega?"

Blue opened his mouth, his eyes downcast, struggling to find his words. "I, I don't know...who Hida or...I don't know them." His voice was so timid and soft. I desperately wanted to hold him.

My father narrowed his red eyes at my omega, the crimson reflecting the flame from the single lantern that still burned. He looked like a demon—the monster from my childhood. I just needed to keep him more interested in me than Blue.

"Are you of age?" my father asked.

"Yes," Blue mumbled.

"Strip," he ordered, standing up abruptly.

"Father?" I stepped toward him, panic pounding in my veins.

"I said strip!" he roared.

Blue flinched, crossing his arms tight across his chest. "Wuh, why?" he asked, tears pouring down his cheeks.

"What the fuck are you doing?" I demanded, enraged I couldn't just beat the old man senseless.

"If this pup is just that, a random omega you came across wandering alone in the middle of the woods," he smirked, "then I can only assume he hasn't been checked for the mark."

I swallowed hard, knowing exactly what he was doing. He was either going to torture Blue or humiliate me. And I'd take a thousand beatings before I allowed even one tear to fall down Blue's face because of this fucker.

I narrowed my eyes at my father, and a small smirk played on his lips. He was getting what he wanted, and he knew it.

I inhaled deeply, preparing to lie. "I've seen every inch of this omega's body," I said with a bite in my tone. "He has no mark."

I prayed to the Moon that my father didn't see the lie in my eyes. I didn't know if Blue held a birthmark or scar that my father might see as a threat, but I wasn't willing to find out.

A disgusted grin split my father's face. "So you *have* been fucking around while my kingdom falls to ruin?"

"He was just something to pass the time while I made it home." Blue's head snapped up at my words, but I didn't look at him. I couldn't. "My apologies, Father. It won't happen again."

"So he doesn't matter?"

"No, Sir." I moved to block his view of Blue. It was a stupid move, and my father's eyes lit up the second my feet moved, but I couldn't help it. I hated his eyes on what was mine. "We have many other important things to discuss. Let us discuss your strategy for this war."

My father leaned back in his chair, his eyes narrowed. "If this omega doesn't matter, can I sample him?"

I suppressed a growl so hard, it physically hurt.

He had no interest in Blue. He was just being cruel. My father preferred his partners to be tiny, female, and, most importantly, untouched. In all my years, I had never once seen him with a male, even though it was common practice for most alphas to be with both genders before settling down. It was an odd preference, but one that was well known throughout the kingdom, but I knew he'd fuck Blue just to destroy me.

"Did you hear me?" My father's voice was loud and cutting. Blue flinched hard at the sound and took a careful step back.

"Yes," I said, trying like hell not to bare my teeth. "I heard you."

"And?" He was playing with me.

"And I'm not giving you permission to touch him."

He let out a quick laugh as if he had won a hard-fought game. "So he *does* matter?" His fists tightened as his eyes flickered to Blue, then back to me.

Fear burned through me. He was going to hit someone. He was bored and needed something to entertain him. I just prayed it was me.

"Leave!" I barked at Blue. "I wish to speak to the King alone."

Blue's whole body shivered, and his feet moved at my command. In a rush, my father was across the room, my omega's arm firmly in his grip. A pained yip jumped from Blue's lips, and I snarled. My fangs punched out, and my claws pushed at my fingertips, heavy and ready.

"Really?" My father smiled, and his eyes widened with excitement. "After all these years of trying to find something to rile you up, something to push your wolf and find your

235

fire," he jerked Blue to his side, "and a fucking omega does it?

"Let him go," I snarled, angling my shoulders forward.

"Or what? We both know you don't have the fucking backbone to do anything about it."

My father glared hard at me, squeezing Blue's arm to the point of pain. Blue's lips trembled, and his throat worked as he began to sob.

"You've never had the backbone to challenge me, never fought back when I raised a hand to you!" A smile settled on his face as he reveled in my rage. "What kind of alpha sits still for a beating?

A burst of distress erupted from Blue, and he pulled at his arm, desperate to break free. His fear was as potent as the flashing light coming off his skin, but my father didn't even look at him, too distracted by the satisfaction he got by abusing me. I had been gone for over a year, and I was sure the old wolf was eager to make up for lost time.

"If you even once pushed back," my father seethed, "I wouldn't have had to worry about the witch's words. I could have let the Moon take me on that glorious blue path to the sky and left it all to you. But instead, I had to murder my people because you are so fucking weak!"

Blue yelped loudly and shoved hard at my father's side, his distress consuming him. My father's trance broke, and his eyes snapped to Blue.

Then, before I could even blink, he slapped Blue.

My body burst apart, my wolf ripping my skin and shoving my bones into place. Blood rushed in my ears, blocking out all other sound, and my vision went red. The last thing I remembered was the taste of blood.

In the Shadows

Tzidal

FEAR LOCKED me in place as Byriel's big, gray wolf launched himself at the King. Blue shook, his eyes wide as he took in the horrors quickly unfolding around us. Byriel punched, clawed, and bit his father.

A violent roar pulled me from my shock, and I grabbed Blue's arm, pulling him into the shadows next to me. I glanced at the tent flap, wondering why the hell no one was racing inside. Surely they could hear Byriel's snarls and growls.

Were the guards here so used to the King's violence that such sounds from his quarters were commonplace?

The hairs on my neck stood up, and I inhaled deeply, preparing myself to fight my way out of here if needed.

"Gua—"The King tried to yell out, but Byriel's clawed hand wrapped tightly around his throat, cutting him off.

I unsheathed my dagger and held Blue tightly to my back,

keeping myself as a shield between him and the alphas. I thought briefly of making a run for it, but getting caught between two enraged alphas wasn't worth the risk.

The King struggled, his voice coming out in stunted grunts. Byriel's big, furry back blocked most of my view, but the splatter of something dark, followed by the thick stench of blood, made my chest squeeze with fear.

The scent of Blue's tears mixed with Byriel's rage. My throat itched from the overwhelming emotions dancing around us.

Byriel leaned into his father's face. There was a muffled sound of a struggle. Then a deafening snap of bone and a gurgle of breath.

Then everything went silent.

The King's hand fell limp onto the ground. I stared at it, unable to move. His fingers curled slightly inward, a bit of blood covering his fingertips. The light from the lantern made the wet substance gleam slightly in the flicker of its flame.

A deep growl left Byriel, and my body went tight. The big, grey wolf leaned away from his dead father. The long claws on his back feet dug deep into the plush carpet as he slowly moved away, settling next to the corpse.

Byriel's whole body shivered, fur disappearing into dark skin, revealing his naked human-form.

Blue whimpered behind me, and Byriel jerked to the sound.

His eyes were consumed entirely by black and red, his fangs still engaged and his claws massive. He was trying to rein in his wolf, but it wasn't working. The man in front of us was still very much a beast.

Byriel inched forward, moving softly on all fours. He stalked toward Blue, his shoulder blades rolling and claws shredding the carpet.

I gripped my dagger and flung my arms out to shield the

youngling. Blue kept sniffling, but I held firm, determined to protect him the best I could from Byriel's approaching beast.

The alpha gripped my arm and flung me away. My strength was nothing to his, and I was easily ripped away from the omega. I landed with a grunt, rolling away from the pair.

Scrambling to my feet, I turned to find Byriel looming over Blue. I raised my blade and lunged, sinking it quickly into Byriel's bicep. I didn't want to hurt him but needed his senses to return.

With his red eyes still locked on Blue's face, Byriel pulled the blade from his flesh. Then he tossed the dagger lazily at my side.

He closed the space between him and the frightened omega, pushing into his neck. Blue's bottom lip trembled, and his eyes went wide, pleading with me to help.

A deep vibrating growl filled the room, and Byriel whispered, "Mine."

I didn't know what to do. Byriel was too lost to his wolf.

Inhaling deeply, Byriel dragged his nose over Blue's trembling arms, then his mouth and nose, all the way up to the omega's dark hair. Blue's scent was so sharp with terror, I was amazed the omega wasn't sobbing hysterically, but he seemed so much calmer now that Byriel was slowly scenting him.

Leaning back, Byriel stared at Blue. The intensity in his eyes made me want to look away, but I couldn't. What if he attacked?

Blue let out a soft, jerky breath—his hypnotic eyes brimming with tears and pain. His cheek held a distinctive red mark from the King's assault.

"I'm sorry," Byriel whispered, pressing a bloody hand to Blue's cheek. "I let him hurt you."

Blue shook his head but didn't speak. He curled his fingers into Byriel's shoulders, holding him closer.

"I'm so fucking sorry I did nothing," Byriel sucked in a

harsh breath through his teeth. "He looked at you and touched you."

Byriel scooped Blue up, moving to hold him.

Blue flung his arms around Byriel's neck. The alpha's big body softened into Blue, and he slowly moved his arms to cradle his omega. Blue broke apart, weeping openly in his arms.

Feeling it was okay to move, I grabbed my dagger and turned my attention to the tent's entrance. It was still closed—no guards or help rushing in. I swallowed hard at the realization that the violent sounds that drifted from the King's tent must have been commonplace to everyone.

I sheathed my dagger and turned to Byriel, knowing we needed to get out of here *and fast.*

The alpha had pulled Blue onto his lap, just holding and caressing him. "Please forgive me," Byriel mumbled against Blue's temple. "Please, Blue. Forgive me, my love."

Blue pulled back, looking over his face. He almost looked too frightened to speak.

"You love me?" His voice was so soft.

I resisted the urge to sneak away. It was so lovely and intimate, but we needed to go.

"You are the only thing I love," Byriel whispered.

"By'" I said. He jerked, seemly surprised to see me here. "We need to go. It's not safe here. We need to find Joon and leave."

The tent flap moved, and the sounds outside became louder.

An impressive female stepped inside. She was statuesque and stunning. A flowing black dress barely covered an impressive amount of cleavage and one long, toned leg. Her eyes went wide as she looked around the destroyed tent, then her attention fell to the King's lifeless body.

Her expression shifted from false innocence to absolute shock to a giddy bliss that set my teeth on edge.

"Oh, baby brother," she said with a husky shiver of excitement. "What have you done?"

Waiting In The Camp

Joon

LEANING AGAINST A WATER BARREL, I stared at the King's tent, waiting. Tzidal hadn't been in there long, but each second felt like an eternity.

Our bond was tense, but she was blocking me out. She was doing it because whatever was happening in there scared her, and she didn't want me to overreact, but it made my wolf a frantic mess.

Lex still laid unconscious behind me, his body crumpled and broken.

A massive alpha loomed over the siren. I growled low at the fucker as he approached. He kept his distance, just snarling at Lex's unconscious form. I understood his hatred of the creature, but I needed him to move the fuck on so I could grab Lex and move him somewhere safe.

Strayton marched across the camp. A few guards flanked each side of her. She stopped just in front of the King's tent.

She hesitated for a moment, then pulled the flap open. Her guards quickly followed her inside the dark tent, securing the entrance behind them, not giving me a chance to see inside.

Groaning, I looked back at Lex, relieved to see the alpha gone. I took my chance. I rolled Lex's battered body, letting him rest on his back. His face was black with thick siren blood.

"Lex," I whispered, touching his shoulder.

He didn't move.

"Lex," I repeated, pressing my hand to his wet cheek. He was hot. Too hot. But his features were still intact.

"You're going to be okay," I whispered, moving my hand down his arm. It was something Tzidal did to soothe Blue. She even did it to me on occasion, and it was always comforting. I just hoped I was doing it right. "Everything is going to be okay. Just don't...die."

Checking around me, I moved to pick Lex up but froze as Strayton stepped out of the King's tent. The deep satisfaction on her face contained an excitement that couldn't be described. She looked reborn and ready to take on anything in her path.

She moved her pleased gaze all around the camp, her eyes finally falling to me. Her lids fell, hooded with lust and violence.

I carefully stood up and moved away from Lex. Strayton looked over his figure at my feet, and she recoiled slightly in disgust.

"Theo!" she called to me. "We need to return to Ossory."

I hesitated.

Leaving with Strayton was an opportunity I couldn't pass up—I could find out what she was up to, possibly find the King's weakness, maybe even end all this madness. But I needed to see my mate first.

I needed to see Tzidal's face.

The tent flap moved again, and one of the guards stepped

out with Tzidal and Blue right behind him. They both looked pale and scared. Blue had a dark streak of blood smeared on his neck and one cheek. I fought the urge to run to them, pushing my claws into my palms to remain steady.

Strayton turned to the guard and spoke quietly.

Tzidal's eyes widened as our eyes locked, and her body jerked as if she wanted to run. But she held firm, gripping Blue's wrist. She opened our bond, letting me feel the dread pulsing through her. It took everything in me not to let my wolf take over, rush to her in a fit of rage, and destroy everything in my path.

But that was how things like this failed—an alpha's inability to control his beast.

"She's okay."

I turned to the unknown voice. A stocky alpha with short black hair stepped up next to me.

"Kenji," he held out a hand, "I'm a friend." He looked pointedly behind me, and I followed his gaze to Jonelle on the other side of the camp. She nodded at me, then walked off.

Turning back, I ignored his outstretched hand, staring once again at my mate.

"Trust us," he said, crossing his arms over his barreled chest. "She'll be okay."

"I know," I gritted out through clenched teeth. I didn't know this fucker, and his assurances weren't helping.

"Then why do you look like you might kill everyone here?"

I forced my eyes away from Tzidal to see Kenji's almost lazy expression. He was calm. Too fucking calm.

"Strayton wants me to escort her back to the palace," I said.

The alpha's eyes went wide, but he quickly reined in his shock. "You have to."

"I know." I stole another glance at my mate.

"I'll watch her," Kenji said. "I'll stay near your mate and your other omega. I'll watch them, and, once I can, I'll get them to safety. I'm lowly enough that no one will notice my absence. Things are too unhinged right now for anyone to really care."

"The siren too," I said, motioning behind me.

Kenji glanced down at Lex. "Really?" His nose twitched in disgust.

"Yes, fucking really," I snapped. "He's important to this cause."

He was important to Tzidal, and that was all that mattered.

"The siren too." Kenji nodded, surrendering to my command.

"Madra," I said softly, looking hard into Kenji's eyes. "If I don't come back, take them all to Madra. My mate has family there."

He nodded. "I'll get them to Madra."

I extended my hand, needing to shake his, to feel the truth in his words. And he quickly grabbed it, giving me a fierce look to seal his promise.

"In the palace," Kenji said, dropping my hand. "If you are able, try to find out where the gate is. We don't know much about it other than it exists, but the letters we've interceded from Strayton's people say it's important."

"Strayton mentioned a gate."

"Yeah?" He shifted his feet at that information, moving a little closer. "This is good. Maybe we can find out where it is and what it is. Based on the way Strayton has talked about it, it could be the difference between her taking the throne from her father or surrendering her reign to another more deserving wolf. And trust me, no one will survive under her rule."

"Theo!" Strayton yelled. "I need you. It's time to go."

"Coming, my Lady," I yelled, giving Kenji a hard look. "Keep my mate safe, or you will fucking answer to me. Understand?"

Kenji gave a quick nod and placed a hand over his heart. "I promise."

I left him, my eyes flickering to Tzidal. Strayton smiled as I approached, then she turned to her guard. "I want these two locked up." She pointed at Tzidal and Blue. My chest tightened, and claws extended.

"And I need the commander of my father's guards here now!" she commanded to no one in particular.

"Lady Strayton," Jonelle was suddenly at my side, "I am headed to Ossory now. It would be my honor to escort them for you."

"That's fine," Strayton nodded, seeming to really not care.

"Kenji!" Jonelle yelled out, motioning for the young alpha to escort the omegas. I resisted the urge to turn and watch Tzidal walk away from me. My wolf spiraled, whimpered, and wailed as the distance between my mate and I grew.

"Theo," Strayton's voice snapped my attention back to her.

Slowly, she moved toward me, pushing into my space. I looked down into her face, her lids hooded with lust and her lips wet as she repeatedly licked them. She whispered, her voice seductive and husky, "You have something I want, and I'm done waiting."

Into The Woods

Tzidal

I FOLLOWED THE ALPHA, Kenji, to the other side of the camp. I didn't want to trust him, but Joon did nothing to stop him when Jonelle handed us over. I could only assume he was an ally...or at least I hoped.

The alpha stopped just in front of a crumpled figure on the ground. A pained gasp left Blue's lips about a second before I realized who it was.

Lex.

He was so grey and pale, his lips busted, both eyes were swollen shut, and thick, black blood covered his arms. I dropped to my knees, but Kenji pulled me back onto my feet, away from my friend.

"We need to hurry," the alpha said, scanning all around us before leaning down to pick up Lex. He hesitated, his hands hovering just over Lex's middle.

A pained shriek echoed through the camp, followed by a

cascade of murmurs and gasps that moved like ripples in a pond. I could only assume the news of the King's death was moving quickly.

This was our moment to make our escape. I leaned down next to the alpha and whispered in a rush of words, "We need to go now."

As if coming out of a trance, Kenji grabbed Lex's arms and flung him over his shoulder. Lex grunted softly as he hit the alpha's hard body. I released a thankful breath. He was still alive.

Risking a glance behind us, I caught sight of Joon. The bonfire illuminated his impressive profile as he spoke to Byriel's sister. The she-alpha spoke with large, excited movements of her hands. She barked out orders all around her. Joon turned his head to me, and our eyes met. I nodded at him, then Blue grabbed my wrist and pulled me away.

I stumbled as we hurried into the shadows of the trees, away from the tents and fires. Turning to look over my shoulder, I was desperate for one more glimpse of my mate, but he was gone.

A slip of pain lanced my chest, and I sucked in a pained breath, refusing to cry.

BITTER, prickling fear raced through my mating bond, and I jerked awake.

Feeling disoriented, I swayed a bit as I sat up, rubbing my temples. The backs of my eyes ached, and my scalp felt too tight. I checked all around me. My movements made the pine needles that covered the dirt pinch into my skin. Blue was still asleep on one side of me, and Lex was unconscious on the other.

Lex's face was so bruised and swollen. It was hard to tell

if he had lost his ability to project or if he was just that injured from the beating he had endured. Pulling the sleeve of my black robes over my hand, I wiped the black blood off Lex's chin and lips, but it was too thick and sticky, not budging.

The sun peeked over the mountains, and the scent of a fresh kill made me move away from the silent pair. Crawling out from under the low-hanging branches, I found Kenji scanning the area with two dead rabbits at his feet.

"Omega," he greeted me without turning around.

"Kenji." I rubbed the back of my neck. I was so stiff.

"You can call me Alpha or Alpha Kenji." His tone was polite as he scolded me, but I still had to suppress the urge to roll my eyes.

For the better half of the year, the only alphas I had spent time with were Joon and Byriel. I never addressed Byriel formally, and Joon never corrected me, letting me call him whatever I wanted.

It was clear I had forgotten how to behave in a civilized society.

"Alpha Kenji," I smiled, trying to sound respectful. He nodded at my words, then motioned to the food at our feet, indicating I should eat. I ignored the rabbits. "Can I ask what the plan is?"

"I'm taking you and your friends to Madra," he said as he scented the air.

"The village?" Blue asked as he stepped toward us. His green robes were fussed, and his dark hair was a mess—the purple streak hanging awkwardly in his eyes.

"What's in Madra?" I asked the alpha, already knowing I wouldn't like his answer.

"Your family?" Kenji raised a brow. "Your mate said you had family there. Is that not right?"

Of course Joon would order someone to take me back

home. I snarled at the ground, searching him out through our bond. Then I jerked as I remembered what woke me.

Joon was in pain.

I couldn't feel it now, but I was sure it wasn't a dream. Wherever my mate was, he was hurt, and the stern alpha in front of me would have to fucking kill me before I'd abandon him and go back to Madra.

"We need to go to Ossory," I said forcefully. Kenji's eyes flashed red at my tone, but I didn't give a shit.

"You need to do as you're told, omega." He crossed his arms over his thick chest.

Remembering the letter in my pocket, I lowered my voice, "I have something I have to deliver. Jonelle said it was urgent. We have to go to the palace."

"What do you have?" he asked, tilting his head to the side and looking me over as if he might see a fib written on my skin.

I clenched my fists and stood strong, already knowing this alpha was the kind that would easily use his dominance over an Omega. "I'm not to say." I braced myself, looking him hard in the eyes, and waiting for him to demand I tell him.

He rubbed his chin, then slowly nodded. "Fair enough." He leaned forward, a smirk splitting his face. "But you're still going to Madra."

"But Byriel..." Blue whispered to me. "I can't leave him. After what he did..." he swallowed hard, "they'll kill him. I have to go back."

Kenji turned to Blue, his eyebrows raised. "Why would anyone kill the King's son?" He almost snorted as he said the words.

"Because he killed the King," I said, waiting to see how the wolf would react.

Kenji stumbled back as if punched in the gut. "No," he whispered, shaking his head. "That's not possible."

"I saw it," Blue mumbled, his fear blooming in the air as Kenji's claws lengthened and his hands shook.

I grabbed Blue's wrist and moved him behind me, then slipped my other hand into my robes, gripping the hilt of my dagger.

The alpha's breath came out in harsh pants as he stared at the ground. Suddenly, as if someone had slapped him in the face, he snapped his head up and rushed me. I drew my blade just as he grabbed my upper arms.

Moving as quickly as I could, I pressed the edge of the dagger to his throat, but he ignored it, leaning into my face. "Do not leave here," he snarled, his wolf moving just behind his eyes. My body shivered at his command, but I didn't answer, simply pressing my weapon a little tighter against his flesh. A slow trickle of blood dripped. "Do not leave here," he looked at Blue, "either of you."

Blue's whole body shook, and he nodded fiercely, promising to stay put. I refused to answer. My wolf was only interested in finding my mate.

"I will be back by sunset," Kenji said. "You had better fucking be here."

Unable to fight off this dominance, I finally nodded. Then, just like that, the alpha was gone. A big, white wolf consumed his human as he raced off into the trees.

I stared into the distance, feeling conflicted as to what to do. I wasn't going to Madra, which meant we needed to move on before Kenji returned, but there was no way Blue and I would get far with Lex in his current state. I just had to hope I could wake the siren and get him fed and better so we could leave.

"Byriel killed his father," Blue said softly, pulling me from my thoughts. His bottom lip trembled as he looked down at his hands. His sleeves were spattered in dried blood. "It, it's..." he let out a pained whimper, "it's my fault."

"Absolutely not," I said loud and clear, grabbing him by the arms. "I was there. None of it was your fault. That unhinged animal hit you, and Byriel did what an alpha is supposed to do." I looked into Blue's eyes, making sure he knew I meant it. "Byriel protected you. What he did has honor in it. Don't take that away from him by blaming yourself."

Blue nodded, a distant look of sadness in his big eyes.

"What will happen to him?" he asked, wrapping his arms around me. His hug was warm and soft.

"I don't know," I said honestly. I didn't have the strength to lie and try to instill any kind of hope.

Blue nuzzled into my neck, pressing his nose to my mating bite. It was something pups did to their parents to deepen their bond and coat themselves in their scent. It was a loving, familial gesture, and it broke my heart. The poor Omega really did have no one else in this world but us. And I wasn't going to let anything happen to him.

"You still hate him, don't you?" Blue mumbled.

"Hate who?"

"Byriel."

I leaned back, trying to see his face properly.

"What makes you say that?"

"The way you and Alpha Joon look at him, the way he and Byriel fight, the fact that Lex is the only one that'll let me be alone with Byriel." Blue let out a long sigh. "It's just really obvious."

"I don't hate him," I said softly, and I was shocked to find it to be true. I didn't know if I was simply grateful to the alpha for killing the King, protecting Blue, or helping Joon and me, but whatever it was, it had eased my opinion of the wolf.

Having no idea what to say, I simply repeated myself. "I don't hate Byriel," I whispered. "He's a good alpha. He's just lost."

The sound of water rushed nearby, and I glanced at Lex.

As much as I wanted to stay here and hold the sweet Omega to soothe both our hearts, we needed to get a move on before Kenji returned, which meant cleaning Lex's wounds.

"Interested in helping me lug an unconscious siren to the river?" I asked.

Blue gave me a half-hearted smile and nodded.

The River

Tzidal

It always amazed me how fear could change time, either slow it down or speed it up, depending on what your mind dreaded more.

The path to the river was fast. Blue hauled Lex over his shoulder, and we walked quickly. I had to help Blue readjust the siren several times, and a few tricky breaks in the path made for some interesting maneuvers, but we were next to the water in no time, the sun slowly etching its way to indicate mid-day.

A strained moaning drifted in the air, and I spun to the sound of Lex's voice. Blue was already on his knees, rolling the siren carefully to see his face better. The swelling around his eyes had gone down a bit, but his skin was still blotched with deep black and purple bruises.

Lex's throat worked as he tried to talk, and I brought my

hand to his lips, quieting him. "It's okay," I whispered. "Save your strength."

"How are we going to get him better?" Blue asked, holding Lex's hand. Lex squeezed Blue's fingers as he began to rouse.

"I don't know." I shook my head. I would think of something, but I needed time and Joon. I searched for my mate through our bond, but it was so muted. He was here but somehow too far to feel anything real.

Blue-eyed the black water. "Lex?"

A soft hum left the siren's throat in response.

"I think we should try to wash some of the blood off of you."

A sharp 'no' muddled by thick fear burst from Lex's lips. His big, grey eyes met mine, terror pouring off him. "Dark waters," he whispered to me.

"Dark waters?" Blue asked, looking at me to make sure he heard right.

"Lex doesn't like dark water you can't see the bottom of." I smoothed down the siren's white hair. It was caked in his black blood.

"Why?" Blue whispered, no judgment in his voice, just curious.

I shook my head, continuing to caress my friend. I had never asked. It was clear that whatever the reason was, it hurt Lex to think about.

"I was killed in dark waters once," Lex whispered. "Me....and my mate."

I paused, thinking over his words. Blue's eyes narrowed in thought, and he cocked his head, looking at me.

"I thought your partners weren't called mates," I said.

"They aren't." Lex shifted slightly against the rocky shore.

Blue's eyes darted to mine, and I returned his confused expression.

"Were you mated to a wolf?" Blue asked.

Lex cleared his throat, the sound rough, almost painful. "Yes," he said, his voice stronger.

I didn't know what to say. So I said nothing. Blue took Lex's hand, squeezing it gently.

"My people didn't care for it. They said it went against nature and our laws. So they killed him." Lex pressed his lips together, smoothing his hand down the front of his bloodied robes.

"I'm so sorry." I kissed the top of his head. Lex closed his eyes, letting me love him for a moment. I wanted him to soak up my tender feelings and let them heal him a bit. I didn't know how siren's worked or fed off emotions, but I hoped it might help. Even just a little.

"What, what was he like?" Blue asked, his voice a little uneasy at asking something so personal.

"Fierce. And mean." Lex smiled with so much pride as a tear fell down the side of his face. It was slightly silvery in color and mixed into the black blood in his hair. "He was perfect."

Blue quietly stood up and removed the sash from his middle. He dipped it into the eerie water before returning to wipe at Lex's chin and neck.

"I saw him near Myphic Village and decided to slip into his mind and see what he wanted in a sexual conquest. I was going to consume him, then move north." Lex narrowed his eyes into the distance as if watching it all play out in front of him. "But he didn't hold any violent lust in him. He wanted love. He wanted a love that had no face."

He smiled wide as he spoke while Blue dabbed at the wounds in his hairline. "He wanted someone he hadn't met yet. I had never met an Alpha that didn't carry a carnal lust for at least one or two other creatures. So I followed him." Lex gave me a mischievous scrunch of his nose, the love he felt in his memory flowing out of him. "Then I talked to him, and I fell in love. One day, I looked into his mind and saw that he wanted me too. But not the fantasy I projected for him. He wanted my mind and humor."

Lex let out a slow breath, his eyes glistening with tears. "I was his fantasy and his passion. I was what he thought about when seeking pleasure."

My chest tightened for the siren and everything he lost. I slipped my hand in his, listening as he continued to speak.

"My people discovered us near the beach, talking, laughing, and making love. We had accidentally wandered too close to Siren Territory." He sucked in a painful breath. "They anchored our feet to steel and pitched both of us into the black reef."

Blue gasped, letting his tears flow freely.

"I was helpless as I watched him struggle for air, his eyes never leaving my face. I held his hand as he died and cursed my body for not being able to die with him. I stayed at the bottom of the reef with his lifeless body for days. What little light that surrounded us only let me see his face. The rest was black. Lifeless, horrible, black water."

Blue's chin trembled as he slowly circled his arms around Lex's neck, snuggling the siren. I did the same, kissing his temple and smoothing his hair. He wasn't an omega, and our comfort probably wasn't what his kind really needed, but it was all we had to give, and he took it graciously.

Silence settled as we sat in our shared grief. For lost mates, wounded packs, and missing loves. We just held each other.

"Blue?" Lex finally said, breaking the soft silence. "Byriel loves you."

The omega smiled at his words, his cheeks going pink. "I know," he whispered, pride filling his face. "He's mine, and I'm his. He hasn't had me yet, but he will. We're going to save him." His big eyes met mine, and I quickly nodded in agreement. "We'll save all of them."

"Tzidal," Lex whispered, slipping his hand into mine. "Joon can't stand you."

Blue let out a burst of laughter, and I immediately smacked Lex's arm. "This is not the time to be funny," I said, still smiling at my terrible friend.

Lex groaned in a slightly dramatic fashion, rubbing his arm. "If you can't laugh at death's door, then you have no business dying."

"You're such a baby." I rolled my eyes, and Lex smirked.

Blue sat up straight, a new kind of energy pushing off him. "We're going to save Byriel and find Joon." He nodded as if he was stating a fact.

"I know," I agreed. I was still too beat to offer much more than a weak smile, but Blue's fierce energy had me thinking about the letter in my pocket, and I suddenly felt determined to make sure it was delivered exactly where it needed to be.

Lex continued to tease Blue, telling him about Byriel's ridiculous feelings for the omega, but I tuned them out. Trying again to feel Joon through our bond, I closed my eyes and concentrated hard, but he was quiet. Deadly quiet.

"What?" Lex gasped, and I snapped my eyes open.

Blue nodded, his mouth pulled down slightly in the corners. "Yup. Byriel killed the King."

Lex bolted up, letting out a strangled cough. Then he grabbed Blue by the shoulders. "Did he really?"

Blue nodded.

"The King hit Blue, and Byriel lost it," I said, not interested in reliving the moment for the second time this morning. "We need to get to Ossory." I stood up and dusted off my bottom.

A mischievous energy poured off Lex. "Of course we do. We just need to get through these woods by ourselves. Sneak into Ossory with two omegas, which will capture everyone's attention. Find Joon. Find Byriel. And kill an evil Queen." Lex shot me a look. "I saw into her mind for a moment before they had a go at me, and that female holds nothing good inside her."

"Do we even know which way Ossory is?" Blue asked.

"You know," Lex said, rubbing at his ribs, "you should go without me. I'm too weak to walk and too heavy for either one of you to carry."

"I can carry you," Blue said quickly. "I carried you to the river."

"You just need to eat," I said, sitting directly in front of the siren.

"That would be great," Lex snorted, "but sadly, the menu is lacking here."

I held out my wrist, eyeing it, then him.

"No." Lex shook his head, pushing my hand away.

"Okay, then we'll go, and you can stay here and die."

Lex grabbed my wrist. "Fine."

I smiled wide as he winked, but I could see the unease in his eyes. My nerves flared as Lex turned his attention to my arm, his pupils dilating as he eyed my skin.

"Lex," I whispered. "Do you have to eat my flesh or...?"

Lex's voice sounded dreamy, almost far away, as he licked his lips. "A bit of blood will do until I can get someone proper. I just need to be able to stand without falling over. Just a bite."

Lex's sharp teeth pushed hard into the fleshy part of my arm, pain punching through my body. It was nothing like when Joon left love bites on my skin. His fangs were just as sharp, but the euphoria that followed his marks left me panting with pleasure. This just fucking hurt.

I turned to Blue, trying to distract the pinching sensation that radiated up and down my arm, making me sway. The omega was staring hard at Lex as he feasted on my blood, and the color drained from his face.

Blue's chest heaved, and the air crackled in my ears as his skin flashed white. Between the blood pulling from my arm and the weird pinch in the air, I was dizzy and nauseous. Lex released me just as Blue's skin flashed with sparks of lightning all over his pale skin. His whole body went tight, then the current stopped, and he fell backward onto the ground.

"Oh, my," Lex whispered, fresh, red blood coating his lips. The swelling around his eyes was already gone, just the bruises left.

I moved quickly to Blue, a little scared to touch him. His skin was smudged as if he had wiped ash all over his face and hands. Moving slowly, I placed a hand on the side of his face, then exhaled when it didn't hurt.

"Lex," I said, motioning for him to help me move Blue into the water. I needed to wash him to make sure his skin wasn't burnt under the ash.

Lex sat next to his feet while I dipped Blue's head into the water. Using the sash around my middle, I cleaned his face off, then cupped my hand and dripped water over his hair.

"Sorry," Blue mumbled, his eyes fluttering open. "I can't, I can't control it." His words were slightly slurred, and I quickly shushed him.

"Save your strength," I said, moving my fingers through his thick, blue-ish black hair. He hummed at the sensation, and I kept caressing him, willing him to be better. I twisted the strand of purple around my fingers, then channeled them up and into his scalp.

Then I froze.

"What?" Blue whispered, watching my face carefully.

"Lex," I said, terrified to move or breathe or think.

Moving just at my shoulder, Lex leaned down, looking at Blue's hair. "What?" he asked with a lazy bit of snark.

Using both my hands, I parted Blue's hair just where the purple strand grew to reveal a dark birthmark. It was circular and red, resembling the crescent of a blushing Moon.

Lex pushed out a heavy sigh. "Well, fuck."

WANT to find out what happens next? Read the last book in the Blushing Moon Trilogy, Broken Stars.

Need More?

Need more sexy alphas? Sign up for my newsletter at kittlynn.com to get access to free content and epilogues of your favorite characters.

THANK YOU FOR READING!

It means so much to me that you read my little book. I hope you enjoyed this story as much as I enjoyed writing it. If you did, it would be so lovely if you could write a short review on your favorite book website. Reviews are so important for authors and even just a single line can make a big difference.

Thank you so much!

Also by Kitt Lynn

The Hund Valley Series

The Casin Series

The Broken Omega Series

About the Author

Kitt lives in Oklahoma with her husband and stacks on stacks on stacks of fantasy books. She writes not-so-exciting technical things in her "real" job but lives for the evenings when she can visit her paper friends in their magical worlds.

She is obsessed with fantasy, folklore, love stories, and horror in general. If you dig these things then you might enjoy her books. You can find pictures of her sweet puppies, her coffee obsession, and the ridiculous things she says to keep herself motivated on her Instagram @kittlynnauthor.

For information on books, signings, and content, please visit www.kittlynn.com